Book 6 in the SEEING JESUS Series

HOSTING JESUS

A NOVEL

By

Jeffrey McClain Jones

HOSTING JESUS

Copyright © 2019 by Jeffrey McClain Jones

All rights reserved. No part of this book may be reproduced in any form by any electronic or mechanical means including photocopying, recording, or information storage and retrieval, without permission in writing from the author.

John 14:12 Publications

www.jeffreymcclainjones.com

Cover Design by Gabriel W. Jones

For the people of Chinese WORD Ministries, who inspire my faith in a Jesus who can do anything.

Chapter 1
Jesus Sitting in Philly's Apartment

The living room had never looked this clean in all the years Philly had lived in his Chicago apartment. The sun broke from the clouds again, splashing into the courtyard. His front windows glowed with the light reflected from the neighbors' windows across the way.

Jesus sat in his favorite armchair with Irving dozing in his lap. How had Jesus settled in and soothed the fluffy gray cat so quickly? Just a minute ago he was helping Philly adjust the angle of the couch.

Philly flopped onto the sunken cushion at the far end of that couch. He had worked hard today without really noticing until he stopped to rest and evaluate the results. Talking to Jesus made everything speed by—even more than listening to the radio. "This part is definitely not gonna last." Philly lowered his chin to his chest. He didn't mean it as a complaint, just a spoken thought that he didn't expect Jesus would contradict.

"Accompanying you wherever you go is my plan for the rest of your life. I'll be right beside you whether you work at home or in the office."

"But moving furniture with you is completely different than just having you invisibly follow me around."

"Sure. The feeling of me lifting the other end of the couch helps you believe I'm real."

"Should it? I mean, am I allowed to want it to go on?" As he glanced toward the front windows, a cloud passed over, dimming the room. He could feel Jesus turning his head to track his gaze.

"Is it me taking the other end of the couch that you enjoy so much, or is it having someone to talk to who doesn't judge you or try to trick you into doing things you don't wanna do?"

Now Philly turned his eyes to the man in the long robe. "Trick me? You gotta admit this whole thing with you in my apartment is pretty tricky."

"You think it's tricky because I don't let anyone else see me besides Irving?"

Nodding, Philly couldn't find energy for any kind of debate. "That part's okay with me. But I just wonder what it'll be like later—when I can't see you or hear you anymore."

"It's okay to wonder about the future, Philly. Everyone does. And wondering how this will work between you and me is normal. But the thing that worries you the most is how you will still believe in me then. Will you remember everything? Remember what I said, or what I helped you to do for others? Will you trust that I'm still real and present even when you can't see me?" Jesus bowed to focus on his long, slow strokes over Irving's downy fur. "That last part is the most important, by the way."

"Remembering that you're real and that you're with me? That's the part I have to get right?"

"It's the part you will need to sustain you through your life. It's not about passing a test, checking all the boxes. It's about staying in touch. You're accountable for what I show you, but there's still no condemnation if you don't get it exactly right all the time." Jesus let his hand settle along Irving's back, the cat deeply asleep. "You're hosting me in your apartment now, and I'm very grateful for your hospitality. But I'm always going to be interested in being with you where you live, wherever that is. Hosting me in those future homes is what will matter to you then, what will help make your life joyful and peaceful then."

The thought that he would live in other places unfurled a strand of Philly's imagination. What sorts of places? When? With whom? But, on his way down that rabbit trail, he recognized the distraction. Real estate wasn't the point of what Jesus was saying.

His guest was talking about something else. Philly hosting him—
hosting Jesus through the rest of his life.

Chapter 2

In a Townhouse in Schaumburg

Philly thumped down the switchback of stairs from the top floor to the entryway, then creaked over the laminate wood floor toward the kitchen. The sliding glass door behind the kitchen table shone bright on this March morning. It had rained yesterday from sunrise right up to when he fell asleep. Remnant drops sparkled now where the morning sun found them on the white-painted railing on the deck outside.

Rounding the corner away from his appreciation of the bright new day, Philly headed for the coffee maker. The first order of business after getting dressed and downstairs was coffee. Recently he had begun to indulge in a cocoa-hinting Italian coffee, making a small pot of it before work. He was playing the part of the rich suburbanite. That's what he called himself, mocking himself, venting a bit of guilt. He had abandoned his "Sweet Home Chicago" for the burbs. His coffee maker was taking the place of the ever-expanding variety of Chicago coffee shops he had enjoyed. That loss was just collateral damage.

"Philly, have you seen my gray jacket? I thought I brought it up here."

Without stopping his scooping of ground coffee, Philly tried to remember where he had last seen that gray wool jacket. "I think it's in the living room."

"What? Can you look? I'm sure I was wearing it last night when we got home."

He warmed briefly at hearing her call their new townhouse *home*. Then he slipped the carafe into place and hit the start button on the coffee maker. "Sure. Just a second." Philly spun back toward the living room, unintentionally confronting a black-and-white cat locked in a stalking pose against the opposite wall. Daisy was imitating a cat statue—kitchen camouflage. "I see you there, cat." He shook his head and kept clear of the tentative feline as he exited the kitchen. Daisy seemed to have reverted to her doubts about him since the move to this new place.

In the living room, Philly spotted the gray wool jacket draped over the end of the couch. "It's here, Brenda. On the end of the couch."

"Oh, okay. Thanks, honey." Her voice rose and dissipated as if she had been standing at the top of the stairs and was now moving away. She was probably returning to the master bedroom to finish her morning preparations.

Philly reversed course back to the kitchen. He checked the clock on the stove and listened for signs of promise from the coffee maker. It gurgled its good intentions. The first aroma of perked coffee steamed the air above the linoleum counter. He had to divert his attention from what Brenda's mom had said about that linoleum—and the kitchen décor in general. Really, he was dodging the feeling that his mother-in-law was trying to stir his wife to regret buying this townhouse, if not to regret marrying this guy.

This guy pulled the bread out of the pantry cupboard and shook off that thought—at least most of it. Brenda coming down the stairs helped. Philly loved the morning routine they had established—in the kitchen together for breakfast before charging out into the world. In a new neighborhood and with two relatively new jobs, each day was still an excursion.

"Hello, dear." Brenda scooted onto the vinyl tiles in sock feet.

Philly focused on the feet and the wife attached to them, and not the fact that the kitchen floor was just vinyl tiles. Mother-in-law, be gone! At least be gone from his cozy morning time with his wife. He kissed Brenda on the lips, the puckery early morning kiss that he was used to by now. She was sparing him her overnight breath with those tight lips. But he generally doubted her breath was really so bad.

"I'm a little worried about the training today." She hesitated for a moment before renewing her track toward the cupboard. She pulled out the plates for toast and mugs for coffee. "I feel so dumb compared to all those young kids in my department."

Having forgotten to turn the timer knob on the toaster, Philly reached over to right that wrong. "You have nothing to worry about. You're bright and conscientious. You'll figure it out."

"Bright? You really think I'm bright?"

"Of course." Philly turned to catch her next to the oval oak table and slipped his hands around her waist.

She set the dishes on a blue woven placemat and entwined her arms inside of his and around his newly slimmer waist.

He noticed his own weight loss most when Brenda slipped her slimmish arms around him. He had dropped thirty pounds, down from over two hundred. It felt good. He looked pretty good in the mirror. But he was most pleased at how he could get closer to his wife without the impeding belly he had carried for so many years.

"I don't *feel* bright." She rested her forehead on his shoulder and sighed into his chest.

"I'll pray for you. What time is the class?"

"It starts at nine."

Philly knew his wife's need for prayer wouldn't begin when the class started, but he was pretty sure it was important to her for him to make promises like that. Neither of them had been church people for the first thirty-some years of their lives. They had just been learning about stuff like praying for each other in the past six years or so. Philly didn't spend a lot of time analyzing Brenda's need. He just knew what she expected and what she appreciated. He pulled out his phone. "I'll set an alarm to remind me. Though I'll probably remember anyway." He hoped to deflect any implication that he needed his smartphone to remind him to care about his wife's needs. It was one of those things that would probably not hatch into actual words from her, but it might incubate for a while inside her mind. He was still spending plenty of mental resources trying to manage the impression he made on other people.

Brenda was now the most important of the spectators in Philly's life. She had a box seat just behind home plate, as it were. He just wished she wouldn't invite her mother to join her there so often. Baseball metaphor. Opening day was just two weeks away.

"Thanks for praying for me. I'm sure that'll help." Brenda continued to set the table.

Philly saw her check the clock—a reassuring gesture. For most of his acquaintance with Brenda, he had worried about her—how she would survive in the hard-and-fast world, given her tendency to drift through. But, more recently, he had been heartened by that brightness of which he had spoken. He couldn't tell for sure whether her more-directed flight through life had anything to do with him. He hoped he was helpful to her in lots of ways. Keeping her conscious of schedules and obligations was a minor example.

They had about fifteen minutes for coffee and toast before Philly would drive their new medium-sized SUV down to Naperville, where he worked as the network administrator in a software development firm. Brenda had a shorter commute up to Rolling Meadows and the pharmaceutical company where she was an administrative assistant, and where she would receive training on new software this week.

Brenda landed the tub of soft margarine next to the toaster. She settled it next to the plate Philly had placed there, one big enough to host buttering four slices. Those slices of bread were beginning to warm the air with their grainy sweetness. "Mondays are way better now that I get to do them with you."

Philly chuckled. Such a simple affirmation from his wife, but such a ringing endorsement. It seemed like a noteworthy accomplishment to make someone's Mondays at least tolerable. He made a stab at calming her fears. "Don't worry about work. You're still new, so it should get better and better as you get more used to it." Philly's mouth was literally watering over the smell of the toast. He would have pulled the slices out now if it were up to him.

But he restrained himself so Brenda could perform her usual morning ministrations with spread and knife.

"It's all so different out here. Not like the city. I feel like I'm working at a college campus. So much sunlight and trees all around the building."

Brenda hadn't finished college, and when she did go for classes, she had attended one of the City Colleges of Chicago many years ago. Philly assumed she was talking about schools she had seen in the movies. Or maybe she was thinking of Northwestern University, in Evanston, where she used to live. Philly had graduated from Loyola University in Chicago almost exactly half his lifetime ago. Now they were both adjusting to being suburbanites.

"Can you hear cars on the thruway from where you sit?" He knew that her employer's corporate headquarters presided over one of the eight-lane interstates that ribboned around and through the city.

"No, the place is all sealed up. And I'm not where I can even *see* the windows most of the time." She had the toast on the plate, and she was playing a rhythm of stainless steel over crisp golden bread.

Philly forced himself free of the hypnotic work of his wife's hands and grabbed the coffeepot. It had stopped hissing and puffing, and the dripping had become scarce and irregular. When he tried to carry the pot toward the table, however, he had to stop abruptly. The cat was angling toward Brenda's legs and had paused between Philly and the table. Philly had apparently interrupted another stealthy slink. "Go on, Daisy. Get out of my way."

"Hey, be nice to her. She's having a hard time with this new territory. She's definitely a city cat."

Philly remembered laughing at Daisy butting her head against the wavy glass of Brenda's apartment window in an effort to get at a pigeon on the ledge outside. That was around the time he had asked Brenda to marry him, and not long after his cat had died of a kidney infection. Philly still missed Irving three years later. He and the fluffy gray cat had shared an easy understanding.

Uneasiness, on the other hand, tainted his relationship with Daisy, the short-haired black-and-white kitty now seeking shelter between Brenda and the pale ash wood cabinet in front of her. "Sorry, Daisy. I know you're out of your comfort zone. But this is your new place. Settle in and get used to watching robins out the front window. No pigeons around here."

"And squirrels. Lots of squirrels around here." Brenda glanced down at Daisy.

Philly noted the cat's head stopped moving as if alerted by the word *squirrel*. "Don't get her too excited. It's still early." Philly set a bottle of sweet creamer on the table for Brenda. The sugar bowl was already there for him. He turned back to the fridge to get the quart of half-and-half for himself. It wasn't just Daisy who was still adjusting to this new territory. Philly was still taking twice as many trips to do anything in the kitchen. How long would it be before he stopped looking in the wrong drawer for the forks and spoons?

Moving from their apartment where they had lived together for eighteen months wasn't so hard, but his Chicago apartment, where he had lived prior to getting married, had been extra hard to abandon. There he had hosted Jesus—Jesus visible and clearly audible. But, then, he had also suffered some devastating losses while he lived in that apartment. One cat. One neighbor. One grandma. And one fiancée.

He had moved on. He was still in the process of moving on, creating a home with his wife of two years.

In their new kitchen, flawed or not, they both sat at the table, crunching toast and sipping sweetened coffee. Philly aimed a chewing smile at Brenda, and she grinned a squinty reply.

Chapter 3
Getting Back Together with Brenda

That life-changing encounter with a visible Jesus had driven a wedge between Philly and Brenda when they were just beginning to date for the second time six years ago. Jesus's presence had been entirely strange for Philly, so he didn't blame Brenda for considering it too much of a stretch for her. But Brenda had started a process of exploration back then, prompted by something Jesus had said through Philly. That was how they both thought of it now—Jesus speaking through Philly—though they didn't talk about it often these days.

In the years in between, Philly had dated Theresa and had eventually gotten engaged to her. She was a nurse in a Chicago hospital where Philly had first met her when his grandma was in a coma. A few months after their engagement, Theresa's work with critical and serious patients exposed her to an infection for which the doctors could find no effective antibiotics. That was what Philly understood about it anyway. His fiancée had died from that infection. It was all he needed to know. He wasn't going to investigate how it all happened, as if he might sue the hospital for contributing to his great loss.

After she died, Philly simmered in a dense soup of grief for at least a year. Grief and confusion haunted him day and night. His confusion swirled mostly around his inability to heal Theresa. Up to that time, he had seen numerous people healed when he prayed and laid hands on them. It was part of the legacy that Jesus's visit had left him. That legacy seemed to expire just in time to watch

Theresa slip from Philly's hands and into a coma. That time, he couldn't wake his loved one out of a too-deep sleep.

Why not?

That he had even asked that question in those days proved how much he had been changed by his encounter with Jesus. He had seen healing. He had come to believe in healing. He believed so strongly that he asked *why* when it *didn't* happen, not when it did. That was true for him until Theresa died. Then he stopped thinking about healing. He willed himself to forget what he had seen.

Of course, Philly still visited his father in the family home in Chicago after Theresa's death. His father's hearing had been fully restored when Jesus was visible. Philly couldn't forget that. He didn't really *want* to forget that miracle. But he did give up trying to reconcile that surprising gift with his great failure.

During those first months after Theresa's death, Brenda had offered him kind words of sympathy in email and phone messages, as had so many others. When he did see her, Philly rebuked himself over and again for receiving Brenda's sympathy as an opening to a renewed relationship with her. That temptation felt like a betrayal of his love for Theresa.

Then, one Friday over a year after Theresa's death, Philly and Brenda had each been invited to a party at the home of one of the church members they had separately befriended.

"Hey, Philly. Meet Brenda. I think she started at the church about the same time as you." Nathan may have made that connection about their start dates as a desperate attempt to bring together two lonely single people he knew. At least, he probably thought of them as lonely. He was happily married with three beautiful daughters—a full house and a full life.

"Actually, we know each other. We've known each other for quite a while, haven't we Philly?" Brenda had raised her clear plastic cup of soda toward Philly, her eyebrows elevated a fraction, as if testing whether he was ready to admit to their history together.

"Yeah. We even dated, back in the day." Philly was as comfortable with Nathan by then as he was with Brenda. He knew Nathan would enjoy discovering the irony of having introduced them to each other at his party.

"Well, there you go. I guess I knew you two were meant to be ... ah ... to be introduced again ... to each other ... at least."

Was he just stumbling for an exit, or was Philly's friend hinting at a bit of matchmaking? Philly was ready to believe either interpretation of that verbal stumble by his usually articulate friend.

Philly and Brenda didn't latch onto each other instantly at that party or right after it. But that odd reintroduction did break the ice between them. Philly needed some time to get over his guilt at being attracted to Brenda while he was still mourning Theresa. But he knew that mourning had to end sometime—he hoped so, anyway.

"So, Philly, how's it going?" Brenda had stepped tentatively into one of the adult education rooms at the church a few months later.

When he saw her, Philly instantly knew that she wanted to reopen their friendship at least as a friendship. And he knew he was free to do it or not. As if a straitjacket had been untied at his back, his arms released to fall to his sides, Philly stretched his arms toward the implied offer. "I'm doing okay. How are you, Brenda?" His return query was in a friendlier tone than what he had offered her the last several times they bumped into each other. Each of those times had featured Brenda making the first move. This time, he returned the volley in a way that he intended to allow for a more relaxed back-and-forth.

Later, at the end of that Sunday evening training session on evangelizing people in a more natural way, Philly caught up to Brenda by the door. "Would you be interested in going out sometime, Brenda?" He winced as soon as he realized that he had looked down at his shoes while he asked her out.

"I would like that." She didn't seem to resent his awkward offer—at least not enough to refuse him.

On Friday of that week, they had sat across a white linen tablecloth, each looking at the menu in a nice Italian restaurant in West Rogers Park. Neither of them had been to this dinner spot before. Philly regretted that he hadn't checked on the prices first. The guy at work who recommended it probably made more money than Philly did.

"It's pretty expensive. Did you realize that?" Brenda didn't look up from her menu, maybe still searching for something she could order without bankrupting Philly.

"Yeah. I didn't check that out. But don't worry about it. Think of it as back payment. I should have asked you out a long time ago." After saying that, he realized it was a pretty insensitive response. But here was one of the good things about him and Brenda—he could be himself with her. And she didn't seem as desperate, nor as fragile, as she had when they'd dated before.

"You were gone for a while there. I didn't see you at church for months, I think." She peeked over her menu briefly.

"Yeah. I had to get away from church. I was kinda getting away from Jesus after he didn't heal Theresa."

"Ah. I wondered if that was it. Hard to understand how you could heal lots of people but then not the one who mattered most, or at least mattered a lot."

"Well, my grandma mattered a lot, of course. And my dad. But my grandma died after a while anyway." He shook his head at that unfinished draft of a reply.

"Hard not to get messed up by all that. You really lost a lot."

"Irving is sick now. I'm worried he's gonna die next."

"Have you tried healing him?"

They had both set down their menus. Perhaps they had both been waiting for this conversation. Philly got the feeling that Jesus had been waiting too. "I guess I prayed for him a couple times. But it's not the same. I'm not feeling like I can still do that healing stuff."

"Why not?"

"I gave up on it. I pretty much closed it down after Theresa." He regretted mentioning his late fiancée yet another time. That, too, seemed insensitive to Brenda, assuming she was interested in more than just being an old friend helping him get over losing the love of his life. Was that what Theresa had been to him? Was there even such a thing?

"I guess Jesus would let us close things down like that if we wanted. He doesn't force us to do things with him."

Philly only nodded. Their waitress arrived back at the side of the table, giving him opportunity to pause the dicey conversation. After they had ordered their meals, skipping expensive appetizer options, Brenda recalled him to the delicate topic. "Do you still talk to him? Jesus, I mean."

"I pray sometimes. Mostly when I need something. I guess that's pretty much like my parents used to do on odd occasions. Not like my grandma though. And not like talking to Jesus in my living room." He looked for some cover. "I guess a lot of church people do it that way, don't they?"

"Yeah, I suppose." Brenda averted her attention to the window behind Philly. "I guess I can understand why you sort of disappeared, then."

"And not just from church. I lost my job at the community center. I just didn't show up for a couple weeks without telling anyone. Not a good way to keep a job."

"You were depressed."

"I was. And then Dave came by and revived me. He even gave me permission to stay in my funk, but I knew that wasn't really what I wanted. And even if getting back to church and healing stuff wasn't gonna happen, at least I got back to work. I started doing some contract work then, out in the suburbs."

"That's funny. I didn't even realize you had changed jobs. But it makes sense, I suppose. It's hard to go back to the same places that remind you of ... your loss."

"It wasn't *that* so much as not really wanting to put in the effort it would take to make things right at my old work. The community center needed to move on, and I'd treated them badly. I still regret that, though I have apologized to my old boss since."

"So, you're working somewhere else now?"

"I'm working as a networking consultant at about my fourth place in the last year. It pays good enough, and I'm getting used to the commutes. My new job is in Oakbrook."

"Oh. That *is* a commute."

"It's not so bad. I'm starting to count on it, in a way. I'm glad for the time to think. There aren't too many traffic jams, especially early in the morning."

"You start early?"

"Yeah ..."

And that was how they began again. Normal together. Just two people comfortable with each other, talking about their lives, getting reacquainted, and learning to trust who each other had become in the intervening years.

Brenda asked him lots of questions, but she didn't seem invested in hearing any particular answers most of the time. That was before the questions started to touch more on their relationship and their future together. There was never one dramatic romantic event where Philly finally asked her to marry him. They just evolved into it naturally. Or so it seemed to him as he looked back.

Maybe that natural transition from friends to lovers to spouses was one reason he could feel their bond deepening still after marriage. They were still evolving as a couple just like they were growing as individuals. They were still giving each other space to grow, and they were growing together in the process.

Chapter 4
Rescuing a Lady in Distress

A cold rain stippled Philly's windshield as he exited the thruway. Condensation framed that windshield. He was still figuring out how to use the accessories on his new car.

As far as he was concerned, he was just minding his own business when a voice interrupted his commute. "She could sure use some help, Philly."

He didn't even have time to formulate the question, "Who is *she*?" before he noticed a woman on the side of the wide arterial road. She seemed older, hunched against the rain. She was huddled near an RTA bus stop. Instinctively, Philly slowed. But that instinct wasn't about pulling his car over to help an old woman. The instinct that compelled his compliance was the need to figure out the source of that voice. Who was talking to him?

But, since he was slowing down anyway, and the light ahead was turning yellow ...

There had been a voice. And now there was an old woman.

It would certainly be annoying to other drivers if he did it, but he could easily pull over. How could he *not* stop and investigate now?

He remembered to put on his hazard lights, which he hadn't found occasion to use in this car before today. And then he remembered to check for traffic before opening his door. He was doing pretty well so far. A white sedan zoomed around him, and Philly was careful not to check for indications of the annoyance level of the driver as that car whooshed away.

The old woman was watching him when he stepped around the front of his car and pulled his collar up around his neck. She wore one of those rain scarves like his grandmother used to have, transparent plastic decorated with little pink and white flowers. This old woman's hair was dark, but he noted strands of gray. She seemed to be Asian, from what he could see of her face where she cowered away from the diagonal rain. She waved a hand down the street and then at the building behind her. "Wrong one. Not here."

Okay. That made sense. She must have gotten off the bus at the wrong stop. Now what? Just wait for another bus? It was pretty miserable weather for that. But maybe there was something more. Philly despaired of finding out more details. It seemed likely that two-word sentences were the best she could do.

The old woman dropped her head and began rummaging in her purse, dark gray with a pattern of light gray flowers. She pulled something out of the pink lining. "Call son?" She held out a small and inexpensive smart phone.

That too made sense. Sort of. She wanted Philly to call her son. But why couldn't *she* call her son?

The woman pulled the phone back. She let her purse strap slide up into the crook of her elbow. She held the phone in one shaking pale hand and tapped it with one finger. Nothing happened. The screen was dark. She shook it and then looked up at Philly, her sparse eyebrows raised on her slightly freckled forehead.

For a second, Philly's heart dipped low at the thought that her phone wasn't working. Then he seized on the likelihood that she simply didn't know how to use it. As someone who made a living using computers, that was one of the things that annoyed him about technology. While the screens and chips were everywhere, they weren't all sufficiently intuitive for lots of elderly people—like his mother, for instance. Philly reached for the phone. He didn't recognize the model, but began to feel around the edges for a power button. Maybe the phone wasn't charged. But maybe it was just powered off. Either would make sense if the woman seldom used it. He found a slender button and held it down for a few seconds. As much as this technology was opaque to an old woman from another country, Philly had guessed how to power on the unfamiliar device. It lit up with a logo from the manufacturer.

"Oh. Yes." The old woman chuckled and nodded briskly. "You do. You good."

Philly couldn't help but chuckle at her simple satisfaction, her obvious relief at getting at least this far in her bid for help. But his work wasn't done yet. And a complicating factor had just arrived. A County Sherriff's car pulled in behind Philly's.

"You can't park here."

"Sorry, officer. This woman is lost and needs some help to call her son to come get her." That Philly hadn't yet figured out if calling the son was a viable option didn't stop him from describing his justification for violating the parking laws.

"She flagged you down?" The officer didn't wait for an answer. "Can I see some identification, ma'am?"

The old woman looked at Philly. Did she expect him to translate?

He turned to the officer. "She doesn't seem to speak much English. That's probably why she needs help."

The cop rested his hands on his belt and twisted his thin lips to one side. He surveyed the road. Rush hour traffic was flowing around Philly's car and the police cruiser, which had blue and red lights flashing. "Okay. I'll sit here for a minute while you try to get through to someone who can come get her." He shrugged slightly and headed back to his car.

"Thanks, officer." Philly was glad he hadn't been required to answer that passing question about whether the old woman had flagged him down. He hadn't yet explained to *himself* how he had heard that request to stop and help.

The phone was lit now, and the woman was holding it and poking at it. She waited after these random pokes, as if she hoped the phone might respond to her need out of sympathy. But the phone wasn't being that generous.

Philly reached for it again. He found the contacts list. "What is your son's name?" The names were a mix of English and what looked like Chinese. "Your son?"

"Yes, son. Michael. You call." Maybe she was uncertain about where she was and needed Philly to give her son the directions. Or maybe she was *that* intimidated by the phone.

He found a listing for Michael Hua. In the notes, it said plainly, "Son." Perhaps Michael had set that up for his mother for just such a situation. After three rings, someone answered the phone.

"*Wei*?"

"Ah, this is Philly Thompson. I found an elderly woman on the side of the road who seems lost. Is this Michael?"

"Oh, Lord. Yes. Is she all right?"

"Yes, she's fine. Just wet and maybe a bit worried."

"Where are you? I'll come get her."

Philly arranged for Michael to come and pick up his mother by the front door of the insurance company building behind where he had found her. That would give Philly a chance to move his car and get the old woman out of the rain.

"You can call her Mrs. Hua, by the way." Michael breathed a laugh into the phone, perhaps intuiting the overall awkwardness of the situation.

Philly handed Mrs. Hua the phone so Michael could explain the arrangements to her.

The Sherriff's police officer pulled away in his cruiser when Philly got Mrs. Hua into his car and headed for the office building driveway just ahead. There they found an overhang in the lee of the building, a much drier place to wait.

"Okay. You go now." Mrs. Hua waved her wrinkled hand toward the driveway. "Go work. Okay. Thank you."

Philly chuckled again, recognizing the old woman's concern for him and his appointments for the day. Fortunately, Philly's work responsibilities included very few appointments, and his schedule was full of flexibility. As long as he kept the network running and secure, his employer wasn't strict about when he arrived or left work. It was one of the advantages of working for a progressive startup firm that needed to attract young software coders. The new generation of workers expected flexibility and freedom. Philly was a beneficiary of that culture, which included the option to work from a laptop while sitting on a couch in the cafeteria. He could certainly arrive at work a half hour later than usual without disturbing anyone today.

Even if he did have a schedule to keep, he wouldn't feel right about leaving the little old woman standing there in the doorway of the big office building. And her son, Michael, had said it would just take him ten minutes to get there. That didn't seem too long to wait, even if Michael was one of those people who tells you it will be ten minutes when that's an impossible deadline to meet.

"You no work?" Mrs. Hua seemed concerned now that Philly might be unemployed, not just late to his job.

"I work soon. Not far away." Why was he speaking in truncated sentences? He was glad not to have to explain that to anyone either.

It was perhaps more than ten minutes after Michael hung up when a silver SUV pulled into the parking lot and slowed next to the building entrance. The rain had let up a bit, but the wind was still insistent and cold. A middle-aged man with carefully styled black hair climbed out of the car. "Thank you so much for waiting, Phil." Michael offered his hand for a shake. He gave Philly the impression of a salesman, perhaps real estate.

"Oh, no problem."

"I'm curious how you knew she needed help."

Ouch. That was the question Philly was hoping *not* to answer for this sharp stranger with his straight white teeth and curious dark eyes. "Uh, well, she was standing there on the side of the road in the rain. She looked a bit confused." All that was true, but he feared it left a misleading impression about the mental health of Mrs. Hua. Philly didn't want to cause her son added concern, so he tried again. "And I just had this idea pop into my head that this lady needed some help. That random thought hit me, and then I saw her standing there. And I just couldn't *not* stop."

Michael was staring at Philly now. "That's interesting. Maybe my mother's angel alerted you." He smiled generously.

Okay. That was even weirder than Philly's explanation. He smiled and breathed a small laugh. "Yeah. That could be it."

Mrs. Hua shook Philly's hand before they all emerged from the sheltered entrance and headed to their respective SUVs. "You good man. You help me. God bless."

"Thank you," he replied. "You are very kind. Bless you too."

And with that, Philly was back in his car and on his way to work. He was driving again less than twenty minutes after he first heard that disembodied voice.

Was it really a voice? Maybe it was just a random thought. Maybe it was just his imagination. Clearly it was some sort of intuitive insight. Mrs. Hua really *did* need help. But it wouldn't have to be a literal voice that alerted him.

To this thought, he seemed to hear another unexpected sound. Cheerful laughter. Just laughter.

Chapter 5
Time for Another Big Commitment

"We need to talk about having children, Philly."

Brenda had draped her legs across his lap, and he was slowly stroking her smooth black leggings down to her bare ankle. Philly kept his eyes on the gas flame in the fireplace, staring as his mind wandered. He was still trying to figure out what had happened that morning with the old woman in the rain and the voice in his head. Brenda's prompt was a wakeup call from reality—the realities of married life. Stopping himself just before sucking in a big breath for a sigh, Philly tried not to give Brenda the wrong impression. "Of course we want to have kids, like we said."

"So, what are we doing about it?"

"What?" Philly rotated his head hard right. "What are we *doing*? Is that your way of saying you wanna go up to the bedroom?"

Brenda laughed and leaned the side of her head on the back of the couch. "Well, we *should* do that. But, I mean, are we gonna start preparing? We should paint the guest room if it's gonna be the baby's room. And we need to decide where guests are gonna stay if they come over after we do that."

Most of their family still lived in the Chicago area, and their out-of-town sisters would each stay with their respective parents when they came to visit, most likely. So it seemed to Philly that guests were a mostly hypothetical consideration. Brenda's old bed had gone in that guest room, and his old bed was in the master bedroom. But that had just been a way to fit the furniture they already owned into the space they needed to decorate. "I think it *should* just be the baby's room. And, if we really want guests to stay over, we can get a hide-a-bed for the basement."

"Your man cave?"

He snorted. "Hey, you watch movies down there too."

"Surrounded by Cubs posters."

"Are you telling me you don't love the Cubs? Are you really admitting that now? And you say you wanna have *kids* with me?"

Brenda leaned forward and butted her head into Philly's shoulder. "God forbid I would finally admit that." She snorted and honked a nasally laugh. "I guess I should call it your bear cave. *Our* bear cave."

"Hey, Bears and Cubs cover most of the year if they can both make the playoffs. What more does a man need?"

"So, does that make you my honey bear in his cave?" She nuzzled his cheek with her nose.

He breathed a semi-silent laugh deep in his chest.

"There you go with that laugh. What? Do you *not* want me to call you my honey bear?"

"What laugh? You heard some hidden message in my laugh?"

"Yes. You laugh like that when you wanna say something but don't actually say it. It's your doubtful laugh."

Then he caught himself doing it again, the same breathy "*Huh huh huh.*" Maybe she was right—maybe it was his uncomfortable laugh. But if he was uncomfortable being called her honey bear, he wasn't uncomfortable with planning to have a baby. And, of course, the preparations for that included some very pleasant elements. "Well, you can call me your honey bear if you come down to the cave with me now." He bounced his eyebrows in that suggestive way he reserved for Brenda.

She didn't hesitate, practically vaulting off the couch and stepping across the room to hit the off switch for the gas fireplace. Perhaps it was the prospect of making a baby together that motivated her. Philly couldn't imagine she was excited about making love amongst the Cubs posters in the basement.

Just briefly, as he trundled down the stairs behind Brenda, Philly returned to his unsettled curiosity about the voice he had heard on his morning commute. In reexamining that unsettled question, he managed to repress one of those uncomfortable laughs.

He hadn't told Brenda about the voice yet. Why was that?

Chapter 6
Meeting Jesus in the Basement

As he slept that night, Philly had one of those dreams that started out with telling himself he was dreaming. Perhaps this disclaimer was meant to be reassuring. Philly could remember doing it in the face of more frightening scenes in the past. This scene was just his basement. He was walking down the stairs to the English basement where they had their TV and two recliners. Of course, it was also the basement where he and Brenda had been together before coming up to bed that night. At the bottom of the stairs, he turned his head. Was Brenda down there? He felt as if someone were there. He wasn't entering his basement alone, or maybe it was that he wasn't going down there to *be* alone. He was there to be with someone. Was this going to be a sexy dream?

The room was dark, the way Philly liked it for watching movies. He had hung room-darkening curtains over the windows. Though he hadn't actually seen it happen, he had the impression that someone had just shut off the TV when he reached the bottom of the stairs. Was that a hand on the remote? Someone else's hand? Philly generally monopolized the remote in this basement—his basement. Who was here?

Out of the recliner on the left stood a familiar person. At first it was a person, not a man or a woman. Was the gender uncertain? Was the identity of this person fluid? No. It was just how the dream unfolded.

"Hello, Philly. I'm so glad you finally came down to see me." Jesus stood in front of him now, grabbing him by his shoulders. Jesus was in Philly's basement.

"Finally?" Whether Philly responded aloud wasn't important. The Jesus in his dream seemed to have access to his thoughts.

"I've been waiting down here for quite a while."

Philly's gaze settled on the arms of the recliner out of which Jesus had just risen. There were worn parts—handprints—on each arm, the dark leather worn through to tan, rubbed down to underlying threads. It looked as if someone had been sitting there a lot, and for a long time.

"You've been waiting for *me*?" Another question, even if it wasn't spoken into the dreamy air.

"Well, I have the TV. At least I get to watch you on that when I'm down here."

Philly's attention turned to the flat-panel display in front of the two recliners. There where holes in the screen—shattered glass and shallow impact craters—as if someone had thrown things at the TV. His heart sank. Someone had ruined his TV.

"I get upset sometimes about what I see you going through out there in the world. I've ruined a few remotes that way." Jesus was holding a remote in his hand now, whether he had been holding it before or not.

In Philly's dream, Jesus was sad and smiling at the same time. Philly could feel his sadness. Jesus's face was tilted down slightly like he was remembering throwing a remote when something bad had happened to Philly. But then Philly saw him smiling in that playful way he used to when Philly could see him in real life. A real smile. Was he making a joke? Was Jesus joking about throwing the remote? Maybe.

When Philly looked at the TV again, it didn't seem to be broken anymore. "Why do you just watch me on TV?"

"Don't worry. I'm not mad at you. I'm not mad that you don't take me out into the world with you these days. I'm not mad that you haven't come down to sit with me. Don't worry, Philly. I'm not mad at you."

The voice was familiar. The feelings expressed by that smiling face were also familiar. This conversation felt real.

"But it's only a dream." Jesus was apparently saying it now.

Even if it was a dream, Philly wanted to understand what was happening, what Jesus was saying in the dream. He suddenly knew that he didn't have to ask any more questions to gain the understanding he needed. He didn't have to ask Jesus to repeat what he had said. That was a good thing about a dream. The story, the message, and the discovery were all neatly contained in his head, and Jesus was contained in his basement—in this dream.

Apparently, Jesus was in the habit of sitting in the basement of Philly's house, waiting for him. He had been sitting alone down there a long time. And he had been watching Philly on TV because that was the only way he could keep in touch with what was happening in Philly's life.

Back to asking questions. "You want me to come down and sit with you here?"

"Would you? I would love that." Jesus seemed younger, somehow. More innocent. Maybe a bit lonely, maybe a little desperate. He reminded Philly of the way Brenda used to be before she started going to church.

But this wasn't Brenda, not the new Brenda nor the old one. This was Jesus. Definitely Jesus.

"You just want me to sit here?"

"With me. The two of us. We can watch together. Or we can talk."

Now there was a fireplace next to the TV. Philly had wished that their fireplace was in the basement instead of on the first floor. That would make it an even cozier man cave. Bear cave. Whatever.

The dream was over now, but Philly wasn't awake. He wasn't fully awake, anyway. He was still hungrily absorbing that dream. Jesus in his basement, as if he had been down there all along without Philly knowing it. And Jesus seeming lonely. Or maybe it was Philly who was lonely. Jesus seemed like he could just sit down there and keep waiting. How long had it been? Had it been since Theresa died? Certainly, if it was really Jesus, then he would be able to go on waiting and waiting. He could be patient. Jesus could keep on being patient. But why make him wait? Didn't Philly *want* to be with him down there, cozy in the basement? Best friends talking again.

Philly considered whether this Jesus in the basement might be related to the voice that had spoken to him yesterday. He had suspected that all along, of course. Did asking the question of who had spoken to him in the car prompt this dream? Was it an answer to his question? Not directly, maybe. He was a little more awake, but he wanted to hang onto that dream. He didn't want to wake up yet. He didn't want to move away from that basement, that room where Jesus waited for him, that place where he could go and find Jesus. Was Jesus really waiting for him to come and sit and talk?

He probably was.

Not in Philly's literal basement, maybe. But that was probably as good a place as any to reconnect with him.

Chapter 7
Sharing the Dream with Brenda

As he shaved the next morning, Philly faced the fact that he hadn't told Brenda about the Chinese woman from the previous morning. He wouldn't mind telling her about his Good Samaritan act, of course, but telling her about the voice irritated him like sharp pebbles in his shoe. And now he was also carrying the dream about Jesus in the basement. He really wanted to tell her about that.

Brenda usually climbed out of bed after Philly, squeezing in a few more minutes of sleep while Philly showered quickly and shaved. He had always taken quick showers, so that worked well. Brenda didn't have to wait long. And, if she was in a hurry one day, she had the option of showering in the guest bedroom across the hall while Philly ran the wet-dry electric razor over his face, a face blurry in the foggy mirror.

Though part of his brain warned him that their breakfast routine wasn't the ideal time for a deep spiritual conversation, Philly couldn't stop himself. Standing by the coffee maker while Brenda prepared some cinnamon raisin toast, he launched into his dual revelations. "There was something I forgot to tell you about yesterday. And then I had a dream last night that reminded me to tell you." He glitched just briefly over the moderate dishonesty of saying he had *forgotten* to tell her about the voice he heard.

"Oh. That sounds interesting." She was pulling the bread from the toaster oven, cinnamon and raisin sweetness saturating the coffee-laden air.

Philly had to overcome the fact that the word *interesting* was his dad's favorite description of things his ma cooked that were *not* his dad's favorites. "Uh, yeah. Really, I was shy to tell you 'cause I thought I heard a *voice* yesterday."

"What, shy? You heard a voice?"

Obviously this was not the best time to tell her. But how could he stop now? "I think I sorta talked myself out of the idea that it was an actual voice and not just a thought in my head. But I saw Jesus in a dream last night, and I think I know now that it really was an actual voice I heard. Probably."

"You heard a voice?" To Brenda's credit, she curated a cogent question out of the disorganized data dump Philly had handed her.

Philly started from the beginning of the story of Mrs. Hua lost in the rain.

Brenda sat at the table and listened with wide eyes.

Philly wasn't surprised when she stopped chewing toast to say, "Oh, Philly, that was so nice of you."

But Brenda did seem surprised that he hadn't told her about it the day before. "That's a pretty big thing to not tell me about."

"I know. I was still trying to figure out what I believed about the voice. Maybe I was afraid you would think I was crazy." But, as soon as he said it, he knew that wasn't what he had feared. What he had really feared was that Brenda would take the voice seriously and raise obvious questions about why Philly wasn't listening for that voice more often, more faithfully.

"You know I never doubted that you saw and heard Jesus. I was just uncomfortable being around that when I didn't have any faith in him at all."

Philly knew all that. They had talked about it many times. They had discussed what happened to him way back then. But they hadn't had to update that discussion with any new experiences lately. Any new voices. The last supernatural thing Philly could remember doing was healing a little girl's toe in a restaurant several years ago. That reminded him of Gladys, the girl's grandmother. He hadn't written to Gladys for a while. But that was a sidetrack. "Well, I don't think I was ready for it yet. I probably wasn't really worried that you wouldn't believe me—it was more that you wouldn't know what to do with it either." He felt like he was muddling the issue, rolling the truth around but not getting a good grip on it.

"Okay. So what was the other thing you said? You had a dream?"

Philly sipped his coffee, extra bitter, probably too strong this morning. His mind had been running on this treadmill while he was supposed to be counting scoops. "Yeah. Huh. I can sort of still feel it, like the dream just happened. Or like it's sort of still with me." He set down his mug and slid the last corner of toast between his lips. He tried talking politely around that small crunchy bit. "It was one of those dreams that seems very real."

"What was it about?"

"Jesus sitting in one of the recliners downstairs waiting for me to come down and sit with him." It sounded pretty simple when he said it that way, maybe not so earth-shattering.

Brenda scowled very slightly. "He was just sitting down there? Not doing anything else?"

"Oh, he talked to me. He thanked me for finally coming down to see him. He said he usually just watches me on TV since I don't come down and see him, and since he can't come with me when I go out into the world."

"Why can't he go with you?"

"I guess I don't let him."

"I mean, I guess that's true for most of us, isn't it? Do I really take Jesus with me in a conscious sort of way when I go to work and stuff?"

Why had Philly feared telling Brenda about all this? She wasn't judging him. Her mother probably would judge him about all kinds of things. But Brenda didn't tell her mother everything. He *hoped* she didn't tell her mother everything. "Well, I think that's where I connected this dream of Jesus in the basement with the voice I heard in the car yesterday."

"It wasn't just a thought in your head?"
"Or my imagination."
"He spoke to you again *aloud*?"
"I think he did."
"It had to be him. Otherwise, how would you have known the old lady needed your help?"
"Right. How could I have known?"

Chapter 8
Let's Go and See Gladys

Philly hadn't even introduced himself to the thought, or the fear, that he might start to hear voices on a regular basis. But it happened again that morning, the sunny morning after he told Brenda about Jesus in the basement.

"Let's go and see Gladys."

Gladys? He had just thought of her that morning, remembering healing the little blonde girl's toe. What was the girl's name? He had forgotten. That encounter had been in Naperville, at a buffet restaurant where he had met Gladys and her granddaughter. Philly had been with Ray.

Now, his relationship with Gladys wasn't just from that one encounter over five years ago. In the interim, they had linked up on social media. The news he remembered about Gladys was probably all old. Her contributions to the social media stream had gotten stirred into the others that he generally ignored—words and pictures about someone's restaurant meal, someone else's exotic vacation, pet pictures, and another old acquaintance surviving some sort of surgery.

Let's go and see Gladys? Where was Gladys now? Philly couldn't even go to the last place, the only place, he had seen her. That whole chain of restaurants had closed, at least in the Chicago area.

Philly arrived at work that morning at the usual time, and he became instantly engrossed in troubleshooting a network issue. The system that connected the conference room reservation tablets, posted outside each of the meeting rooms, wasn't working.

Several of the tablets had lost their link to the internet, where the web-based service monitored room availability. It was a minor crisis. It was the sort of thing that consumed an entire morning of trial and error, testing and documenting. Finally, it was working again, and Philly was hungry.

He took the stairs up to the cafeteria on the sixth floor, carrying a laptop. He planned to eat lunch and do some personal computing. He'd brought a sandwich Brenda had made, and he planned to supplement it with fruit and a snack bar from the break room. His employer provided free snacks, many of them healthy. Though Philly still had to be careful to keep his calorie intake low, to maintain his new lower weight, he often grabbed one of those free snacks.

Parking himself, his company laptop, and his food at a table by a window overlooking a nearby forest preserve, Philly wondered if it was warm enough outside for a walk later. A sidewalk connected this office complex to paths that meandered through the trees in the county parkland on two sides of the commercial development. He was thinking about that when he hit the shortcut to his social media account. He was logged into that computer as a local user in order to protect his work profile and the company network from any infections lurking in non-work-related sites. He considered this social media site relatively safe.

A message awaited him when the site finished opening. It was probably Brenda sending him a cute video of a cat or a baby. Cats and babies were big parts of their lives these days.

At first, he didn't recognize the name on the message. It wasn't Brenda. It was someone called 'GrandmaGladys'. Was that just some kinky spam?

No, wait. *Gladys.*

Hi, Philly. Been a while since we wrote each other on here. How are you doing? I just had this odd notion that I should contact you. Any idea what that might be about?

Philly nearly swore out loud. A shiver wiggled him from belt to neck, and then from shoulder to shoulder. "Whoa!"

Someone was laughing. Was that Jesus?

Philly realized it was Tahaan, one of the project managers he knew by name, who was laughing. Apparently the younger guy had notice Philly writhing over his laptop.

Tahaan was still chuckling. "Find something freaky online, Phil? A scary video?"

"Ha. No. Just a scary coincidence. Freaky. Not really scary." He stopped himself before he said too much. He had spilled that much in an unguarded spurt. Having lost one job over his odd spiritual experiences, he was particularly cautious about appearing too religious or too strange at work.

"Serendipity? Is that what you mean? A convergence?"

"Oh. Well, I don't know about that. Just someone I haven't heard from in a long time, and I was just thinking I should contact her."

"Ah. An old girlfriend."

"No. She's a grandma. Just a friend, and old." It was a weird thing to say. But this whole conversation was weird. And it was distracting him from an important point. Gladys was feeling like she should contact *him* on the same day that the mysterious voice had told Philly to contact *her*. He shivered again but tried to cover it with a surge toward his lunch bag, as if he were suddenly really hungry. He *was* pretty hungry.

Philly chewed and swallowed, drank some Vitaminwater, and thought for a while before responding to Gladys. He wondered if he should talk to Brenda first, but that precaution might have only come to mind because of Tahaan's wayward guess about an old girlfriend. Of course, Brenda would tell him to answer GrandmaGladys right back.

Did her granddaughter, that little blonde girl, set up this account? GrandmaGladys.

He wrote her back after he finished his sandwich.

Hello Gladys,

Funny you should contact me today. I thought I heard a voice tell me I should go and see Gladys. Totally out of the blue. What do you think about that?

Philly

He paused for nearly a minute of reading and rereading before he sent it. He was chewing slowly on a fiber-rich snack bar. The worst-case scenario was that she would think he was crazy. But she had started this. Well, that voice had started it. Gladys was just an accomplice. And who knows? Maybe she had heard a voice telling her to contact him. He hit the send icon. Then he finished eating and went back to work.

Philly managed to resist checking his social media page all afternoon—until just before time to head for home. He checked his phone for a return message. One was waiting.

Philly,

Oh, that's exciting. I wasn't going to tell you that I heard a voice tell me to contact you. At least I was pretty sure I actually heard it. Not always easy to tell. Come visit me any time. I live here now ...

She included the address of a retirement home right there in Naperville. For a moment, he thought about driving straight there from work, but that seemed too risky and impulsive. Risky and impulsive wasn't his style. But, more than that, she might not have meant that he should come right away. He would want to warn her when he did come and visit. Surely she would appreciate that. That's how he talked himself out of an immediate visit. Instead, he answered,

Gladys, I actually work in Naperville now. I could stop by on my way home from work tomorrow. Is that okay with you?

Philly

By the time he got home that evening, Gladys had replied, and it was all set for him to visit her after five the next day.

"Wow. This is getting really exciting." Brenda was looking over his shoulder at the kitchen table, reading his conversation with Gladys. "It's almost like back when Jesus told you things to tell other people."

Philly didn't say anything. He was restraining his hope like it was an overly friendly dog lunging against its leash. For now, he would just try following these prompts from *the voice*. This was the second message involving an elderly woman, by the way. What was the significance of that?

Maybe this would be the extent of it—just hearing voices and doing what they said. Maybe the voice would only lead him to talking to a couple of lonely grandma types. Even that much sounded pretty crazy. But it wasn't so wild compared to what he had done back in the days when Jesus was walking right next to him.

Chapter 9
When Jesus was More Real

He knew it wasn't strictly right, but Philly thought of those days back when he could see and hear Jesus as when Jesus was more real. He was *realer*. Was that a word? Philly's life was full of words from Jesus back then—encouragements directed to him exclusively and guidance for healing others. And then Jesus went invisible. But the words and healings continued for a while.

His pastor, Dave Michaelson, had continually encouraged Philly to use the gift he had received from the living and breathing Jesus. Jesus hadn't taken that healing gift away with him when he went into stealth mode. And Dave had tried to instill in Philly a sense of responsibility to steward and grow that gift. He put Philly into all kinds of healing situations. Back in those days, Dave taught classes on using spiritual gifts, and he would invite Philly to attend the week when they discussed healing. The church that Dave pastored favored a show-and-tell style of teaching. Or maybe it was more like *tell and show*. Dave taught, then it was Philly's turn to show what Jesus had shown him.

Philly still clearly remembered one night nearly six years ago. Dave had issued a call for church people to bring sick and injured folks to the class so the students would have people to experiment on. He actually said it that way, not particularly religious about even supernatural healing. Dave's relaxed and natural approach fit Philly, including the notion of experimenting. As long as Philly knew he was just there to *try* and cooperate with Jesus's desire to heal people, he felt less pressure to perform. It was *less* pressure, but not a complete absence of pressure.

The usual suspects had taken Dave seriously and had invited their most sick or injured friends to the meeting. Philly could tell it was an unusually large group by the fact that he had to stand at the back of the room during the teaching. He could see no chairs available when he arrived a few minutes late.

"That'll teach you to be on time." Dave had teased him in front of the whole group—maybe forty or fifty people. But Philly, standing in the back and shrugging, was used to being teased by Dave, who was determined that no one should take themselves too seriously, including himself.

Even before Dave finished the teaching portion of the evening, Philly began to feel his attention drawn to a man in the front row— a man with a bald brown head ringed with a thin gray crown of hair. That was all Philly could see of him from the back. Philly assumed he was being drawn to the guy because he was supposed to try to heal him. He often got a sort of preview of what Jesus wanted to do, an idea coming to him through an intuitive part of his brain.

But the second time Philly felt his attention drawn to the man, Philly thought he saw something hovering over that bald head. It was a ghostly image. Was that a good thing? Philly had assumed he was getting a prompt to offer the guy healing. Healing would be a good thing. That the man had some sort of ghost thing floating over him didn't seem so good. Checking a third time, Philly realized that the faint image hovering over the man reminded him of Jesus. Maybe it even *was* Jesus.

This was after Jesus had officially gone invisible to Philly. Jesus himself had explained to Philly that this was normal. Invisibility mode was going to be the default for Jesus in his life. So why was he now seeing a visible hint of Jesus over that guy's head?

Dave interrupted Philly's hamster wheel of questions by calling him forward to start demonstrating his gift of healing.

By this time in Philly's relationship with that church, he had realized it was false humility to try and cast doubt on his gift. The evidence was clear. In any given church meeting, he could pick out at least one person who he had seen healed by the power of

Jesus flowing through his hands. He had stopped pretending that he didn't expect anything to happen when he tried to bring healing to people. Though all that was still a work in progress, of course.

He tried not to be self-conscious about the way he walked to the front of the room with a hundred eyes locked on him. But the thing about trying not to be self-conscious was that it's impossible. That was another thing Philly had been learning to accept in those days.

When he rounded the end of the front row, he was startled from his preoccupation with trying to look confident. There, in front of the man with the bald head, stood Jesus. It was like a faint copy of Jesus. This ghost Jesus was standing there smiling right at Philly.

Philly just missed tripping over the woman sitting at the end of the first row and didn't resist staring at the spot that contained the hologram of Jesus. Then Jesus disappeared. The disappearance was as startling as the appearance. And his gawking clearly made folks around him uncomfortable. Their lingering stares had mostly turned to confused scowls by the time he arrived at the front of the room and turned to look at the group.

Fortunately, Dave recognized what was going on. "So, Philly, I'm thinking you already know where to start with the healing."

Philly wasn't in the habit of saying anything even close to *Duh*. But he was having exactly that feeling right then. How could he possibly miss where he was supposed to start? He didn't even look at Dave. He just raised a hand toward the man in the front row. And, as he made that gesture, he thought he saw a picture of Jesus's hand resting on the man's left foot. This made Philly drop his gaze to the man's shoes. He managed to avoid dropping his mouth open as he did so. "Uh, sir, what's your name?" This was a successful start, as far as Philly was concerned. Dave's coaching was paying off. At least Philly remembered that much in his befuddlement.

"Rollins." The man's neatly curved eyebrows were about halfway up his forehead.

Philly hurdled over wondering whether Rollins was raising those eyebrows because he was baffled by Philly's attention, or because he was impressed that Philly had figured out what he needed. "You have pain in your left foot?"

"Ah, no. Not really. I came here tonight because I have heart palpitations."

"Oh, okay. Well, maybe I missed it, then." Right there, Philly had to decide what to do next. Should he try to heal the heart palpitations based on his certainty that Jesus wanted to start the healing off that evening by touching Rollins? Or should Philly give up and move on to someone else because he had been mistaken regarding Rollins's foot?

"I mean, I do have some discomfort in this foot." Rollins indicated his left foot. "But really I was hoping to get my heart healed."

Dave helped out. "Okay. So, here's a good lesson. Philly, you saw something specifically about Rollins's foot?"

"I saw Jesus put his hands on the left foot."

"Oh. Well, that's pretty clear. Do you usually see Jesus like that?" Of course, Dave knew all about Philly's experience of seeing Jesus, so he was just asking a methodological question about healing in the post-seeing-Jesus era. At least that's what Philly assumed.

"Uh, no. It's really rare for me." Philly looked hard at Rollins, hoping for some more visual aids from Jesus. But he saw nothing.

A woman in the second row chimed in. "I thought I saw a sort of a glow over his head—this gentleman in the front row."

Rollins put a hand to his shiny pate and laughed. "You sure you wasn't just seein' the shine off my bald spot?"

Dave and Philly laughed with him.

"So, I think we should start with the foot, since Philly saw a pretty clear indication of that, right? It was a pretty strong leading?" Dave kept things moving.

"Yes. That's what I was feeling when I asked him about the foot." Philly thought maybe Dave could interject a lesson here for those who wanted to receive healing—something like, if someone picks out an ailment you actually have, don't freak him out by saying that you don't have it. But that was just what Philly would do. Dave was the expert at this sort of training.

"Rollins, is that okay with you?" Dave proceeded with characteristic deference to the person needing the healing.

"Sure. I have some bone spurs in this foot, which only bother me when the weather is cold, or some such."

"Okay. Do you feel pain now?" It was a cold and wet day in Chicago, though still early autumn.

"Yeah. I suppose I do." Rollins slid forward in his chair and stretched his left leg to adjust the angle of his foot on the hard gray carpet. "Yeah. It does hurt a bit when I do that."

"Well then stop doing that." Dave got the crowd laughing. Then he nodded to Philly to go ahead.

Between Dave and Jesus, Philly had all the direction he needed. And he was used to healing coming in a variety of styles and sizes, so he stepped forward and knelt in front of Rollins.

For whatever reason, Rollins seemed to recoil a bit. Maybe he didn't expect the healer to drop to his knees.

What came to mind for the method of this particular healing was to try and emulate Jesus's hand in the way Philly had seen him touch that foot. So he scooted to one side and used his right hand to cover the top of the left shoe. Then, without any further ceremony, he said, "In the name of Jesus, I heal this foot. Bone spurs, be gone." The run-up to this healing was unique, but that didn't mean Philly had to do anything unusual to cooperate with that healing.

At the time, Philly was still transitioning out of seeing and hearing Jesus with him day in and day out, so anything he did to heal people after that seemed relatively reasonable.

It was a lesson in the adaptability of people, perhaps. Because, looking back on it these years later, it all seemed very bizarre to him. Philly couldn't imagine doing any of that stuff now. He was hearing Jesus give him instructions again for the first time in a long time. But he was having trouble even trusting his ears and admitting that he was hearing it.

When Rollins's foot was healed that night long ago, the heat he reported feeling, the test Dave had him do by standing and stamping his foot on the floor, and his subsequent dance of celebration, all fit into Philly's reality. But Philly's reality had changed after that—when he failed to heal Theresa.

Because of Theresa's death, Philly had given up on healing. He had given up on hoping. And he had given up on seeing and hearing Jesus, even if only a faint ghost of Jesus hovering over a guy's bald head.

Part of the charm that drew Philly back to that memory about Rollins was the way Jesus had also healed those heart palpitations, as if he wanted to build some faith by starting with the foot and then working his way up from there. That had been Philly's impression at the time, anyway. It was only an impression. But, these days, an impression of what Jesus might be thinking would be a revolution in Philly's mundane life.

Maybe Philly had opened some kind of new door in his ordinary life.

Jesus seemed to be getting more real again. Realer.

Chapter 10
Meeting at Gladys's New Place

After work the next day, Philly set his phone GPS to take him to a retirement living community a few miles from his work. He had been in this current job for six months, but he still didn't know much about the town in which he worked.

Philly's impression of Gladys's life in Naperville, gleaned online, was of a very busy woman now eighties. She reminded Philly of his Grandma Thompson, a church lady who devoted as much of her time to her church as to her family. Gladys had moved at some point to be close to her daughter and granddaughter. At least, one of her granddaughters.

Philly's grandma had never moved to one of those retirement homes. In a sense, she had died with her boots on, refusing to be warehoused even when she was slowing and wearing down. But the place Philly now approached looked nothing like a warehouse. It looked like a charming suburban community, not a lot different from the townhouse-lined neighborhood in which Philly and Brenda lived.

Pulling into the asphalt parking lot next to the building in which Gladys lived, Philly squinted into the late afternoon sun. As he turned his car toward an empty parking space, he slammed on his brakes, startled by the appearance of an old lady right near his chosen parking spot. He shaded his eyes with one hand and figured out that he hadn't been in any danger of running over the slightly hunched woman with a small cloud of white hair.

The woman was Gladys. She had come out to meet him.

When he stepped out of the car, Gladys was standing with her hands clasped behind her back. She was wearing a medium-weight red jacket. She seemed smaller than he remembered, though he had been sitting down for that one earlier encounter. And she seemed a bit frailer, though the big outdoor setting might have contributed to that impression.

"Philly, so good to see you again." Gladys extended a hand to him, and he took it before stepping up onto the curb.

"Hi, Gladys. I'm glad to see *you*." He hesitated a second and then jumped right in. "I guess Jesus wants us to get together. I think it might have to do with us both seeing him before. I seem to need to kinda get back into that sorta thing."

Gladys just nodded. She didn't look confused by Philly's hasty opening remarks. Stepping back from the curb to give Philly room to join her on the sidewalk, she motioned to her right. "You wanna go for a walk? It's time for me to get some exercise."

"I could sure use some exercise." He steered himself into the space beside her.

The grass next to the walkway was already green and cropped short like the first cut of fringe next to a golf fairway. Philly had passed a golf course on the way in, which might explain the analogy.

"How have you been? What have you been hearing from Jesus these days?" Gladys accelerated to a fairly brisk pace for her shorter legs. Philly guessed this was meant to match his normal gait, or at least find a middle ground.

"I've been okay. I've been through a lot since Theresa died. Sort of a journey of trying to figure out what's going on with me. I haven't really been hearing much from Jesus until just this week."

"Oh. Why this week, do you think?"

Philly shrugged. "I really can't say. But that was always how it seemed to me. I was sure Jesus had reasons for when he did certain things, but I wasn't gonna necessarily understand his reasons."

"You've been in church these days?"

"Yeah. My wife, Brenda, and I are going to a kind of modern church that puts a lot of emphasis on reaching your neighbors and being relevant to the culture. We like the sort of casual atmosphere there."

"I did see that you were married. I don't think I sent you a congratulations at the time. So, congratulations." She chuckled, maybe a little uncomfortably.

"Oh. Thanks. I thought I saw that you were dating someone there for a while."

"Yeah. That was some time ago. I gave it a try. He was a nice man. He passed on last year. But we weren't really a couple by the time he got sick. He had moved back to be with his kids in Texas toward the end. And I moved down here for the same reason."

"So, your family lives nearby?"

"Yes. Katie, my granddaughter, could ride her bike over here. It's just a mile or so. Not that she has time to come over here very often."

"Oh. Sure." Philly didn't know what to say about the hint that Gladys was being neglected by her family.

"It's not just her that's busy. I keep myself occupied pretty well. I moved here to be close to the kids, but also to get my daughter to stop bugging me. She's a worrier. Of course, she got some of that from me. But I just thought I may as well make it easier for her by moving close. Worrying is easier at a shorter distance, I guess."

"That makes sense to me."

"But I didn't wanna move in with them like she was offering. My oldest granddaughter's bedroom is available now. She's grown up and gone off on her own. But I still wanted some independence. And I was hearing Jesus tell me to think of this place as my mission field. I sorta joke with him that it's like with the apostle Paul ministering to the guards while he was in prison." She chuckled some more.

"Fortunately, this doesn't really look like a prison." Philly surveyed the wide lawns and tidy buildings of the graduated care facility, and the comfortable houses on the other side of the quiet street on which they now walked.

"Indeed. I've met a few folks around here who talk like they'd been sent away for some kinda crime, like getting old is a crime. But lots of my neighbors who live in their own apartments by me are plenty happy. It's a nice place."

"So, you're still hearing Jesus? He's telling you ways to minister to people around here?"

"Yes. I volunteer over at the part where some older ones are confined to wheelchairs and some are kinda losin' track of things, ya know." She gestured toward a large two-story building across the lawn to their left. "Jesus tells me things to say to them that bring some encouragement." She suddenly cackled. "I even helped a man find his teeth that he misplaced. I tell ya, Jesus can be pretty handy with things like that."

Snorting at the way she laughed, Philly was getting curious. "You sound like you still see and hear him just like back before I met you."

She shook her head. "No. Not just like that. But he showed me then that I could quiet myself down sometimes and listen inside for his voice. I still do that. I even sit on my couch like he showed me. Not that the couch is magical or anything, but just 'cause I got into the habit of doing it there, and 'cause it works. At least, it works for me most of the time." She glanced at Philly, as if checking whether she had lost him with any of what she was saying.

He knew what it was like to be so sure that his experience was real while also knowing that most of the people he told about it didn't fully believe him. He smiled at Gladys and allowed himself to slide back into those days of a thoroughly visible and audible Jesus. That fueled his smile more intensely still.

She turned the tables on Philly. "But you've been hearing from him lately, then? Even though he's not sitting on your furniture and eating your pancakes."

"He never did eat with me. It blew my mind when I found out he ate with you."

"Maybe it's just because us grandmas like to feed people. He knew it was important to me."

Philly laughed. "For me, he just kept stretching my budget by suggesting I go out to restaurants all the time."

"Maybe that's why he didn't eat with you. He didn't wanna run up the restaurant tab." She squeaked a little laugh and raised her dark gray eyebrows in an impish way.

Philly laughed harder than he had in a long time. Then he remembered that he hadn't answered her question. "Oh. Yeah. Well, I think he *has* started talking to me again. I wasn't really sure about it until I had a dream the other night. And in the dream, he met me in my basement."

"Oh, really? What was that like?"

Philly recounted the dream. And, just as when he told Brenda about it, he noticed more about it in the retelling. "I couldn't help notice the way the arms of the recliner were all worn down, as if he had been resting his hands there for years and years. But he really didn't look angry or seem tired from all that waiting."

"Well, sure. He's not ever gonna get tired. But the things of earth will get old and worn down."

"The things of earth?"

"It's from an old song I learned in church as a girl."

"Where do you go to church? Do they teach about Jesus talking to you there?"

Gladys tipped her head to the side and then shook it briefly. "I've been taking seriously what Jesus said about my mission being here at this place. So, I've been going to the services they have over at the chapel there." She indicated the larger building toward which they had just turned.

Philly glanced that way through the long shadows of budding trees that were portioning out stripes of sunlight. "I guess what they teach there has to be kinda generic."

"Yes. Generic and geriatric." Gladys laughed at her own joke. "It has to be kinda slow moving, and the chaplain has to repeat herself pretty often."

Philly's laugh was more restrained than hers. He didn't feel as free to laugh about the limitations of old people as Gladys clearly did. She was a spry eighty-something, but clearly spent lots of time with people older and more limited than her. That raised a question. "Are you doing any healing stuff?"

"When I get a chance, I do try. I like to tell folks about my hips being healed. I walk without any pain now. Never could've done this walk with you before Jesus straightened that out." She raised her hands slightly as if to turn her ordinary walk into a demonstration.

"Does that convince them?"

"Oh, you know, some folks are just never gonna be convinced. Maybe some get convinced that I'm a nut or a liar, but I don't mind. I just offer to pray. And I don't make any guarantees. I don't see 'em healed most of the times I try. Unless it's a little headache or something like that. I find that one prayer and two aspirins are pretty effective." She chuckled a bit, then seemed to cut herself short. "But, hey, you healed Katie's toe just like that. Are you doing any more of that sorta thing?"

Philly allowed himself a confessional sigh. He wasn't going to hide anything from Gladys, but that didn't mean he was anxious to admit the disappointing truth. "When Theresa didn't get healed no matter how many times I tried to heal her, and no matter how many other people from church prayed for her, I had a real crisis. It seemed like Jesus had abandoned me all over again. My pastor tried to explain how it's the enemy who makes people sick and not to blame God. But still, I was devastated that Jesus didn't do anything to keep Theresa alive."

Gladys just glanced at him, allowing some space for him to say more.

"Maybe that's what's changed now. I'm married, and I'm not depressed like I was about losing Theresa. Maybe I'm more ready to listen now. But I doubt I'll get to do more healing. I pretty much rejected that. Your granddaughter was the last person I even tried to heal."

"You feel like you disqualified yourself?"

"Sure. I guess so. Didn't I? I mean, God is patient and all, but he's not gonna ignore me sayin' I'm done with it, and that I'm mad at him 'cause he didn't heal when I wanted him to."

Gladys was staring into the blue sky above the big nursing facility as they turned again to follow the sidewalk around the lawn. "I had this friend who moved to the mission field in Africa this year. But, when we were still meeting on a regular basis, she said something to me that stuck. She said this thing about a mistake so many folks make about God. We use words like *holy* to show that God is totally different than us. But then, when we start to feel guilty about something, we start thinking of God as being just *like* us. Her point was how God is way better at forgiving and forgetting than any of us humans are. And we shouldn't ever assume it's so hard for him."

"So, God could forgive me for being mad at him for not healing Theresa?"

She cocked her head sideways to get a look into Philly's face. "Is it you who's mad at God? Or is it you thinkin' that God is mad at you?"

"Maybe both. Maybe neither now, though."

"Well, it sounds like he's still talkin' to you."

"He told me to come and see you like the three of us were old friends."

"Well, I am old. And I'm glad to be your friend, Philly."

Philly laughed a bit more comfortably this time.

Chapter 11
A Visit with His Parents

Philly's parents still lived in the same house on the north side of Chicago, a gentrifying neighborhood where single-story ranch houses were being supplanted by four- and five-bedroom homes that bulged in the small lots. Philly could tell that his ma was trying to keep up with the upscale neighbors.

"Those are really nice curtains, Ma." Brenda had her arms crossed and an iced tea propped in one hand as she examined the heavy floral print drapes in the living room—a new addition.

"I had to twist your father's arm to pay for those—like I was asking him to put in a swimming pool or something." Philly's ma said it with only a little acid in her voice and a small smile as punctuation.

"I heard that." Philly's dad was in the kitchen getting the Sunday meal ready to put on the table. His comment from the other room was countered by the pipe-like bark of the highly vocal Lhasa apso in the dining room. The little dog was pacing back and forth, monitoring both the man in the kitchen and the three folks in the living room.

"He hears everything. Him and that dog." Philly's ma was maintaining her contention that the dog belonged to his dad and not to both of them. That was her position this time. Their previous dog, a fat old Scottie, had died of obesity-related illness. Dad had been the primary provider of fattening food for the old terrier, and Ma was clearly protecting herself from getting too attached to another furry critter in the house.

Philly liked the new dog, Sparks, almost as much as he had liked Blacky, their previous dog. "C'mon, Sparks. No more barks, Sparks." He leaned down and reached for the little dog. The little mop of a mammal pranced toward Philly on shaggy feet. The dog panted his satisfaction at garnering some attention from one of the guests. He seemed to like Philly more than he liked Ma, at whom he uttered a low growl occasionally.

Brenda was still on the curtains. "Maybe we should get some of these, Philly. I think they would go well with our couch. And they could cut the sunlight when it gets too sunny."

Philly thought that *too sunny* was an impossibility, but he guessed that Brenda was accounting for their living room being a southern exposure. Winter sun could never be too much, he was pretty sure. And anyway, he really didn't like his mother's cream-colored curtains with their swirls of yellow, orange, and aqua blue. He couldn't tell if Brenda actually liked them, or if she was just trying to butter up his ma.

He didn't have to answer Brenda's appeal for new drapery. Dad interrupted with a call to Sunday dinner.

"The dog goes in the bedroom." Philly's ma laid down the law, though Philly had heard it before. He just happened to be holding the little animal as he walked toward the dining room. Diverting toward the guest bedroom, Philly set Sparks down with apologies and shut the door behind him. But not before an indignant look from the dog for this betrayal.

That was one of the reasons Philly didn't want a dog of his own—he felt their pain too deeply. Cats were much better for him. Clearly, the average cat had no pain, and if it did have, a cat would never stoop to sharing its feelings with an unreliable guy like Philly. He was fine with that arrangement.

Seating himself at the table between Brenda and his dad, Philly absorbed the savory steam of the green bean casserole along with the homey aroma of mashed potatoes, gravy, and especially the blade roast, which his dad had cooked to crumbling tenderness. But his culinary reverie was interrupted by a weak moan from Brenda. For a moment, he wondered if his wife had suddenly become a vegetarian. The big, singed roast would have turned the stomach of vegan and vegetarian alike. "What's up?" He said it in the lowest voice that could possibly reach her amidst the sliding of chairs, the clattering of dishes and flatware, and his dad's habitual humming in appreciation. Just because he cooked the meal didn't mean Dad couldn't enjoy the anticipation of eating it.

"Uh, I don't know. My stomach suddenly feels sorta queasy."

"Are you pregnant?" Philly's ma hadn't missed their covert conversation. She was leaning slightly forward on the opposite side of the table. Her relaxed gaze and the level set of her head betrayed nothing about whether she was joking.

If she hadn't said it, Philly wouldn't have suspected that pregnancy was the reason for Brenda's sudden queasiness.

"Oh. I don't think so. I mean, well, I don't know. The food looks so good, but suddenly I just can't imagine eating any of it." Then Brenda turned her head toward the little relish dish filled with olives—black and green in separate compartments. "Except the black olives. Those look so good."

"You're pregnant." His ma definitely wasn't joking this time.

Brenda just popped a black olive into her mouth and stared at her mother-in-law. "Hmm. Well, we'll see." Then she loaded half a dozen more of the shiny black orbs onto her plate.

"I'll let you off this time." Philly's dad had been watching from the head of the table. "But you better bring us a grandbaby soon to prove it." He grinned his usual joking sideways smile. Then he surprised Philly. "Maybe we should start dinner with a prayer, given the occasion."

It was an unusual suggestion, but Brenda being pregnant would be an unusual circumstance. How praying before the meal followed the prospect of a baby on the way would have been hard for Philly to explain. But he didn't argue.

"Well, Lord, thank you for this meal, this really good food, even if not everyone is feeling like eating it. And thank you for family and the prospect of new life. And, anyway, help Brenda's tummy to feel better. Okay, thanks. Amen."

Talking to Jesus face-to-face had shaped his style of praying more than anything else. This family very rarely prayed before a meal. No one complained about the method or contents of his prayer.

Only after he "hung up the call," did he stop to seriously consider that Brenda might actually be pregnant. That churning uncertainty stunted his appetite quite a bit, though he indulged in more than just the black olives.

They bought a pregnancy test at a pharmacy near Ma and Dad's house. Brenda called to leave a message at her gynecologist's office while Philly drove them up Interstate 90 toward home.

"What if I *am* pregnant, Philly?" Brenda's voice quavered a little.

"That's what we wanted. That would be good."

"But I'm getting so old. I have old eggs. What if they can't hatch?"

"You're not a chicken."

"Women have eggs too."

"But they don't hatch."

"That's not the point."

Philly snickered. "That's good, 'cause I don't want a kid who hatches out of an egg, old or otherwise."

"Philly! I'm serious."

"But you were the one who said that thing about old eggs."

"That's a serious thing."

"It is? I mean, really, you're not that old. Not even forty. Lots of women have babies these days when they're forty. We talked about this already."

"But that doesn't mean I'm not scared."

Philly let that settle in. Of course he wasn't going to argue Brenda out of being scared. Instead, he thought of a better option. "Well, Jesus, please give us courage and confidence that you are going to take care of us, whether we're two or we're three of us—or more. Thanks, Lord."

Brenda stared at him. But the look on her face was neither confusion nor disdain. "Thanks, Philly. That was good." She looked ahead at the dry gray highway. "But I'm not agreeing to have twins, just so you know."

Philly laughed, pretty sure he didn't need to amend his prayer.

Chapter 12
Getting Ready to be Parents

That week, when they received confirmation from the doctor that the pregnancy test and the black olives had been accurate, Philly thought of all the people he wanted to call and tell the good news.

"But we should wait until it's farther along, Philly. There's no need to get people all excited about it if it doesn't come to term."

That sounded like the gloomy Brenda of an earlier time in his life. But it also sounded reasonable. He had heard of other couples waiting a while before they spread the baby news. When that was all settled in his mind, he felt a knot of emotion fill his throat. They were at home now, landed out of the shock of the big news at the doctor's office. Philly stiffened his back against the full weight of that news. The urge to cry seemed to have something to do with the prospect of a little guy or girl calling him *Daddy*. It had to do with the knowledge that he was going to share the whole transformative experience with Brenda. And it came wrapped in the feeling that he wouldn't be alone in his life, that his bond with Brenda was lasting, and that their bond would be extended to include another person.

"You were never alone, Philly."

He was standing in the kitchen refilling a water glass for another long drink. A salty lunch had left him thirsty, and the trip to the gynecologist had blanked out all lesser priorities such as thirst. But now all of it, even thirst, got lost behind another one of those crazy moments. A voice in the kitchen. A voice giving him a small reassurance.

"I'm so hungry. How about we celebrate by eating out and going to the bookstore for some baby books on the way home?" Brenda had clearly put some thought into how she wanted to celebrate their good news.

"Okay." Philly was off balance after that rise of emotions and then the apparent intervention by *the voice*. He even briefly forgot the fact that he had already eaten out for lunch, which was good reason not to go out for dinner on most days. He didn't change his vote, however.

They were sitting in a Japanese restaurant, Philly scooping the last of his beef teriyaki and Brenda slurping the last of her sushi, when he heard the voice again. "That man could use some healing."

Maybe it wasn't an actual voice from outside his head, but the words were so clear and understandable that they may as well have been spoken by a man sitting across from him. It was Brenda who was sitting across from him. His wife had wanted sushi in her pregnant state. It seemed a doubtful choice for a squeamish stomach, but she insisted that sushi sounded wonderful to her. It was only Philly who it made feel queasy.

Now the top of his stomach twisted under the sort of anxious twirl that came with someone asking him to do something dangerous—even more dangerous than eating raw fish. Part of what felt so dangerous was that he knew which man *the voice* wanted to heal. The man facing Philly at the table across from them looked slightly green, with darker green circles around his eyes. Philly had noted that condition before the man ordered sushi. And he was pretty sure the guy wasn't pregnant. Philly had no idea why the man looked so sick, and he had harbored no intentions of finding out. In fact, even after the input from that voice, he wasn't feeling any ambition for finding out the cause of the man's ill complexion, nor any ambition to heal whatever it was.

"You okay, Philly? You look a little sick." Brenda was staring at him with her metal chopsticks poised over her plate.

Was the man's sickly complexion reflecting on Philly's face? He shook that thought away and answered half-heartedly. "I was just noticing how sick that guy looks over there." He muttered it under his breath. "Don't look." He stopped Brenda from turning all the way around.

"He looks bad enough to make you lose your appetite?"

Philly had slowed his eating, but that was because he was realizing how much he had violated his diet already today. Flagging down the waiter for the check, Philly just shook his head. He hoped she would think he was cutting off the conversation out of discretion regarding discussing the health of someone at the next table. He doubted he had completely fooled her.

In the car, he found evidence that his wife was conspiring with *the voice*. "Do you think you were supposed to try and heal that guy?"

He inhaled and held that breath for a second. "Maybe. But I'm still not feeling like I can do that anymore."

"You might have to try it sometime to find out."

Brenda was like that more so these days than when they first worked together in Chicago. She was wise. She was also prone to stating the obvious. And that obviousness was obvious because it was wise.

Philly knew he would have to try it in order to find out if he could heal anyone these days—if Jesus could still use him, at least for small things. He drove away from the restaurant thinking that the man with the green complexion probably had some *big* thing wrong with him. Maybe his deadly disease wasn't a good place to start trying to heal people, especially in a public place like that.

By the time they pulled into the parking lot in front of the big bookstore, Philly had managed to discard his worries about whether he had dodged a chance to try healing again. He wriggled free of the feeling that Jesus had spoken to him and that he had ignored his invisible friend. After all, the voice hadn't told him that he *should* heal the green man.

Philly was still fretting over it, obviously, but baby books were the agenda once they entered the store. Brenda pulled Philly's focus along with hers. Baby name books, baby parenting books, and books to read to babies. It was like a whole baby culture. Philly was about to embark on a cross-cultural experience. He was entering the land of the babies.

In contrast to Philly, Brenda had an expansive capacity for browsing. She was a seasoned shopper. More a shopper than a buyer. Philly was more interested in purchasing, getting it bought, and getting home. Brenda was more interested in the journey, the wonder of exploration, the careful examination of every item on a given shelf.

Philly gradually drifted away. He noticed the Christian book section across the wide aisle. Glancing at Brenda, he made his escape as she reached for yet another volume on baby names. She had half a dozen books cradled in one arm. Philly was carrying two more. He assumed they wouldn't actually buy all of them.

He snuck across the wide demarcation between the land of babies and the land of God, or at least books about God. A lot of the books in that other land looked like self-help books—being the better you and stuff like that. Then he noticed a Christian fiction section. That category of books had never occurred to him. Christian fiction. It seemed an ironic category. Wasn't Christianity all about truth? How could you have Christian fiction? He could imagine atheists laughing at the black-and-white sign on the end of the stack of shelves. For them, Christianity itself was fiction. Christian fiction was a redundancy.

But he stopped the prattling critique inside his head when a title caught his attention. *Jesus Beside Me.* He picked it up. The book cover showed a guy who was probably supposed to be Jesus sitting in a chair in a living room across from another guy. The angle of the portrayal was from behind and to the side of Jesus, so Philly couldn't say whether the artist had faithfully captured the real Jesus. But there was something familiar about what Philly could see of this living-room Jesus. He read the name of the author. Jason Stivers. Then he read the back of the dust jacket on the hardback cover. "Imagine finding Jesus in your living room, just sitting there waiting for you to join him for a friendly conversation." Philly allowed his eyes to roll over the rest of the words of the blurb, but he wasn't taking in any of it. He blindly opened the book and read a scene in the third or fourth chapter where the main character was trying to decide if he was crazy, or if he was actually seeing the real Jesus. Philly's palms were sweating. His head was swimming. He might fall over at any moment.

"Philly? What's wrong? Now you *really* look sick."

He turned to Brenda and grinned at her.

She wasn't grinning back, probably fearing for his sanity.

He held the book out to her, at a loss for words.

Chapter 13
Is This the Right Church?

Philly and Brenda were like most couples planning to start a family. Church felt like part of a responsible parent's toolbox for preparing their kids for the world. They had selected the church they now attended at the recommendation of a woman in Brenda's women's Bible study in Chicago. They were still in the getting acquainted stage when they attended that next Sunday.

With little previous experience in church, Philly was pretty close to starting from scratch with this new congregation. That the externals all looked familiar helped him make that start, but he could sense that the internals might be somehow different from his church in Chicago. The faithful arrived in casual attire, and the crowd was diverse but tending toward young and professional couples with a significant group of singles. The worship was contemporary and somewhat expressive, though maybe a bit more restrained than in his previous church. Many of the songs were the same ones, and the central faith of the preachers seemed to also be the same. It was all about learning to live as a follower of Jesus.

But in none of the half dozen or so services they had attended had Philly heard anything about healing. No teaching, no testimonies of sicknesses vanishing or bones rapidly restored. Philly knew, somewhat vaguely, that there were a variety of ways to be a follower of Jesus. His experience in Pastor Dave's church had been purely that, an experience. He had attended lots of classes there, and he had learned a lot. But he had learned hardly anything about the alternative sorts of churches out there. Or out here—in the suburbs.

Hints about the possible difference between this new church and his old one began to worry Philly a bit, especially as he considered that Jesus seemed to be nudging him back toward offering healing to the people around him. Where he had balked at offering to pray for that stranger in the restaurant, he was hoping for a more hospitable environment for his first forays back toward that ministry. Church had always been that friendly environment for Philly and his gifts—back when he felt like he had gifts.

All this came into fine focus on this Sunday. The sermon on pathways to freedom from fear and shame had ended, and the folks around Philly and Brenda were milling toward the aisles of the large auditorium. Sharp laughter cut through the sound-dampening of the plush seats and carpeted floor, and through a babbling chatter of little greetings.

Philly and Brenda had just reached the aisle when he overheard a welcoming conversation between someone apparently new to the church and someone with a longer history there. Names had been exchanged, at least first names, but Philly didn't catch all that. What he did catch was a question and a resounding silence in response.

"Hey, so Salma and I met this guy at this restaurant, and he prayed for her and totally healed her breathing problem. He told us we should go to church. And we heard that people do that same kinda healing thing in church. So, who do I see here about getting healed?"

This church identified itself as seeker-sensitive, open and inviting to those who were lost and who were seeking an easy on-ramp to God and Christianity. As Philly had noted, that invitation hadn't yet included offers of healing. The sermon this morning had mentioned emotional healing, and the pastor had advocated forms of therapy that would lead to freedom. Perhaps that had sounded like a healing invitation to this new guy.

Apparently, Brenda had overheard the question as clearly as Philly had. She gave him one of those patented wifely elbows in the ribs that would probably cost her royalties paid to whomever held that patent. Perhaps it was Eve, in the garden. And, of course, Philly knew the meaning of that poke in the side.

He was, however, currently preoccupied with the tongue-tied nonresponse of the guy who had greeted the new couple. The gray-haired man, with stylish, wire-rimmed glasses and a button-down pink shirt, seemed to be trying to read some small print on the visitor's forehead.

The visitor, a younger guy with longish black hair and intense stubble on his face, blinked in apparent confusion. The dumbfounded reaction of the friendly church member was anything but welcoming.

Observing this apparent breakdown tweaked a bit of guilt in Philly. He had long ago realized his tendency to feel guilty for other people's misdeeds. When they were kids and his sister broke something in the basement, he had stood by with his face turning red as if he had been the clumsy assailant against his mother's floor lamp. Similar experiences had rerun many times through Philly's life. Right now he was feeling the embarrassment of the gray-haired man, who might have an answer to the question about healing, but seemed very reluctant to admit what that answer was.

"Philly, go ahead." Brenda added vocabulary to her thump in the ribs.

"Uh, hi. My name is Phil." He and Brenda had both coasted right into the middle of the three-way greeting in the crowded aisle. A stream of people were flowing past the little clot that was now corralled to one side. The gray-haired guy welcomed the interruption with an unmistakably grateful smile. But he might not have been anticipating what Philly was about to offer.

The new guy shook Philly's hand and introduced himself as Sergio. With him was a slender woman with caramel skin and black hair. Her name was Salma. The gray-haired man was Matt. These introductions only delayed Philly's obligation to reveal the reason for his intervention.

His elevating heart rate and increasingly shallow breathing were distracting him. "I know this might be unusual here, but I actually have, uh, done ... uh, given ... uh, prayed for ... some healing ... sometimes ... uh, in the past."

So, it wasn't his best opening line, but the new guy looked relieved.

Peripherally, Philly thought he noticed a grimace on Matt's face. But he chose to ignore that for the sake of propping up his wobbly courage.

Brenda helped. "He's being humble. He's seen lots of people healed." His wife was pushing him forward, though no longer physically pushing. She added that clarification in a voice that was confiding and apologetic, not bragging or pushy.

Sergio nodded. He didn't seem confused or discouraged. Instead, he lifted his right hand toward Philly. "I fell and sprained my wrist, and it's been really slow to heal. It's been affecting my work. I'm a web developer and use this hand for controlling a mouse and typing."

Philly could relate. And he had seen several people healed of wrist pain related to computer use. He remembered here, in the midst of his windstorm of emotions, that an injury from an accident could be approached in a specific way. "Okay if I touch it just lightly?" This introductory question was another piece of healing protocol he still remembered.

Lowering his hand toward Philly, Sergio agreed. Salma drew closer, offering Philly a little extra shelter. He was glad for the cover. He looked at Salma, who had apparently been healed of something recently. "You wanna put your hand here too, on his, to help me?" He was hoping to leverage any faith she might have as a result of her own healing experience.

Salma bugged her eyes and shrugged. "Okay. Sure." She gently touched Sergio's wrist with three fingers.

"Okay. So, in the name of Jesus, I command this wrist to be free from all pain, and for any swelling in any parts of it to go down and go away." Philly probably said all that a bit faster than he needed to, but he had noticed a passerby craning his neck to see what was going on in the little circle of lingerers. Philly looked at Sergio's face. "You notice any difference?"

Shaking his head slowly, Sergio pulled his wrist back and began flexing his hand back and forth and then in circles. He stopped shaking his head and arched his eyebrows. "Well, maybe. It does kinda feel better."

Philly took a deep breath and allowed himself a preliminary grin. "Okay. Let's try again." And he repeated nearly the same command. But he remembered the part about the accident this time. "And, by the Holy Spirit, I break off the power of the trauma done to this wrist."

At this point, Matt said, "Huh." It was a notable break from his silence, which Philly assumed meant that something he had just said had disrupted the older man's reserved judgement. At least, that's what he had been reading into Matt's silent observation.

"Hey. Oh, yeah. Oh, hey, that feels good." Sergio was flexing his wrist again. "I was gonna have to take unpaid leave this week, and we have lots of bills due. I didn't know how we were gonna make it. I was desperate."

Salma clapped her hands in a small rapid rhythm and squealed, bouncing on her toes.

"Huh. Yeah. Maybe that's why God healed it. Because you were desperate." Those were Matt's first full sentences since Philly intervened.

Philly wasn't totally comfortable with Matt's interpretation, but he felt unqualified to question it. He surrendered now to the warm rush of relief flooding through him.

Brenda elevated that good feeling with a grateful grin she aimed at him. "Thank you, Jesus." She offered praise that would have been common in their church in Chicago, and very common in his grandma's old church.

But Philly saw another scowl cloud Matt's face.

As if sensitive to Philly's attention, Matt softened a bit. "Well, I've never seen anything like that. That was something." He sounded about thirty percent enthusiastic. Which probably wasn't really enthusiastic after all.

Philly appreciated the effort, nonetheless.

Chapter 14
Going Back to the Basement

Sunday afternoons at their house had become quieter since the end of the football season. Brenda often spoke with her sister in Spokane for some large chunk of the stretch between lunch and supper. And Philly usually noodled around fixing things—tight doors or loose handles, dripping sinks or stained toilets. But he had finished lots of those little projects before this Sunday. And the healing at church had unsettled him, like a house shoved off its foundation by a passing tornado.

The dream in which Jesus was waiting for Philly to come down to the basement to talk to him came to mind as he treaded down the stairs, past the front door, to his man cave. Brenda was up in the living room dialing her sister. Lunch was still settling in his stomach, leftover pork tenderloin from an early season attempt at grilling on the narrow deck off the kitchen. Now he was hoping to get back to that dream about Jesus in the basement.

It hadn't exactly been *this* basement in the dream. The recliners were different. Philly's chairs were plush microfiber and not leather. But he could still feel a bit of the scene of that dream coming to life as he stepped onto the carpet. There wasn't carpet in the dream, and there had been a fireplace. Those were just distracting details.

Normally, Philly would have been coming down here to watch a game. He had a computer desk wedged in the corner, and might come down to do some remote work for his employer, under certain circumstances. Those were the usual distractions that would have acted like virtual reality goggles over his eyes, preventing him from sitting down to talk to Jesus.

Of course, any place could be a place to meet with Jesus. Philly had been grateful that Jesus never followed him into the bathroom back in those days when he was available in full 3D with surround sound. But Jesus had reminded Philly then that not seeing him in the bathroom didn't mean he was excluded from any room of the house.

Philly tried to focus on the here and now. He stood looking at the two recliners. Jesus, in the dream, had worn out the one on the left. For continuity, Philly sat in the one on the right. It was his usual spot. He looked over at the other recliner and imagined Jesus sitting there. He closed his eyes and pictured it. And when he did, he thought about how Jesus hadn't been trying to get him to meet for some kind of important talk. It was more like inviting him down here to hang out. The Jesus who had visited him those years ago had been very good at hanging out, though he certainly did have lots to say, whenever Philly felt inclined to listen. Would things be any different now?

He pictured Jesus leaning back in the recliner, his feet up, a smile on his face. Philly leaned back, flipping the lever on the right side of the chair. It didn't feel like he had to imitate Jesus's imagined posture, but reclining next to Jesus seemed the friendly thing to do.

Once he had reclined and closed his eyes, the inevitable began to happen. Lunch still settling, the house quiet except for very faint music from the neighbors to the east, and Brenda's cheerful and inarticulate tones upstairs, Philly began to drift. He flung his eyes open and groaned. What a failure. Here he was trying to reconnect with Jesus, and all he could do was take a nap.

"Naps were one of my favorite things, back in the day. I could even take a nap in the middle of a lake on a small boat in a storm." That was *not* Philly talking to himself.

Jesus?

What was he saying?

As usual, Philly had to get over the fact that Jesus seemed to be talking to him before he could begin to absorb what Jesus had actually *said*. A nap? A storm?

The most familiar thing about what Jesus had said was his tone. The tone wasn't angry. Jesus wasn't mad at Philly. Even if Philly had tried to swap hanging out with Jesus for taking a Sunday afternoon nap, Jesus was still willing to cut him some slack. And, actually, Philly had not been trying for that swap. It just happened.

"Only natural."

Was that just from himself, or from Jesus? It could be either.

Was it true? Sure, it *was* natural to take a nap after a substantial lunch on a quiet Sunday. Philly had even faded from a few Cubs games to snooze for a few minutes. If he could fall asleep during the Cubs, certainly he could fall asleep while hanging out with Jesus. That was Philly's thought. He could imagine Jesus laughing at it.

The time with Jesus visible next to Philly, sitting at his kitchen table playing chess with him, or sitting on the couch with the cat on his lap, had made Jesus more believable to Philly. That experience of seeing Jesus made it easier to imagine Jesus here now. In fact, Philly had a feeling that the dream of Jesus meeting him in the basement also helped him to sense his presence in the real world.

"Dreams are real, in their way."

Was that from Jesus, or was Philly just talking to himself again? It was hard to tell, but maybe that was just normal. Most things in Philly's life were less cut-and-dried than he wanted them to be. Life was more than strict dictionary definitions. And weren't there even a whole list of definitions under each word in the dictionary? His lack of certainty regarding the origin of each thought passing through his head was consistent with just about everything else in his life. So, why worry that he couldn't always tell if a thought came out of his own head or from the Spirit of Jesus hovering invisibly in the room?

"I don't really do hovering, usually."

There it was again. Not exactly a voice, but it felt like a voice because it seemed different than his own thoughts. It probably had happened entirely inside his head, but it felt like something that might have come from a visitor inside that head. Did that make sense? Maybe. Good enough, anyway.

So, was he doing it? Was he hanging out with Jesus now? Or was he just sitting down here thinking about hanging out with Jesus? He was busy wondering if he was hanging out with Jesus. That wouldn't be the same thing, would it?

"Relax. Don't overthink it."

Was that golfing advice, or was Jesus reassuring Philly that he could just sit back and enjoy at least thinking about meeting with him in his basement? Even if it was pretty unclear what was happening, he still felt like he was sort of hanging out with Jesus. Probably the great saints did it in more saintly ways. They probably didn't have recliners to sit in. But this experience might qualify as something suitable for a lay person like himself.

Maybe Philly was just reassuring himself, just giving himself excuses. But it seemed like something that would at least make Jesus smile at him.

Philly smiled back as he imagined that forgiving and loving smile—the one he had seen with his actual, physical eyes years ago.

Chapter 15
Philly Being a Supportive Husband

Philly had never lived with a pregnant woman before. Brenda hadn't either. She was, like Philly, the youngest child in her family. So, neither of them had even lived with their own mother while she was pregnant, except in utero. Which had to be different, Philly figured. Anyway, Philly was adjusting to Brenda adjusting to being pregnant. That they were withholding the news from even their immediate family made the pregnancy seem less certain. Philly had managed to offer a sort of "no comment" reply to his ma when she called to follow up on Brenda's queasiness at Sunday dinner. He was pretty sure his ma knew. She could sniff out a nondenial with practiced ease. But he was sticking to the plan for waiting as long as possible to make an official announcement.

In contrast to that feeling of uncertainty around delaying the announcement, Philly was experiencing some very certain changes in Brenda on a daily basis. The speed with which she shifted from nauseated to famished on a given day was startling. They had both been watching their calories during the past year, and both had lost a significant amount of weight. But half the time now, Brenda acted like she was in a speed-eating contest.

"You're *not* a pig. You're a mother-to-be, eating for two." That was Philly being a supportive husband, holding Brenda back from the edge of tears over her out-of-control appetite. He was really just thinking aloud when he said, "Maybe we should tell our families. I think my ma already knows. We should tell your sister and your mother. Then they can be supportive." By this he meant that then he wouldn't have to carry this alone. He felt like he was hanging onto Brenda's hand as she dangled over a precipice, kicking her feet and looking down at the lava below. Philly hoped to keep Brenda from falling into hysterics now, if not into actual lava.

"Yeah, I think that would help. Maybe I should just call my mom and tell her over the phone. Or should we have her over for dinner?"

"Maybe we could take her *out* to dinner. Go ahead and see if she's available this week." Philly was glad to avoid his mother-in-law's critical perusal of their little townhouse. It felt especially little when she set her assessor's eye on it. Brenda's mom had actually been an auditor in a county assessor's office before she retired.

"Good. And I can call Sharon tonight and tell her on the phone."

"Yeah, let's not fly her out here to tell her."

Brenda scrunched her face in the way that marked one of Philly's failed jokes. But she brightened up and patted his cheek. "Thanks, Philly. Good idea to let them help us bear the burden."

"Bear the burden and share the good news." He could at least try to cover the fact that getting some help with supporting her had been his first motivation.

While Brenda talked to her sister for the second time that week, Philly checked his social media stream on his phone. He found two friend requests related to church, the mutual acquaintance being one of the assistant pastors he and Brenda had met in one of their first weeks attending. One of those requests was from Sergio, who was pictured with Salma. Philly accepted the connection. That led to a conversation back and forth. Eventually, they agreed to have lunch together after church on Sunday. The four of them.

"Supper with my mom tomorrow night. She says she has some big news for us too." Brenda looked tired, as if her entire face were already asleep, except for her eyes. Philly loved to watch her sleep, so he knew what that looked like. Her eyes were almost there now.

"Lunch with Sergio and Salma Sunday too. Don't forget." He had checked with her even as she was still laughing at something Sharon had said about being pregnant. Her sister had two kids, a little blond boy and girl.

"Oh, yeah. I almost forgot I agreed to that."

"Is it okay?"

"Sure, yeah. That's fine."

They met her mom for dinner at a Chinese restaurant that turned out to be a bit too authentic for their little party. They struggled to find something on the menu that they recognized. And then all three of the entrées turned out to be different than they had expected. At least the egg rolls and fried rice were recognizable.

In general, Brenda's mom looked a lot like a future version of her daughter. She was a bit heavier than Brenda, and could probably prove all her sixty-eight years with lines and wrinkles. Her eyes and her curvy small mouth reminded him a lot of Brenda. Her nose was larger than Brenda's. Brenda had apparently gotten her nose from her dad. Philly had barely met her dad, though he had only died three years ago. Philly's relationship with Brenda had just gotten to the meeting-the-parents stage by then.

At dinner with her mother, they had just finished ordering when she issued the first exclusive headline of the evening. "So, I said I have big news. I hope you're not gonna be upset, but I've decided to move out to Spokane to be close to Sharon and her kids."

Without a moment's hesitation, Brenda blurted her news in response. "But Ma, I'm pregnant. We're gonna have kids too."

Philly had never seen his mother-in-law frozen like that, locked in place like Han Solo encased in carbonite. It would have been better if Brenda had blurted their news first, probably. But Philly did momentarily enjoy the carved-statue silence into which his mother-in-law had been trapped by the unfortunate correlation of their news alerts.

When she finally said something, it wasn't really a word. "*Wallahufaa.*" That's what it sounded like. Maybe it was a few real words knotted together into one nonsense sound.

Brenda was shaking like a washing machine in spin cycle. Letting loose the restraints that kept her from crying all day every day, she clutched her paper napkin to her nose and mouth. For a moment, Philly worried that she had poked herself in the nose with the disposable chopsticks wrapped in it.

"Oh, baby, I'm sorry. I didn't know." Her mother huffed a little laugh. "I mean, what are the chances? Really? Well, congratulations. I mean, I'm glad, of course. I'm gonna be a grandma again. Huh!" That last sound was accompanied by some intensified blinking and a deepening of lots of those lines on her stunned face.

"It's only been a few weeks at the most." Philly felt obligated to stop just watching all this as if it were a very compelling romantic comedy unfolding in front of him. He tried to smooth things. "We were trying to hold onto the news as long as possible to be sure the pregnancy ... that it ... would, you know ..." But maybe he wasn't being very helpful.

Brenda's mom waved him off. "Oh, I understand. She's not even showing yet. I'm not upset about that. It's just so unfortunate that I already called the realtor, and I already told Sharon I'm coming out there."

Unfortunate, true. But that didn't mean she couldn't change her plans now. Philly didn't say this. He wasn't the least bit tempted to debate his mother-in-law.

She was poking at her champagne-colored hair and staring at her daughter, who was starting to slow her sobbing. "Huh," she said again.

Brenda was recovering from the tragic irony of their competing headlines. "But—but, I have old eggs. I'm gonna need all the support I can get."

"Old eggs?"

Philly was out of his territory and out of his depth at the same time. But he tried to help again. "She read that somewhere—about her eggs getting older. I guess that's a thing."

Brenda's mom shook her head as if freeing it from a pestering fly, and reached for her water glass. "Well, I don't have to move right away. Who knows how long it'll take to sell my house. I can even keep the price up if I'm in no hurry to get outta there."

Were either of the women calculating the fact that Sharon had two kids and Brenda had less than one, or at least an extremely small one? Pound for pound, Sharon had way more grandkids on her side of the scale, her side of the continent. But all that might have just been the kind of thing Philly would think of, not something Brenda or her mom would consider.

He kept those thoughts to himself. And he tried, instead, to consult Jesus somewhere inside. Grabbing one of the eggrolls that arrived on the table, Philly tried to guess what Jesus would say to all this.

The evening got better from there, though nothing was resolved. Maybe it was just that Brenda's hunger overtook her despair about her mother moving. She discovered how much she liked duck that night, as far as Philly could tell. Though the Peking duck didn't look like what he expected, he did nothing to discourage Brenda from eating most of it.

In and out of that entire evening, Philly kept wondering what Jesus was thinking. By the end, he wondered whether it was Jesus who had stirred up that question. Was Jesus trying to hint that he had something to say about all this? Philly expected he did have some input to offer. But Philly couldn't hear that input amidst the near tears and voracious eating from Brenda, his mother-in-law bouncing between ecstasy and chagrin.

At least the word was out, and they had dropped the awkward burden of keeping a secret from their families. Philly knew for sure that he would just tell his ma over the phone. It wouldn't be the same, of course, but that evening with Brenda's mom had blasted them like a midwestern thunderstorm. And Philly didn't want to repeat that any time soon.

Chapter 16
Lunch with Sergio and Salma

The following Sunday morning, Brenda had a hard time getting out of bed. Daisy saved the day, however, by insisting on kneading Brenda's butt where she lay face down, ignoring Philly's encouragements to rise and shine. When she did finally rise, she didn't start shining before three eggs and two pieces of toast, washed down with orange juice and herbal tea. She was trying to go caffeine free during the pregnancy.

"Besides, we have lunch with that guy we healed last week."

"*We* healed? Who's *we*?" Brenda's voice squeaked.

"Well, it wouldn't have happened, probably, if you wouldn't have pushed me." Philly was rinsing scrambled egg from a plate before slipping it into the dishwasher.

Brenda sat at the table sipping her tea. "I didn't push you." She chuckled. "I just nudged you."

"Ha. Is that what you call it? Okay. But I still give you at least an assist on it. And I'm pretty sure that's how Jesus would see it too." As soon as he added this spontaneous side-comment, Philly felt the truth of it.

"Hmm. Well, maybe that's my job. Maybe I'm supposed to pick out the times you're supposed to heal people." Brenda was turned in her chair, watching Philly's hands working in and around the sink.

The idea that Brenda could be in charge of directing him to heal someone didn't sit well with Philly. It would be easy for her to say, "Go ahead, Philly, and heal that woman with the missing leg." It would be much tougher to actually do the healing. Or, at least, that's how it felt when she first proposed this new teamwork idea. He offered his usual noncommittal response. "Hmm." But then he thought there might be something to what she was saying, something more than just a wife making excuses for bossing her husband. Brenda's contribution the previous week *had* been helpful—just the right touch.

They arrived at church on time that morning, and Brenda seemed quite chipper. Philly hoped it wasn't the high before the plummet into an uncontrolled catharsis. But he kept that thought to himself. His attention was required elsewhere.

"Phil, this is Robin. She has this growth in her throat that isn't cancer, but it's starting to grow too big, so they have to operate on it." Sergio had barely prefaced that healing request with a hello.

"Oh." That was all Philly said. He was distracted by Robin, an unusually tall woman with elegant posture and a neck like a gazelle. Her almond eyes seemed sad to Philly. Those eyes contained an even more compelling request than Sergio's medical summary.

"Philly would be glad to try."

When he heard *glad to try*, he first thought Brenda was doubting that he could actually *do* it. Or maybe she was also distracted by the appearance of the tall, dark-skinned woman. On second thought, he felt a sort of assurance that Brenda had said just the right thing, just what Robin needed to set her at ease. Brenda's reply was, in fact, very much like what Philly might have said himself if he hadn't been tongue-tied.

He resisted looking at his phone to check the time, but he was pretty sure they only had a couple minutes before the service started. He couldn't see a clock from where they stood in the central aisle of the main floor. "Okay if I put a hand on your shoulder? I don't really need to put my hand on your throat."

Robin seemed relieved at this news. "That's fine." Her voice was soft and smooth as honey, whether that was the sound of the restriction in her throat, or her natural voice.

Philly assembled a standard healing prayer and added a command for the lump to disappear. As usual, he went at it again when Robin confessed to noticing no real difference after the first try. And, as he expected, the opening song started, interrupting the process. A string quartet had been added this week to make it even more impossible for the little group gathered around Robin to say anything after Philly's second attempt.

He had seen a pensive look on Robin's face, her head tipped up, and her eyes beckoned by some distant object, before they had to break it up. And that was when Philly realized that several people near them were watching. That was unsettling, though he wasn't sure if he was obligated to keep his healing attempts undercover. What would Jesus say about that?

"Don't worry about it."

That was either a response from Jesus, or from a part of Philly's head that was more mature than the rest of him. At least less anxious.

They slipped into seats and waved mute goodbyes to Salma and Sergio as well as Robin. Brenda looked pleased with herself. She leaned into Philly's ear and explained that churlish look. "I really think I do know what to say to get people to feel comfortable with you healing them. It's like it just pops into my head."

Philly turned to get a look at her little grin and nodded, allowing his smile to fully blossom. Her contribution had seemed well measured for the situation. If she had been a more naturally gregarious and articulate person, Philly would have been less impressed. But it seemed like Brenda's words had flowed easily and had hit the right tone in two healing situations now.

When he was singing one of the worship songs, Philly glanced toward a guy at the end of the front row. With the curve of the theater seating, one of the church staff had an easy line of sight to Philly, and he was checking Philly out. Philly had met that assistant pastor early on, and had told him about the church he and Brenda had attended in Chicago. The pastor had seemed intrigued, but he'd said nothing substantive about Philly's former congregation. Now he turned his attention back to the stage after having been caught watching Philly worship.

At lunch after church, Philly had to surrender to Sergio's insistence that he pay for the meal. "You saved me tons of money from not missing work."

That didn't make Philly feel comfortable. Whatever anyone else thought about it, Philly couldn't imagine receiving any kind of financial compensation for healing someone. Not even lunch.

"It's okay, Philly. We'll pay next time." Brenda was either less concerned about the remunerative implications of the free lunch, or she was sensing one of those leadings about the appropriate thing to say in an uncomfortable situation.

Philly shrugged his acceptance of the offer.

Several times during that lunch at a small Mexican café, Sergio apologized for his language. He was excited about what had happened to both him and Salma, and the whole idea of church seemed to have him cranked up. Even more, he was amped up about Robin's healing that morning.

"She said she can hardly find where the lump is, or where it used to be." Salma was all smiles.

Apparently Robin had been uncertain of the extent of the healing until after the service ended. Perhaps the improvement was gradual.

"That's great. God is so good." Again, Brenda led the praise for the miracle.

Philly didn't mind her talking like that, though it was definitely new for Brenda, adopted from her friends at their church in Chicago. He, on the other hand, was unaccustomed to verbalizing so much religious fervor. For him, most of his relationship with Jesus happened in the privacy of his own head. In there, Philly was very grateful.

"It must be freaking awesome to be able to do that kinda stuff." Sergio didn't actually say *freaking*, and he apologized once again for his language. "I've never been a church guy."

"Don't worry about it." Philly tried a reassuring grin, though he was mostly preoccupied with the usual discomfort over eating with strangers. "This church stuff is all new to me too. I only started going about six years ago, and got sidetracked for quite a while since then."

"Oh, yeah. What happened to you, if you don't mind me askin'?" As part of yielding the floor to Philly, Sergio chomped down on a burrito the size of a Saturday newspaper.

Philly set down his own burrito. "I was doing the healing stuff, and then someone I knew got really sick and died. I couldn't heal her."

Sergio chewed, swallowed, and swore again. "Dude. That sucks. Yeah, that would mess you up big time. But I guess it makes sense that it doesn't always work. I mean, even doctors can't always cure you."

To Philly, Sergio's response lacked theological sophistication, maybe. But he could imagine Jesus saying to the guy across the table, "You are not far from the kingdom of God, Sergio."

Brenda and Salma had been carrying on a side conversation between pausing to listen to Philly and Sergio and discussing their jobs and families. "Right now, I'm just getting used to being pregnant. I haven't even started thinking about how it will affect my job."

This tripped Philly on two levels. First, Brenda was spilling the beans outside of the family circle. Had they agreed to that? Had they agreed *not* to do that? He wasn't sure. And second, he hadn't looked at the numbers yet on how long Brenda could take unpaid leave from her employer. He let go of his burrito once again and sighed. It was too much—the burrito and the influx of new things to think about. He felt like taking a nap in front of a Cubs game now that the season had started.

"Oh, you're *pregnant*?" Salma nearly howled. "Congratulations! How exciting. We've been talking about it too, not sure if we're gonna go for it." She toned it down just one level. "I suppose we should get married first."

Brenda nodded. The rate of her nodding and the rate of her chewing didn't change, even though Philly thought he saw her blink more rapidly for a second. Perhaps Salma had missed that telling sign.

"We'll do that if we decide to stick with this church stuff." Sergio grinned at Salma, but then turned a more serious gaze toward Philly. "We gotta decide if we're gonna give up some of our wicked ways first."

Philly tried to imitate Brenda's neutral nodding. He hadn't been a very adventurous sinner before he started church. There weren't any major vices he found he had to give up when he decided to be part of the faith community. But that was probably more because of his social awkwardness and timidity than any moral high ground he held. It came from not wanting to hear his ma telling him what a screw up he was if he did drugs or slept around or something. Emerging from that internal walkabout, Philly thought he suddenly knew what Sergio was struggling with. "You want me to pray for you to get free of any addictions?"

Brenda barked an odd little gasp when Philly said that.

Sergio pouted his lips and nodded. "Yeah. Give it a try. That sure would make things easier."

Philly had done this before, back when he was more active in healing ministry. In the context of the restaurant, he didn't get into any details. He just placed both hands on the table, as if he could communicate healing power through the butcher block to where Sergio's hands were similarly spread in front of him. "In the name of Jesus, I command addictions to be gone from Sergio." He glanced at Salma.

She lifted her head and lowered it slowly.

He read that as permission. "And you leave Salma alone too. Addictions, be gone!" He had said all that in as close to a normal voice as possible. Philly wasn't used to acting cool when something big was going on, but he had trained himself to pray for people in public in a way that wouldn't embarrass them, not to mention embarrassing him.

"Okay, then. Well, we'll see if that does anything." Sergio inhaled audibly. "Thanks, man. We're really getting our burrito's worth." He grinned and picked up the last corner of his lunch and bit it in half. His grinning and chewing seemed sincere and natural. Sergio reminded Philly of Jesus, just then.

Chapter 17
I Heard Something About You

Wednesday of that week Philly received a message in his social media feed which probably explained why that assistant pastor had been staring at him in church. Perhaps it took the pastor until Wednesday to find out how to reach Philly. He had spoken to the pastor in person, but Philly hadn't given his email or phone number to anyone at this church yet.

I heard something about you praying for the sick. I wonder if you would be willing to visit one of our members who's in the hospital?

Philly showed Brenda the message. "Okay, if you're the one who's gifted in how to respond to people who need healing, or whatever that superpower is, help me with this one."

She wagged her head side to side. "Oh. Well, maybe *you* can go there with him. I sure don't wanna go to the hospital." She put a hand on her belly as she replied, though that belly wasn't yet showing clear signs of a baby on board.

"Yeah, I could. So, you think I should go over there and try? I was thinking how the last time I tried to heal someone in the hospital, it didn't work."

"But it *did* work times before that, right?"

"Yeah, but that was when Jesus was with me, or soon after."

"Shouldn't it be all the same?"

He sighed. That sigh constituted the end of his energy for a serious discussion. Part of his hesitation about going with that pastor was plain old shyness. He didn't know the guy very well.

He had met a total of three church staff members, and this young pastor was the one he had talked to the least.

Brenda was looking at Philly the way a mother does when she's trying to decide if her son is going to be sick. "Don't worry. It's him asking. And he's probably desperate. He's not gonna yell at you if nothing happens."

That was sort of comforting, but Philly thought he probably shouldn't be comforted by a pastor's lack of expectations or anyone's lack of faith. That would make it sound like his main concern was how all this made him look. Philly knew for certain what Jesus would say to *that*. He didn't need to go down to the basement to find out. And he didn't need Jesus to meet him on the bus on the way to work.

After receiving some details before bed, Philly agreed to meet Stanley Hardwick, that assistant pastor, outside one of the big suburban hospitals in the area.

They met on Thursday evening. "Hello, Phil. Thank you so much for meeting me here. I've prayed for Thelma several times and seen nothing change. Not that I've seen much change other times I prayed. But I heard from one of the other pastors how you prayed for a guy and his girlfriend and they both got better."

Philly could tell that Stan was confusing some of the facts, but he didn't feel obligated to connect all the data points. He was still trying to climb out of the pit of his own timidity. "Uh, well, I have seen some people get better. Though I've also seen some go ahead and die." He hoped the bitterness of Theresa's death had stayed out of his voice just then.

"I suppose that's normal. I mean, only Jesus is perfect, right?"

Nodding as they entered through the wide automatic doors off the parking lot, Philly felt a bit like he was exploring this hospital with his eyes closed. What were this pastor's expectations? What was the situation with this woman? "So, did the doctor's say what her chances of recovery are?" Philly had heard about the tumor growing in her brain and some of the failed treatments, but Stan had left out a bottom-line prognosis.

"Uh, well, I kinda thought it would be counterproductive to focus on that, right? I mean, if we're gonna have faith for this healing, we should focus on the positives." He puffed once. "At least that's what I figured. I'm not really an expert. I was just Thelma's pastor when she was diagnosed with this tumor."

"Yeah. I don't really feel like an expert on it either. I've just sort of followed along as I feel like Jesus leads me. He doesn't always stop to fill me in on all the rules or principles. I guess that's been okay with me. Maybe principles and rules would be discouraging or intimidating."

Stan grinned and twisted his neck to get a square look at Philly. "Sounds perfectly understandable to me. I mean, whatever works, right?"

Clearly, Philly wasn't the only one blindly feeling his way down these broad, shiny hallways.

When they arrived at the intensive care unit, Philly had to wait while Stan went in to tell Thelma's daughter they were there. The hospital's rule was no more than two people visiting an ICU patient at a time.

"This is Carrie." Outside intensive care, Stan introduced a woman in her early twenties with straight auburn hair and freckles across her nose.

"Thank you so much for coming. You probably know we're desperate. Anything you can do would be great." Her words came in little surges, breathy and constrained. What Philly sensed from her was tired resignation. Perhaps the idea of someone coming to pray for her mother's healing was foreign, but the desperation of which she spoke had apparently opened the door to the unimaginable.

Philly just shook her hand and nodded, trying a reassuring smile. But he suspected fear was mostly what she saw on his face. That's what he was seeing from the inside of that twitchy face.

Leading the way through the big double doors, Stan glanced toward Philly a couple times before they reached the curtain that provided a little privacy for Thelma. Maybe Stan was looking for

Hosting Jesus

signs that Philly had changed his mind. Or maybe he was looking for some of that reassurance Philly wished he could exude.

After Stan had slipped in behind the curtain, Philly released a sigh and a simple prayer. "Help, Lord." It was as sincere as any prayer he had ever uttered. How had he agreed to this? What made him think he could do anything here?

He shook off those thoughts and followed Stan through the opening in the curtain. Philly focused now on the woman in the bed. She was pale and yellowish, a white bandage covering the top of her head. She seemed thoroughly sedated.

"Carrie said Thelma has been unconscious all afternoon. The pain meds are pretty strong. The hospital is just trying to keep her comfortable." Stan cut himself off abruptly.

It was clear to Philly that he was the last hope for this woman if the hospital staff had resorted only to pain management. This was familiar to Philly. Too familiar. Theresa's brain had become inflamed with the infection that had invaded her central nervous system. Toward the end, she was unresponsive, under the influence of heavy sedation. *"I don't control this. I don't understand everything,"* Philly reminded himself inside his head.

He seemed to find a response in there. "That's right, Philly. Thanks for giving it a try. Thanks for trusting it to me."

There was no doubt that this reply had been entirely internal, sheltered from Stan. But Philly looked at the pastor, hoping for something from him. Like what?

Stan met his gaze. "You go ahead and take the lead. I'm here to support."

Maybe that was what Philly had been seeking. Permission, and a bit of assurance that he wouldn't be judged for what he did here. This was intensive care. This was a critical, life-threatening illness. This was all outside of normal circumstances, outside the normal rules. Even if he was loading too much onto Stan's permissive words, Philly took courage. "Okay. Well, the first thing I want to do is banish a spirit of death. You get off of this woman, death. You are a defeated enemy. Go away, death. Leave her right now." He didn't look at Stan. He just watched Thelma, a woman who must have been in her forties or fifties. She seemed to be swollen to the point that her skin was tight and shiny. On the nearly translucent skin at the side of her head, he thought he saw a faint twitch. Was that anything? Was it real? He wasn't going to say anything about it. But he wasn't going to stop there.

"To this tumor, I curse you and command you to shrink. I command you to leave this body and allow total good health." He felt as if he were rerunning tapes from his prayers for Theresa. It reminded him of those times when Dave had been with him, along with some of the more experienced healing people from his church. Philly had absorbed a lot of their language and attitudes even if he didn't understand all they were doing. It had all seemed fitting and inspired at the time. But, of course, it had ultimately failed.

He glanced at Stan, who was focused on Thelma and muttering something under his breath. What exactly he was saying wasn't important to Philly. He could sense that Stan was in this struggle with him, on the same side.

"Now, I bless Thelma with healing. Complete restoration. Let it come. Let health and wholeness come to this woman. Thank you, Lord, for life, for this person, for her family, and for what you have in store for her. We trust you to win this fight and give her renewed life." The hope in those words was more than Philly had expected to bring, more than he felt he could take credit for. That surprise package of hopeful words felt like a gift.

Again, Philly thought he saw some sort of movement on the side of Thelma's head. What he didn't know was whether that was normal, whether it meant anything. He resisted imagining good news where there was no clear sign of it. That was familiar too. False hope had stung him deeply before. Now Philly was simply waiting. He was waiting to see if something happened with Thelma, and to see if he was supposed to do anything else.

Footsteps outside the curtain warned of a person approaching. The beige curtain parted, and a woman about Philly's age stepped in, dressed in light blue scrubs. Her focus pushed past the two men. She stared at Thelma, and then at the monitor next to the bed. "Looks like our girl is resting a bit easier now. Her blood pressure has let up a bit. Maybe she's feeling less pain." The nurse was still addressing the two men only peripherally, keeping her eyes on Thelma and the monitor. She checked the drip of one of the IVs and touched Thelma's forehead lightly. Then she used an in-ear thermometer to take her temperature. "A bit of relief, I guess. Temperature is normal. She's been feverish all day." The nurse only glanced at Philly now, turning back toward the opening in the curtain and disappearing as unobtrusively as she had done everything else.

The two men made eye contact for a second. Philly guessed that Stan was asking the same questions he was asking internally. Had their prayers been effective? Should they do anything else?

When Philly had stood next to his fiancée's bed those years ago, he had always answered that last question in the affirmative. There was no such thing as too many healing prayers. So, he often redid the same prayers or experimented with whatever new variations he could concoct. But this felt different. Of course, this was a woman he had never actually met. That was different. But he sincerely felt like he had done what he had come to do. Would saying more be a sin? That didn't seem likely. But why go on restating what had already been stated, trying what had already been tried?

It might have been his imagination, but Thelma looked more like she was simply sleeping in that hospital bed now. She no longer struck him as a suffering patient in critical condition. She was just a woman getting some needed rest. But all that might have simply been influenced by what the nurse said.

Stan interrupted those thoughts. "Thank you, Lord, for blessing Thelma with better rest. We trust her into your hands to keep up the improvement and to give her relief. In the name of Jesus we pray, amen."

As far as Philly could tell, Stan's closing prayer came from more than a pastor's obligation to have the final word or from a responsibility to wrap up this little gathering. It felt like meaningful closure for what they had come here to do.

Philly led the way this time, out through the slit in the curtain and down the long corridor past other identical curtains and the medical equipment parked outside them. A momentary urge to stop in and pray for an anonymous person behind another curtain submitted to his good sense and faded behind him as Philly exited the heavy electronic doors guarding the intensive care unit.

Stan sighed expansively, as if he had been holding his breath while in that hospital unit. Philly shared in the relief of leaving that repository of so much suffering and impending death. He was also trying to slip free of guilt that he had resisted the urge to pray for other patients behind the row of curtains he had brushed past. What if not praying for those other folks had disqualified him from healing Thelma?

That didn't feel like something Jesus would have pressed into his heart, even if Jesus had been the source of that passing urge to heal others in there. Philly tried to console himself with this reminder about Jesus's constant mercy and grace.

"Thanks again, Phil. I really appreciate your time and effort here. It sorta seemed like it did some good." Stan curtailed his voice when Carrie came into sight. She had a tall young man walking with her, holding her hand and attending to her with lowered eyes.

Philly wasn't surprised at the mundane and subdued conversation that passed among them there in the lobby. Desperation isn't the same as expectation. Carrie had confessed the former and not the latter. Even a measure of hope might hide beneath a shell of fear about jinxing it by speaking good expectations aloud. He had heard others say things like that. And he had recognized the same in himself, and not only with Theresa's sickness.

"Thank you so much for coming out. I really appreciate it. Bless you." Carrie held onto Philly's hand a bit longer than he expected. And he might have felt a blessing come from her across that warm connection. Her hand was warm. His was freezing.

That was Philly's normal state when nervous. She seemed not to notice.

Before bed that night, Philly checked for messages on his phone. He pulled an extra pillow up behind him so he could sit up to read a long message from Stan.

Brenda stopped her baby book reading to turn toward her husband. "What is it?"

"A message from Pastor Stan." Philly could feel his head rotating side to side involuntarily. "He says Thelma woke up and spoke to her daughter. She was cogent and peaceful. Then she went back to sleep. The doctor examined her and said there's evidence that the swelling in her head has lessened. They postponed a plan to open her skull a bit more to relieve the pain. Dang. I didn't know anything about that part. I'm glad they didn't tell me."

"Wait. She's better? She's getting better?" Brenda's voice hit that little piccolo note that came with her surprised questions.

"Maybe. It sure seems like good news. I guess we can't be sure if she's totally healed, but it's all good news. There sure wasn't any sign of anything like this when we got there." Though he was reserving some of it from his words, Philly was feeling excitement at the possibility. Even if they had only relieved her pain and given Thelma a chance to communicate briefly with her daughter, wasn't that a blessing?

"That's great, Philly. I had a good feeling about it. I'm glad you agreed to do it." Brenda slid close to him and leaned her head on his shoulder.

Her endorsement reminded Philly of a secret he had been harboring. "I sorta felt like I was supposed to pray for some others in there—in intensive care. But I told myself that was inappropriate, and I just hustled out of there. Maybe I should have done it anyway, even if it would've been awkward."

Sighing deeply and nuzzling her head closer to his neck, Brenda offered a sleepy reply. "I don't think you should beat yourself up about that. Maybe next time. You're just getting back into this stuff."

"Yeah. Maybe next time."

Chapter 18
Taking a Chance at Work

Baseball season had started cold in Chicago, at least where weather was concerned. Sunday evening, Philly had watched the Cubs on TV, playing in long sleeves and with steaming breath, under the lights at Wrigley. The Cubs were probably glad for their traditional Monday off. It was even colder that day.

At work, Philly sipped dark hot chocolate he made from a pricey powdered mix available in the kitchen, one of four cocoa choices provided by his employer. What greater luxury could they offer their employees? As a matter of fact, he was also enjoying his ergonomic chair, which flexed supportively with all his movements. He was enjoying all this luxurious comfort after surviving an interview with a potential summer intern. He was supposed to hire someone to help him with upgrade projects.

The potential intern's name was Anya Minsky, the daughter of immigrants from the old Soviet Union, as far as he could tell. Throughout the interview, Philly had managed to avoid staring at the elaborate piercings around one eyebrow and along the cartilage of one ear. Her hair was shaved on that side of her head to make all that penetrative jewelry more visible. She seemed intimidatingly bright, a student at the University of Chicago. And he knew that her avant-garde adornments wouldn't disqualify her in the minds of any of his bosses. One of the operations executives wore a prominent nose ring.

This company developed logistics software that was being used by some of the leading names in order processing, warehousing, and shipping. And they had thrived by attracting top talent with their nurturing and open minded personnel practices. When they hired him, Philly had joked to Brenda that he was probably meant to be the token middle-aged white guy in the internal support department. He was only half joking.

"So, how was she? Pretty smart, right?" Balraj, Philly's supervisor, stood just inside Philly's office leaning on the doorpost. Philly was one of the few employees with an actual office and door—for added security around his network access and the equipment installed behind his office.

"She seems smart, that's for sure. And she seems like someone I could work with." Philly had spun his chair to face Balraj, who was wearing a bright peach colored shirt. "You look like you're expecting spring or something."

Balraj laughed and looked down at his shirt. "We can always hope."

"If I wore that color, I could probably get sick leave based on looks alone."

"It's not in your beauty palette?"

"Do I *have* a beauty palette?"

His supervisor laughed again. "Well, do you agree, then, that we should offer her the position?"

"Yeah. She's obviously bright. And there's not much risk. It's just for the summer."

"Okay. I'll contact HR about it. Thanks, Phil."

"Thank *you*. I'll be glad for the help."

To keep up with his workload, Philly had been fudging on his self-fulfillment time—the time in his day when he was supposed to be pursuing something just for fun. It was company policy. But he had been logging that time as spent studying "cybercriminal behavior patterns in a modern post-industrial context." He had extracted that phrase from a university website somewhere. Balraj hadn't challenged him on the obfuscation yet.

When Balraj moved on and Philly turned back to the array of monitors in front of his workstation, a thought passed through his head. "You can be a big help to Anya with some issues she needs to have healed."

"*You can be? Who can be? What?*" Philly managed to not say all that aloud.

"Of course, you could also go down the hall *now* and ask Alvin about his blood sugar issues."

Philly had never been particularly prone to random thoughts like these skittering through his mind. His mind often wandered, that was true. When he was working on monitoring the performance of various internet connections, he might be thinking about the sandwich he had packed for lunch. While updating security software on servers, he might be wondering who the Cubs were playing over the weekend. But he had never just suddenly decided he should heal some unknown ailment in one of his coworkers—not without outside input.

Impulsively, he let the springy ergo-chair spin away from his desk and assist him to his feet. The body-hugging responsiveness of that chair hinted that it might want to spring come with him when he left his office. But Philly's chair stayed where it sat, spinning slowly in front of his desk. He let his office door close and lock behind him. Walking down a hallway with the dim lighting set somewhere between energy saving and sedated, he aimed for somewhat brighter lights over a cluster of cubicles.

Alvin's desk was about ten yards from Philly's. Alvin was one of the testing managers with whom Philly interacted most often, usually around deploying beta software and backing up crucial data before launching new versions of internal applications. One of the few people on that floor who was older than Philly, Alvin looked like he could have been a Chicago bus driver in a previous career, only he didn't dress as well as the average bus driver. His assortment of tan and gray rumpled T-shirts generally sported a stain or two, not to mention a rockslide of crumbs. Alvin was heavier than Philly had been when he concluded he needed to lose weight.

Philly decided to try a trick on Alvin. "So, what's this I hear about you having blood sugar issues?"

Alvin had taken off his over-the-ear headphones when he noticed Philly approaching, and he had spun his chair halfway around to investigate. "Who told you that? Balraj?"

"Not sure exactly where I heard it. Are you seeing a doctor about it?"

"I'm seeing them, and they're seeing me."

Philly was trying to ignore the dents the headphones had left in Alvin's medium-length Afro, but he didn't know where else to look to avoid facing the duplicity in his sneaky approach to offering healing. He dug deep and tried a more direct tack. "Did I ever tell you why I got fired from my job at that Chicago architect firm?"

"High blood sugar?"

Snorting and still glancing only briefly at Alvin's round face, Philly wrinkled his nose. Between him and Alvin, awkwardness was not an issue, it was a bond. It was their native language. "No. It was because I started doing this sort of spiritual healing. And some folks actually got healed. So, that caused a stir."

"You did what?"

"Actually healed a few people."

"Was it like the Reiki thing they do at the massage place up the road? Or are we talking TV preacher stuff?"

"Do I look like a TV preacher?"

Alvin laughed. "Yeah, you look like one who lost his yachts and limos and had to go into a witness protection program."

Philly snickered some more. Then he forced himself to make real eye contact, looking squarely at Alvin's face. Such eye contact between them was generally reserved for serious stuff, like debating the ending to the latest epic sci-fi movie.

"What if I tried praying for your blood sugar thing?"

This stopped Alvin's usual swaying and shifting. Leaning back in his ergo-chair, he returned that eye contact. "Uh, I guess so. It prob'ly wouldn't hurt to try. Did you learn this in church or something?"

"Yeah, something like that." Philly suddenly wanted to laugh this off as a joke and sprint back to his keypad-secured office. What was he doing? Risking another good job?

Alvin seemed to read into Philly's hesitation. "Don't worry. I won't tell anybody about your secret identity." A joke and a serious promise all in one.

Shifting his weight from one foot to the other, Philly decided to make it short and simple. "Okay. Well, thank you, Jesus, for your healing power. Let it come now to fix Alvin's blood sugar level. Make him whole, according to your will. Thank you." He had lowered his voice for this recitation of an average healing prayer. He didn't edit the wording for the environment, nor for what little he knew about Alvin's religious leanings. Over the past several months, they had spoken much more about Klingons than about God.

For a moment, Alvin seemed to be waiting for more—maybe the part where Philly palmed him in the forehead and knocked him off his chair. Then Alvin just smiled and shrugged. "Thanks. I've been a bit frustrated with the doctors and with my lack of will power when it comes to eating."

"Well, I bless your will power too then." Philly twitched his head slightly and backhanded a small gesture toward his friend. He was going for a "nothing unusual happening here" sort of presentation. But he couldn't tell if Alvin was buying it.

"Now go and work your magic on the network."

Philly laughed. "Yeah. I'm gonna go lay hands on that wonky router now." As he walked back to his office, it felt nothing like the retreat he had envisioned a moment before. But he did meet a fear sneaking along that hall—a fear that Alvin would never look at him the same in the future.

"I guess things could be awkward between you two now." Was that Philly, or was Jesus making a joke?

When he unlocked his door and stepped into his office, Philly could imagine the warm pressure of rubbing shoulders with Jesus as he entered the room. Maybe just his imagination?

Chapter 19
Let's Try the Basement Again

They hadn't really agreed to designate a weekly date night, but Friday had become that on most weeks since Brenda and Philly got married. Still, Philly didn't say anything to discourage Brenda from going out with some girlfriends to celebrate her pregnancy that Friday. He was a little worried about her driving from Schaumburg to Chicago during the last half of the evening rush, but that drive was more likely to be annoying than dangerous. Brenda was a cautious driver, having done little driving all those years she lived in Evanston. In those days, she mostly walked to the train and to the grocery store from her homey little apartment.

Philly would be alone in their homey little townhouse this Friday. The Cubs had played already that afternoon, six to nothing winners. Another shutout, and a good start to the year, which was already promising another run at the pennant. He could watch a movie, of course. They had several options for streaming the latest films.

Stopping at a soup and sandwich place on the way home, he had picked up a combo. A minute in the microwave reheated the soup, and he pulled out a medium-sized plate from the set they had received for their wedding, unwrapping his half a chicken salad sandwich on it. The combo probably wasn't too many calories.

That thought recalled what he had heard from Alvin that day. "I don't know about my glucose level, or whatever, but I have been able to resist those chewy snack bars in the kitchen this week. I was eating about four a day."

"That's a lot of calories." Philly had allowed an impressed curve to his lips, but he wasn't inclined to fist-pump over such a marginal report of healing. Nevertheless, Alvin's report inspired a bit of hope. More than that, Philly was relieved to find that Alvin was still talking to him as if Philly were still the same guy who had worked with him all along.

Philly sat down in the kitchen to eat at the oak table even though he was alone this evening. It felt somehow healthier than eating in the basement in front of a movie. Maybe he had seen something like that back when he was reading online about how to lose weight. Maybe. So much of what he had learned about anything in his adult life felt like it was absorbed. His brain was porous, but he rarely had footnotes for the sources of what it soaked up.

After finishing his soup and sandwich, Philly pulled a bottle out of the fridge and poured himself a beer, his dessert and his cocktail for the evening. Never more than one beer. That was the deal with Brenda, and not a hard deal to keep. No one in his family had ever been a heavy drinker, though maybe Eileen drank more than anyone else. She had always been the family's party girl, always the rebel.

That reminded Philly that Eileen was coming into town to visit. She seemed to be coming to evaluate Ma and Dad's ability to continue living independently, her covert purpose beneath what she probably told them was just a friendly visit. As he walked down the basement stairs, Philly followed that thought to an idea that he should pray for Eileen and for his parents. He was reviving an occasional habit of walking and talking with Jesus. Mobile prayers, just like a real conversation.

The only time he had ever knelt with his hands folded for prayer was on the most desperate day of Theresa's illness. It seemed the thing to do at the very bottom of his despair, though it didn't seem to have helped.

This tripped another thought about what he had been hearing about Thelma. The latest was that they had reduced her pain meds even further, and she was recovering some of her motor skills. Their aggressive attempts at reducing the tumor were getting credit for this recovery, from the doctors. However, Stan reported that at least two of Thelma's nurses called her recovery a miracle. Carrie had apparently taken the latter view of her mother's improvements.

I just wanted to thank you again, Mr. Thompson, for praying for my mother. I'm sure those prayers were answered. I can't tell you how grateful I am for all the improvements I've seen over these last several days. It is truly miraculous.

Thanks again,
Carrie

Stan had forwarded that message to Philly just the night before. "It looks like an answer to prayer for sure." That was the pastor's assessment. Maybe it wasn't a radical statement of faith in Jesus's healing power, but it gave Philly a small hope that his gifts might find some room in his new church.

Sitting in his recliner, he hit the combination of buttons on the various remote controls required to open a streaming app and select a movie for the night. A blink in his mind, like a mental muscle twitch, weakened his determination to find something to watch. Even a pair of action movies he had been planning to see when Brenda wasn't around were looking unappealing tonight.

When he reached for his beer, he glanced at the recliner next to him. It was generally Brenda's place to sit when they watched a movie together. They were still debating about getting a loveseat to replace the recliners, but the budget wasn't offering any obvious openings with baby expenses mounting.

Tonight it was Jesus sitting in that recliner that flashed onto the movie screen inside Philly's head. Of course, it hadn't been exactly that recliner in the dream. But why remind himself of that? Or was that himself?

Still fiddling with the remote, he allowed the selector square on the TV to pause over *Fight Club*. Maybe it would be worth it to watch that movie again just to remember what the young Edward Norton and the young Brad Pitt looked like in those days. But then he remembered all that blood and decided he wasn't in the mood. When Philly tried to advance to the next row of movie choices, the screen froze. He tried up, down, left, and right. It was stuck. Then he looked at the cable modem on the floor near the TV. One of the lights was out. Presumably the one that indicated a good internet connection. *Blast!*

That wasn't the actual word that filled Philly's head. For the unedited word that popped up, he briefly repented.

"We can just hang out together." That was the alternative arrangement offered by either a part of Philly's brain, or perhaps a *Fight Club*-worthy imaginary companion. Laughter followed that last thought.

"Did you break my internet connection so I would hang out with you instead?" That question seemed like something Philly could own as a native thought.

"Would I really do that to you? Besides, we could always watch a movie together."

"Really?"

"Of course. But it would have to be a very spiritual movie. And rated PG at the worst."

Sorting the source of these ideas distracted him from their humor, if that's what was intended. "Am I just thinking all this stuff up myself?"

"What do *you* think?"

This time there was laughter, and it came from Philly, no doubt about it. "I think I'm talking to myself."

"You remember the part in the Psalms where the writer says, 'Bless the Lord, oh my soul'? Talking to yourself has a long and honored history."

That was definitely Jesus. Philly remembered hearing that part of the Bible before, but he didn't remember anyone saying anything about the Psalmist talking to himself.

"You didn't just make it up. It's an idea that's been out there among my people for a while."

Philly's mind rattled with all this like someone shaking a box to figure out what kind of gift was contained inside. In fact, he suspected he had some loose pieces in his head that would actually rattle if he shook it hard enough.

"Don't try that. It would hurt."

That was Philly protecting himself from brain damage, right? But now he wanted to gather all those thoughts together and sort what he had been saying and hearing. Had he spoken aloud? He couldn't recall for sure. But he was home alone, so that didn't matter. The neighbors on either side wouldn't know he was sitting in his basement talking to an empty recliner.

From there, Philly wandered off to thinking about Eileen's visit that weekend. But that felt like a distraction. Even a betrayal. He didn't need to solve anything about Eileen on this Friday night. He should stay focused. It was more than just a funny joke to think of hanging out with Jesus in the basement. It had become more than that to him.

He sipped his beer and relaxed a bit more. The cable modem was still missing one of the status lights, and the TV screen was black, in sleep mode probably. Philly discarded the urge to hit a button on the remote to wake up his flat-panel display. "What were you saying?"

"Nothing quote worthy, really. Just saying we could hang out together."

"Is that just something that's generally good to do, or is there a purpose behind it? I mean, like, do I have some issues I need to deal with?"

"You think you might have issues?"

"Don't I have issues?" Philly paused to wonder why he had grabbed that as the motivation for him and Jesus getting together. "I mean, I might need to run some sort of questions or concerns by you."

"Like a prayer list?"

"I never really wrote one of those."

"But you pray for certain things pretty often. Things you're concerned about."

"Is that okay?"

"Of course. Bring me everything that's bothering you."

"But should I just leave them with you and not keep praying the same things over and over?"

"Sometimes that's possible. But life just keeps happening, so it's not surprising that similar things keep coming up in prayer."

"I'm worried about being a dad." Philly hadn't said this even to himself before.

"It's a new adventure for you. Of course you're worried. But I can help you with it, you know."

Philly was thinking that Jesus had never been a father, but he didn't form that into an actual reply. And besides, Jesus could always consult *his* Father before providing advice. But then ...

Philly grabbed for his beer and took another sip. He did that to try and snap his head out of that weird little side conversation with himself. "So, you're gonna help me with being a father? Brenda will be glad to hear that."

"You think she's worried about you?"

"She does worry, sometimes."

"She's doing so much better than before, though. Remember, she used to worry a lot more."

"Yeah. That's true. But this is gonna be a whole new class of things to worry about."

"She's changed, Philly. And you've had something to do with that."

"Really? I helped her not to worry so much?"

"You helped."

"But I supposed you helped more."

"Sure. And she helped herself. And women at your old church did too. She could use some encouragement to get in touch with women at your new church, by the way. She's already thinking about it. She could use your cooperation in making it happen."

Brenda was out now with women she knew from her old employer in Chicago. She had been laid off from that job, forced to find work in the suburbs. But she had kept some of her friends from before. Those weren't the faith-filled friends who had helped her stop worrying so much. He supposed Jesus was just telling him that an opportunity for Brenda to meet women at church would come up soon, and that he should pay attention so he didn't miss it. Philly ran out of mental mojo at this point. It had been a long week.

"You wanna watch a movie now?"

The internet light on the modem was illuminated again. "With you? Sure." Philly hit the remote to wake up the TV.

Chapter 20
Eileen Visiting from New York

This weekend would be busy with a dinner at his parents' house and taking Eileen out to dinner another night. Philly and Brenda were also doing some shopping for baby things on Saturday—things they probably wouldn't get at a baby shower. Philly was a lot more nervous about Eileen's visit than about the shopping, as little as he enjoyed the latter.

"At least I don't feel like she looks down her nose at me anymore." Brenda was examining a baby bed made of real wood, apparently a premium item these days.

Philly was a few feet away trying to figure out the motor in an electronic mobile. "Uh, well, that's because you two got to know each other better. I knew you would like each other once you really got to know each other."

"Maybe she's more tolerant these days, and I'm more confident."

"That could be it too." Philly joined her by the big white crib and kissed her on the cheek.

"Can you really imagine us being parents, Philly?"

"Imagining is probably easier than actually doing it. I hope we're not too old. I don't look forward to waking up at all hours of the night."

Brenda ran her hand along the puffy pink bumper in the crib and nodded distractedly. "Maybe we'll get one of those kids who sleeps all through the night. Your ma said you were like that from pretty early on."

"I was probably already worried about upsetting anyone." That facetious reply squirted out of him, but Philly didn't retract it. It struck him as a funny interpretation after he said it.

Brenda didn't seem to notice. "You think this is too expensive? What's our budget for something like this?"

Philly kept the family books, though he had never been a natural accountant or budget manager. He had done purchasing at work before, but that was different, more defined and finite. The possibilities for domestic spending seemed nearly limitless, stretching to the horizon in every direction. And Brenda was especially impulsive about spending, which had already prompted a few marital conflicts. "Uh, this is too much, I think. In fact, everything in here is too expensive, really. The last place was more reasonable. And you liked that yellow crib back there." Philly flipped the price tag of the luxury crib.

"I suppose. But this one *is* so beautiful."

"Yeah."

Fortunately, there had been fine and functional furniture at the previous store, so Philly didn't have to make more of a case for abstaining from this princess-quality bed. Though they didn't make any big purchases that day, they did figure out some of their shared tastes, and they discovered where best to shop for the big items.

Philly had to wrestle himself loose of the nagging money worries raised by that shopping trip in order to try and enjoy dinner with his sister. He had finally convinced his ma to let the siblings go out to dinner on Saturday, and then for her to have them all over to her house for the usual Sunday dinner.

"You seem more relaxed these days." Philly was leaning back in his chair at the rather pricey place he had selected to impress his sophisticated sister. He had resisted recalculating how much it was worth to impress her as he ordered his salad and steak.

"Getting older and more tired, I think." Eileen tipped her head toward Philly, the overhead light catching reddish highlights in her medium-length brunette hair.

Brenda was entirely engrossed in a crunchy roll included in the basket of bread before the salads arrived. She gnawed and nibbled like a starving little animal. Philly thought it was cute, but wondered what Eileen was making of this eating preoccupation.

"How far along are you exactly?"

Lifting her eyebrows first, then her eyes, Brenda seemed to wake to Eileen's presence. "Oh. Well, we think it's about eight weeks now."

Philly knew she was feigning more certainty than the doctor had provided. But, give or take a couple of weeks, they didn't need to know the precise due date. They were also delaying learning the gender of the baby. They were attracted to the old-fashioned way of doing that, at least in theory.

"You starting to notice clothes not fitting anymore?"

Brenda shrugged and grinned a little as she kept chewing.

That Eileen would think of pregnancy in terms of the inconvenience to her wardrobe was no surprise to Philly. This evening she was wearing a black suit with no lapels and a sparkling golden necklace over her deep red blouse. As usual, she left Philly feeling underdressed.

"Do you still think of having kids some day?" It wasn't a calculated question from Philly.

"I think old and tired are disqualifying things when it comes to having kids. Remember, I'm even older than you." She lifted her wine glass and took a sip as she pointed her forehead at her little brother.

"Even older." Brenda laughed. She wasn't drinking, of course, but her nerves often caused her to sound a bit tipsy.

Eileen just smiled generously at Brenda's giggly comment.

His big sister really did seem less prone to criticize these days, but Philly couldn't help assuming that she was thinking less than generous thoughts about Brenda, who seemed to see herself as a damaged daisy next to an American rose when Eileen was around. Philly reached over and took Brenda's free hand, the one she wasn't using to forage in the bread basket.

"Are you still doing any of that healing stuff, Philly, now that you're back in church?"

Philly choked a bit, though he had been staying out of the dinner rolls. A swallow of water helped him recover. "In fact, I have done a bit of that."

"But not seeing Jesus walk around with you anymore?"

"No, not really *seeing* him." Philly felt the presence of the people at the other tables, as if they were leaning toward him when he mentioned seeing Jesus. He lowered his voice. "But I have been feeling like he's talking to me in a way."

"Oh. How does that work?"

"I just ..." He hesitated, then decided not to take another sip of water. "I just take some time to sit still and kinda imagine that he's there and that he's saying stuff to me. And it sorta feels like he does."

Eileen contemplated the deep red wine in her glass for a moment. "You must miss it—him being so real to you."

"Yeah. But I believe he's still real. I feel like I've sorta found a way to keep him real by going to a place where I've seen him before and then just letting my imagination connect to that thing I felt before." Philly noticed that Brenda was listening more intently to him. He probably hadn't said all this to her in the same way.

Eileen dabbed a finger near the corner of her mouth as if checking for stray lipstick. "I remember what it felt like in Ma and Dad's dining room when I was convinced that he was really there. I guess that feeling stayed with *me* for a while too. It helped me get things straightened out with my relationships back then, among some other things."

"I bet you could just sit with a cup of coffee and remember that feeling, and maybe it would come back." Philly paused to wonder how bold he could be in challenging his sister. "I also had a dream recently that reminded me of what it felt like to have him right there with me, and it's helped me to reconnect some. Though I gotta say, I'm not always exactly sure that I'm not just talking to myself."

"Sometimes that can be healthy, though." Brenda was buttering a roll this time, as if she had staunched her starvation enough to allow the luxury of preparing the bread before scarfing it down. "Don't the psychologists say you can tell yourself good things in place of where you might be saying bad things to yourself? I know that helps me—to try and replace some o' what my dad used to say to me when I was little."

Nodding and grinning at his wife a bit sideways, Philly breathed a small laugh. "Yeah. So, even if it's not Jesus himself talking to me in the basement, at least it's me saying good stuff to myself." A relief that he hadn't yet allowed to organize in his head boosted Philly for a moment, as he added something new to his appreciation of his wife.

Brenda grinned back at him with a bit of butter in one corner of her mouth and a tight constellation of crumbs in the other corner.

Eileen was apparently ignoring Brenda's pregnant eating patterns. She seemed inspired. "I think I'll try that. Life is so dull and depressing without that sort of input—real spiritual input, not just old stories and famous sayings." Though the momentum of her voice had implied she had more to say, she stopped there.

The rest of the evening passed less profoundly and more cheerfully, as if the three of them had established a new level of trust.

Chapter 21
Sunday at Ma and Dad's

It took a bit more verbal resistance to get his ma to agree that Brenda and he could go to church that morning before Philly joined his family for the Sunday festivities.

Philly was glad he had insisted on going to church, because that's where he ran into Carrie and Pastor Stan. They approached him and Brenda after the service, all smiles and even a hint of happy tears. Stan's wife, Holly, was with them.

"I just wanted to update you on Mom." Carrie looked about to burst.

Holly chuckled, as if the joy bubbling out of Carrie was tickling her.

Brenda bounced a little, visibly restraining a happy clap.

"We were gonna make an announcement about it from the stage, but ran out of time." Stan inserted this as if to apologize for something. But, somehow, it raised more questions than Philly had before that.

Philly ignored this diversion and focused on Carrie. "She's feeling better, then?"

"Better? Oh, yes. So much better. They scanned her and found the tumor much smaller than last time. I even think that she's being completely healed, but the doctors are slow to believe it. And so is she."

Brenda inserted a tangential question. "Have you been coming to this church all along?"

Carrie maybe blushed a little, but she also laughed. "No. I started coming when Mom started to get better. This is *her* church. I just wanted to thank people here." She made a one-handed tossing motion toward Philly. "But now I'm getting hooked. I really like it here."

"That's great." Brenda had probably found just what she was hoping. She was a great fan of Philly and Jesus healing people. And she was quick to catalog the possible side effects of that ministry.

"So, she's home now?" Philly was still excavating the health news.

"Yes. They were hesitant to let her, but she feels so good that we talked 'em into releasing her to home care. And yesterday the visiting nurse just popped in and popped back out. She calls Mom her miracle patient. I think she just came by to be encouraged, like we all are." Carrie leaned forward for half a second and then seemed to restrain herself.

Philly got the impression that she was holding herself back from grabbing him for a celebratory hug. He was probably blushing at the very thought of it, a little heat rising to his face.

Stan looked like he wanted to say more, but he glanced at his wife and maybe deleted whatever he had in his queue. Instead, he just showed lots of teeth.

The news about Thelma produced an emotional high that propelled Philly and Brenda toward his family home. Though things had lightened up there since Jesus's visit, Philly still appreciated an emotional boost when going to see his ma. She often seemed depressed. She was less likely to grouse and complain these days, but was not really happy with her life, as far as Philly could tell.

"Oh, let me look at you." Ma greeted Brenda with more cheer than Philly expected.

Brenda stood awkwardly with her hands away from her sides, as if waiting to be fitted with a new dress.

"Not showing yet, are ya?"

Shaking her head loosely, Brenda seemed to be trying to get her smile started. "Not much, I guess. I sure am eating a lot more."

"Well, that's to be expected. Don't let anyone tell you otherwise." Ma waved a hand at her as if to swipe away imagined criticism. Then she lowered her head and seemed to revert to another character, like an actress on a stage. It was an unusually rapid transformation, but the dour persona his ma was now playing was a familiar one to Philly.

"How ya doin' kiddo?" Dad came in for a hug, and Brenda complied. This hugging was a new thing for Philly's family. Brenda had inspired it in Dad. Philly had no objection. He patted his dad on the back as a form of spectator participation.

Eileen stood in the door of the kitchen, where all this greeting was going on, holding a glass of wine and accompanying Sparks as observer of the festivities. Sparks barked. Perhaps he resented being overlooked in the greeting rituals. He did follow his bark by commencing his own ritual of sniffing ankles, being too short to sniff other parts of the visitors.

Philly ventured a brief, one-armed hug of Eileen on his way into the dining room and toward the living room. No one in the family ever entered the living room through the front door. That left guests to make their way past the food preparations in the kitchen and around the table setting in the dining room. "How's the visit?" Philly spoke softly into his sister's ear as she turned to follow him to the living room.

"It's okay. I've seen a few things." Her words accompanied him to a seat in his favorite chair.

"What are you two muttering about?" Ma was looking at the dog but talking to her children, apparently. She wasn't far behind.

"Nothing, Ma." Eileen kept her back toward her mother.

Philly could guess that Ma was starting to wear on Eileen's nerves by now, over twenty-four hours into her visit. And he knew that when she said she had "seen a few things," Eileen was referring to evidence of their parents' decline. He harbored suspicions that Eileen was too anxious to declare Ma unfit. But, mostly, she was probably just anxious over the prospect of some crisis that would require her to fly out from New York on a moment's notice.

"What time's your flight tomorrow?" Philly looked up at Eileen, who had remained standing and was looking out the front window.

"She just got here yesterday." Ma had planted herself in the middle of the room. She had scooped up the dog in transit.

"She's a busy executive these days, Ma. People are depending on her to get back and keep 'em on track."

"She hasn't been too successful at getting me on track yet."

Apparently Ma was aware of Eileen's self-appointed role as her health auditor.

"That's just because I'm old enough to know better and smart enough to not give a whit." Eileen actually selected slightly different wording for that last phrase.

"Oh, don't be crude. We're fine here. You don't need to worry about us. So what if your dad forgets a thing or two? Who doesn't? They're not gonna put him away in a loony bin just 'cause he forgets to bring the dog in once in a while." Ma stopped abruptly, as if suddenly realizing she had said too much.

"What happened with the dog?" Eileen dropped her arm from where it had been propped across her chest. She sloshed her wine a little, though probably not spilling any on the dark brown carpet.

Ma pivoted toward the armchair behind her and lowered herself slowly into it, a huff and a hiss serving as sound effects for the effort.

"Your back bothering you again, Ma?" Philly was filing away a list of concerns now, one of which was the ongoing tension between Ma and Eileen. Another was Ma's increasing back complaints.

"Nothing to worry about. I can still get up and down. I don't need one of those lift chairs yet." She looked at the dog in her lap. "Do we Sparks? We're not dead yet."

"What if I prayed for your back, Ma?" Philly wished Brenda was in the living room to help with this part, but he was feeling bold because of the news they had heard about Thelma at church.

"Oh, you know I don't believe in any of that."

Philly stood up. "You don't have to believe. Just let me give it a try. It doesn't cost you anything."

"That's good. I'm pretty sure my Medicare won't cover it. I think it's a donut hole service."

Philly laughed. That was a pretty good joke. He would hang onto it for future healing situations. But he was serious about offering to help his ma. "I'd like to at least try."

"Why not, Ma? Just let Philly try." Eileen's support might have had more to do with her default tendency to oppose whatever their ma said, but Philly knew his sister still believed at least a little.

Brenda had pulled herself away from Dad in the kitchen and ambled into the brewing controversy. "Let Philly try what? Do you need healing, Ma?" She assessed the parties in the living room. "You should hear about this woman with a brain tumor from church. Philly went to pray for her after the doctors had totally given up on her. Now she's back home and feeling fine, with the tumor shrinking. From death's door to feeling totally fine."

A relieved guffaw got as far as the back of Philly's throat before he clamped it down. Brenda was a shameless promoter of his healing work now, willing to make the most of any bit of good news. Though the news about Thelma *was* pretty compelling.

"Well, I ain't got no brain tumor, so you don't have to worry about that."

"That's not the point. Philly can do this kind of thing, Ma. Why don't we just let him give it a try?" Eileen sounded like she was offering to join Ma in taking the risk.

Philly wasn't really worried about her motives. He was feeling a nugget of confidence that something might happen if he touched his ma's back. He had sidled over next to her chair, checking with Brenda as he maneuvered. She seemed to recognize the move.

"You don't even have to do anything. It's not about you believing, necessarily. Healing happens in all kinds of different ways." Brenda distracted Ma as Philly slipped a hand down to her shoulder, bending slightly at the waist to reach her.

"Yeah. I can feel this sort of push to do it, Ma." Philly risked piling on his ma. "It seems like Jesus is wanting to heal you, like really ready to do it. So, I just say let it come. I welcome healing for Ma's back pain. Let all tension and ... and, uh, bitterness be gone right *now*." He hit harder on the last word. The idea of bitterness being involved had sneaked into his healing command, but he had heard it used before with an arthritis sufferer. He didn't understand everything about that, but it felt relevant to Ma's situation.

"What was that?" Ma leaned forward a little and strained to look up at Philly.

He stepped back a foot to make it easier for her to see his face. "I just did a quick healing prayer, sort of just welcoming what Jesus wants to do."

"Huh. I don't know how you can do that." She twisted her neck a bit more. "And you said something else."

Years of ducking the wrath of his ma urged Philly not to clarify what he had said, but it seemed too important to avoid full disclosure. "I think there might be some kind of bitterness that's, like, knotted up in your back."

"Might be from when your mother disowned us." Dad was standing just behind Philly. Dad sometimes seemed a bit confused lately, but his proposed explanation for the root of bitterness in Ma was one of the clearest things Philly had ever heard him say.

"I don't know what that has to do with anything!" Ma practically shrieked her denial. No one in this family ever came even close to shrieking. Grumbling and complaining were common, but no one raised their voice like that. This fact wasn't lost on Ma. She spoke in a small, childish voice now. "Oh, my. What do you think that was about?"

Philly had an idea what it was about. He squatted down, placed both hands on the arm of her chair, and looked in Ma's face. "Spirit of bitterness, come off Ma, right now."

Simultaneously about four things happened.

Eileen said, "What?"

Dad said, "Ha!"

Philly felt a chill run over his arms and up through his head. And Ma belched.

Brenda gasped and then giggled.

"Oh. Excuse ..." Ma's eyes froze where they stared straight ahead. It was the look of someone who suddenly notices a sensation they can't name. "My back. What *is* that with my back?"

She was leaning forward slightly, so Philly stood and slid his hand down behind her. "Your back is hot."

"It's like massaging. It's swirling. And it's warm." That girlish tone had settled onto her voice. "It's nice."

"Does your back feel better, Marge?" When Dad's hearing had been restored, he had retained some of the habits he accumulated during his years without it. But he wasn't the only one who was still hoping to hear a clear and definite update from Ma.

"It's better, then?" Brenda spoke up.

But Philly knew that warmth wasn't always the end of the process. He felt like something more was required. With his hand still on Ma's back, he said in a simple and calm voice, "All pain, leave. Healing, come."

"Thank you, Jesus!" Brenda said it just before Ma reacted.

"Hey. Hey, Philly. Oh, hey! I felt that. Wait a minute." Ma turned and looked at her son. Her movement, though small, was much less inhibited than the way she had twisted when she looked up at him before.

"Better?" Philly was restraining a grin.

"Are you healed, Marge?"

Rocking forward and letting the dog jump down to the carpet, Ma pulled on the arms of the chair and stood up. "Oh, whoop." She laughed at herself. "I mean, yup. Sure enough. What do you think about that? Oh, my!"

Instead of insisting on a more articulate answer, Dad just stepped up and put his hand on his wife's back and chuckled deep in his throat. "Now look at you. Lost for words is it?"

They all laughed then, and Sparks joined in with a single bark.

Chapter 22
Another Visit to Gladys's Place

During the the following work week, Philly was in touch with Gladys. He mentioned the healing victories he had seen, and she told him about an old man she often visited. He was suffering from severe back pain. She told Philly she had prayed for her fellow resident's healing many times. Then she finally asked Philly directly if he could stop by to try to do something for the old gentleman.

Ernest Bowers sat up in his hospital bed with his mouth open half an inch, staring at a TV mounted high in the corner of the room. The room was in the comprehensive care unit in the graduated care community where Gladys lived. This was near the opposite end of the spectrum from Gladys's independent apartment. Philly wasn't surprised that Gladys had gravitated to helping the neediest folks in her community.

"Hello, Ernie. This is the man I was telling you about." Gladys spoke loudly as she led Philly into the room. Then, more quietly, she spoke to Philly out of the corner of her mouth. "He may not remember, but we won't let that hold us back."

"Ah, uh, oh?" The old man's tone was clearly a question, but Philly didn't recognize any words.

"Hello, Mr. Bowers." Philly could see the patient's full name printed on a white board on the wall under the TV. Gladys had told him the man's last name, but Philly had forgotten.

"Ah, uh." The old man didn't move his lips much, his mouth still propped open when he responded.

"He's on some pretty powerful pain medications, you know." Gladys tipped her head compassionately at Mr. Bowers. "You should just go ahead and do what you can. I don't think he'll mind."

Healing his ma that previous Sunday had felt a bit like Philly was slipping in under the fence before the healing began. So maybe this would be the same. Maybe Mr. Bowers would get more lucid once the healing started happening. Philly accepted Gladys's invitation to go ahead and hoped that Jesus would fill in the rest. Keeping a smile on his face—out of a combination of discomfort and artifice—Philly waited for Gladys to round the bed to the other side.

He stood on Mr. Bowers's right with his hands in his pants pockets. "I understand you have some back pain. Pretty severe, I hear." He would at least try to keep the patient informed of what he was doing. "I just saw my ma's back healed pretty much completely this last Sunday. And I'm glad to give it a try for you." Philly was talking loudly and regretting the kindergarten-teacher tone in his voice. If Mr. Bowers was at all cogent, he would probably think Philly was a moron. Philly puffed and shook his head at himself. He caught Gladys's eye and straightened up. "Sorry. I'm not sure how much you understand me, but I'm glad to try and heal your back pain."

For the first time since Philly entered the room, Mr. Bowers turned his head. He settled his eyes on Philly, but those eyes remained wide and blank. His watery blue gaze seemed completely void of feeling or recognition. That empty stare drained some of Philly's faith.

But he had soldiered forward many times before when faith had seemed to vanish entirely. Healing Thelma in the intensive care unit was mostly like that. So Philly continued. "I'll just rest my hand on your shoulder, if you don't mind." His voice cracked. "And I'll say a little prayer."

Usually when Philly said *prayer*, what he meant was a healing command, like the ones he had heard Jesus use. But, this time,

Philly actually paused to offer a short prayer for Mr. Bowers's healing before trying a couple healing commands.

Nothing seemed to click. Mr. Bowers just stared past Philly with those unblinking eyes.

Gladys stood with a sort of sympathetic, but dissatisfied, tilt to her face.

And Philly felt nothing—no confidence, no healing heat, nothing. "Have you ever really heard him talk to you?" Philly wondered whether Mr. Bowers was cogent when he *wasn't* on pain meds.

"Not much. I've seen him come down off the meds a few times. Then he usually closes his eyes and moans a bit."

This renewed Philly's compassion for the suffering of the poor man. "Be healed in Jesus's name. And all bitterness, leave his back right now." It was a recycled and patched version of what he had said for his ma, but Philly wasn't feeling inspired at all. Perhaps the catatonic condition of his patient was distracting him too much. Or maybe Philly was just tired at the end of a long week. He was looking forward to Friday—the next day—already.

"Are you hearing anything from Jesus?" Gladys asked this in a throaty tone that either implied she was embarrassed to have to remind Philly about it, or embarrassed that she hadn't thought of it herself before that.

"I'm not really hearing anything specific. I just feel like Jesus is always in favor of me trying to heal people."

Gladys nodded, perhaps willing to yield to Philly's more extensive experience.

He briefly regretted this. He would rather have her correct his errors. Surely he didn't always hear Jesus, or hear him perfectly. But Philly didn't tell Gladys any of that, and she didn't offer any divine revelations to help him heal Mr. Bowers.

"Okay. Well, thanks for tryin', Philly. I appreciate you coming out at the end of your workday."

Maybe Gladys was hearing from Jesus that it was time to stop. Or maybe it was just obvious that Philly lacked the energy to make anything happen here tonight. Except, making something happen was supposed to be Jesus's job, wasn't it? Philly tried to listen for a response to that thought, but didn't feel like he heard anything. "You're welcome, Gladys. Glad to try. Sorry nothing seemed to happen."

Over dinner at home that night, Brenda tried to console him. "But look at it this way—if any of the Cubs had as good an average as you do, they would never lose." Brenda didn't really know much about baseball, but Philly didn't mind her stretching a comforting hand his way.

"Unfortunately I wasn't just trying to drive Mr. Bowers home from third base with a ground ball." He was twirling his spaghetti and still picturing the blank look masking the old man's face. "I was pretty tired. And maybe kinda intimidated by how out of it he seemed."

Brenda had rested her fork on her plate. "Yeah. That sounds hard."

He turned and smiled at his wife. "How are *you* feeling today, by the way?" He had been neglecting his wife with his focus on trying to heal other people.

"Oh, I'm starting to feel better. I'm not so frantic about eating. And my mom told me that eating was probably a natural defense mechanism against morning sickness."

"'Natural defense mechanism?' It sounds like she's been watching the Discovery Channel or something."

"Could be." Brenda smiled, taking it as a mild joke.

Just before bed that night, Philly read a short series of messages from Gladys. She had remembered something she'd heard from a preacher once, and had gone back to Mr. Bowers's room. She prayed for him, told confusion to leave the room, and then tried to heal his back. The last thing she reported was that he was sleeping peacefully.

Philly messaged back that Mr. Bowers's peaceful sleep reminded him of what happened with Thelma, hoping this observation would encourage Gladys. Her news encouraged him in a way, giving him hope on behalf of the suffering old man. But it renewed his questions. Had he missed something? Did he do something wrong? Was there something he should have been hearing from Jesus?

Clear instructions didn't always seem necessary for healing to happen. Sure, Jesus was the one providing the healing, but he seemed to trust Philly to carry out what he had shown him already, no further instructions needed. Philly suspected that there *had* been further instructions required to heal Mr. Bowers. He had obviously missed those. Gladys had, perhaps, heard them after Philly left.

Resolved to get back to the basement that weekend, he would see if he could get an explanation from Jesus. Clearly, he had more to learn.

Chapter 23
Jesus Chases Away the Darkness

The Cubs were playing a late game on the West Coast that Saturday, which left the afternoon open for Philly. He and Brenda had ordered some baby things online, so they restrained themselves from doing more in-store shopping that weekend.

"I'm gonna go down to the basement and meet with Jesus."

Brenda stopped her sorting of the baby clothes her cousin had sent her and stared at Philly. Was she trying to remember Philly mentioning this to her before? Was she wondering if she could join Philly and Jesus down there? She restarted her industrious folding and stacking. "Okay. Have a good time."

Philly carried a bottle of root beer with him this time, creaking down the stairs over the worn and stained beige carpet. This was the most embarrassing stretch of flooring in the house, a house that could use a lot of new carpet and tile. Those were projects for a later day—or year.

"Have you thought of asking for a raise? Your six-month review is coming up this week." That was Jesus, apparently in his career-development role.

"Would they really give me a raise?"

Silence. No answer.

Philly sat down in his chair and tried to imagine Jesus's answer. "Sure, Philly, it's guaranteed. Just ask and you shall receive." Or maybe he would say, "You know, Philly, you should learn to be content in all circumstances." But would Jesus really avoid the issue like that? Wouldn't he offer some correction and

Hosting Jesus

then some kind of piercing revelation, an answer that made Philly understand his own life better? That was more like Jesus.

The question at hand wasn't about a raise, as far as Philly was concerned, although he did plan to tuck that idea away as he approached his job review this week. No, what Philly wanted to ask Jesus about was what had happened with Mr. Bowers's healing.

"Are you wondering why Gladys got to do it and you didn't?"

"Yes and no. I mean, I know I wasn't really listening to you when I tried. I was all caught up with what the old guy was thinking, how much he was aware of. I pretty much forgot about you, most of the time. Which is pretty crazy, because how am I gonna do healing stuff without you?"

"It is possible to do. Some gifted people do it some of the time. I'm so committed to people getting healed that I don't always let the imperfection of the vessel hold me back."

Okay, that sounded like Jesus, because Philly would never make that up. But had Jesus ever said things like that to him before? As little as it sounded like something Philly would invent, he wasn't completely confident that it was an idea Jesus would endorse.

"Do I love people?"

"Of course."

"Do *you* want the people *you* love to suffer pain?"

"No, of course not."

"Then you can be sure that *I'm* not going to want my loved ones to be sick or in pain. And sometimes there are no perfect healing vessels available."

"Healing vessels? I don't remember you saying anything about that before."

"It's just a metaphor. We could talk about being partners. We're always working together. I bring some things to the partnership. You bring some things. Sometimes I can only find imperfect partners, so we work out the best deal we can."

"Is this still about healing and not about asking for a raise?"

"Was that a joke?"

"If you have to ask, then it wasn't a very good joke."

"Mm-hmm."

Philly snorted. Was he telling himself bad jokes? That seemed possible. Even likely. But Jesus had often joked with Philly, as if the place in Philly's heart that laughed at jokes was the best place for him and Jesus to meet.

"That's a good way to think of it. Wish I had said it."

Shaking his head and remembering his root beer, Philly took a swig.

"About Mr. Bowers."

"Yes. Tell me about him."

"There was a lot going on there, and Gladys was more familiar with all of it. It was natural for you to focus mostly on healing his back. It's still not entirely healed, by the way. Just improved. His meds will be reduced this weekend." That sounded like Jesus confiding in him. "But you were overwhelmed by his mental state and how thin and transparent his skin looked. Gladys was used to all that, and she was better able to hear me about the spirit of confusion oppressing him."

"I *was* freaked out by the way he stared at me. And you're right about the rest. My grandma was old, and her skin looked old, but she was more alive, so it didn't seem so awful."

"I know. She says hi, by the way."

This stopped Philly. "She's with you?"

"Of course."

"She can send me messages?"

"Let's not go there, Philly. I was just reminding you that she's with me. She's part of the great cloud of folks up here rooting for you and your teammates."

"Teammates?"

"The church."

"What about my church?"

"They aren't yet ready for your gifts, Philly. I'm working on them, but there's no guarantee that they won't be put off by what you do. It's outside their comfort zone."

"I was getting that feeling. There isn't gonna be a celebration of Thelma's healing like there would have been at my church in Chicago, is there?"

"No. Not the same."

Philly wanted to hear more, but he didn't even know what to ask. He was overwhelmed like he had been in the comprehensive care unit with Mr. Bowers. He didn't understand much about churches, and he had little personal experience with churches that were uncomfortable with Jesus healing people. But he did settle on one very personal question. "Should Brenda and I stay at that church?"

"It's okay for now. The jury is still out. And that will be something you and Brenda need to work out together."

"Sure. Yeah. I know that." Philly suddenly felt very tired.

"It's okay to be tired. Take a rest. It's been quite a week."

Whether that was Philly giving himself permission or Jesus offering his usual mercy and grace, it felt like good advice, a welcomed bit of freedom to tend to his own needs. Maybe someone preoccupied with other people's healings needed to pay attention to resting once in a while.

He must have dozed off. Philly first noticed that he was barely holding his root beer bottle upright. He tightened his grip and lifted the bottle over the arm of the chair to set it on the little table between the two recliners.

The next thing he noticed was that he wasn't alone in the room. At least, it seemed like someone was looming over him. He glanced at the other recliner. Brenda wasn't there. No one he could see was there. But there was a presence in the basement. It wasn't Jesus. It was meaner, heavier, cold. It reminded him of something he had sensed in the frozen face of Mr. Bowers. Philly shivered. He tried to cry out but couldn't, like in a nightmare. This might just be a dream. It wasn't really happening. But, whether real or a dream, that sinister shadow was cranking his adrenaline level through the roof.

Was it a nightmare? Maybe it was the opposite of the dream he had where Jesus was waiting for him in the basement. Philly had come down here to meet with Jesus. And that was what he got for trying to hang out with him—terror, sheer terror.

Something evil was in that basement.

Maybe that was what happened when you opened yourself up to spiritual things. Not all spirits are good. Maybe meeting with Jesus in the basement was weird. Too weird. Maybe Philly had made himself vulnerable to other spirits, and now they were surrounding him. A desperate moaning started in his throat, as if beyond his control. And it escalated and articulated into a cry. "Jesus, help me."

For a second, the picture became still, a photo of the moment, like a crime scene recorded for the authorities to study later. Then he knew he wasn't the only one under attack. Surrounded by the threatening presence that seemed to control every corner of that basement, someone was with Philly. It was like when that person appeared inside the fiery furnace with those guys in the Bible. Someone was there to help Philly.

"Jesus, help me." He said it again. This time he spoke consciously.

A new current of fear crossed the room. But it wasn't Philly's fear. His internal terror had become muted. Jesus had stepped into the space it had occupied. But now Philly was sensing something else. He felt terror, but it was not *his* terror. The dark presence in the basement was afraid. It was afraid of the other occupants of that room. It was afraid of Jesus ... and of Philly.

"Thank you, Jesus." His voice quaked. Philly was awake now.

"Philly, are you okay down there? Is that the TV?" Brenda sounded like she was at the top of the stairs.

He reached up and scratched at something on his cheek. He was sweating. It was cool in the basement, but he was sweating. He was fully awake now. He was safe. But he could still feel that gut-level change in the room, from when the looming evil turned to run. "It's okay, dear. I just fell asleep. And I had a dream."

Chapter 24
Lunch with Holly and Stan

Before the second service started, the service Philly and Brenda usually attended, Stan searched them out. "Hey, Phil, Brenda. How are you doing? How's pregnant life?"

That greeting poked Philly like a pine needle slipped inside his collar. He was remembering an apprehension from Brenda. "*I don't wanna just become this big pregnancy.*" Comments like Stan's were certainly behind Brenda's sentiment.

On the other hand, Brenda seemed sufficiently enamored with the attention from one of the church staff to ignore any offense in his question. "Oh, we're doing great. I feel good these days. I think I'm having it easy." She was looking past Stan to his wife, Holly, who was shadowing him.

Brenda had edited that response pretty heavily, as far as Philly was concerned. She had begun complaining to him about body parts swelling, and he had shared in the fruit of numerous mood swings. There was an ongoing dispute between them about whether she had actually growled at Philly once that week. No neutral witnesses to the incident had yet been identified.

Philly shook Stan's hand and just smiled. When it came to Brenda's pregnant state, he often felt that the less he said, the better. This was Brenda's time to shine, and it was his time to nod supportively.

"Say, would you two happen to be available for lunch after the service?"

Pretty sure that Brenda had blushed with delight at the offer, Philly thought he heard Stan's voice quaver slightly. But he pushed past those considerations and declared that they had no plans. That led to arrangements for the four of them to meet at a nearby sandwich shop after the end of the second service.

He and Brenda hadn't made many friends yet at their new church. Their affiliation with the church in Chicago had been separate and distinct from each other. They had only a few friends there who had known them both well. A new start at a new church seemed like a chance to build friendships as a couple.

As interested as Philly was in finding friends he and Brenda could share, he wasn't sure they would fit with the elite couples of this church, such as Stan and Holly. They looked like models from an outdoor clothing catalog—not the slicked back models in chic designer catalogs, but the healthy, outdoorsy couples with tans and golden hair, that hinted at woodland nymphs prepping them each morning. Stan's teeth seemed unusually white, intimidating Philly into keeping his coffee-stained enamel concealed behind his lips.

At the restaurant, after a church service that he forgot as soon as it was over, Philly had a hard time focusing on anything right in front of him. He had parked too far from the little lunch establishment and had neglected to open the car door for Brenda.

"You seem nervous." Brenda scuttled to catch up with him in the parking lot.

"Oh, sorry. Yeah, I know. Don't let me ruin it for you. I know you wanna make friends here. I'll get over it."

She slipped her hand into his, huddling into his side. Clouds were blocking the sun's efforts to warm the spring day.

Brenda's proximity warmed Philly inside and out. He sighed and started to crank up an effort to relax. He held the restaurant door open for Brenda and rehearsed a breathing exercise he had learned several years ago.

"I'm right here with you, Philly." That felt like something Jesus would say.

But, as Philly wound his way toward a table that Brenda was targeting, he worried about *why* Jesus needed to accompany him to lunch. Was something wrong that Jesus was here to address? Philly snorted and then tried more of those relaxing breaths.

"This looks good, right? We can see out the window, and we're not too far from the counter." Brenda slipped her pale blue jacket off and settled it onto the rounded back of a chair.

Philly wrestled his tan spring jacket off his shoulders and took stock of the room. The shop was pretty full, and this table looked like the best one available. Right now, his primary concern was breathing. Seating selection would have to be handled by someone with more bandwidth available.

Before he sat down, Philly caught sight of Stan and Holly in the parking lot leading two girls, about eight and ten years old. So, this wasn't going to be just the two couples.

When the family of four bustled through the door, Brenda rose from her seat and joined in the handshakes, the name exchanges, and the apologies from Stan and Holly. Arrangements for the girls had fallen through, so they had come along. "A special surprise," Holly said.

"Oh, it's so nice to get to meet your girls." Brenda remained standing.

More smiling, more silent nodding, and letting Brenda speak. Philly was in a sort of virtual social interaction zone. The hard part would come later when he was expected to speak for himself. He assumed that would be necessary sooner or later.

After everyone had trooped to the counter, ordered sandwiches and salads, and picked up their trays by the cash register, the six of them settled at two adjacent tables. A departing couple had freed up one of the spots near where Philly and Brenda had settled their jackets.

With chitchat fading and first bites swallowed, Stan startled Philly with his practiced and formal tone. "What we wanted to do here today is get a sense of how you two are doing at the church, to see if you have questions, and to provide some information about the church's vision and mission."

Philly raised his eyebrows and regretted having taken such a big bite of the Reuben sandwich he was holding in two hands. A glance at Brenda found her in a similar state, several sweet potato fries preventing her from responding articulately. She nodded and made affirming, muffled noises.

Holly just stretched her brightest smile, proving that she and Stan used the same stellar dentist.

Philly swallowed and cleared his mouth with a hard sip of his iced tea. "It's good. Ah ... we're still new, but we're meeting a few people. And we signed up for one of the Tuesday Bible studies."

"Oh, that's good. We really want everyone to take advantage of the midweek offerings. That's where the church's life really happens." Stan was leaning over his sandwich and nodding through every word. His medium-brown eyebrows hunkered with an intensity that scared Philly a little. Was Stan worried about them?

"Yeah. And I'm gonna go to that class for new mothers on Saturdays. That looks perfect for me right now." Brenda had finished her big bite and washed it down with a slug from a plastic water bottle. This was the start of Brenda and Philly tag-teaming the task of answering questions while still eating. The pregnant woman wasn't the only hungry one at that table.

In contrast, Stan and Holly ate with such a pedestrian pace that Philly wondered if they had eaten lunch with someone else already.

Next, Stan began an overview of the programs offered by the church, perhaps launched by Philly and Brenda checking the boxes about their group sign-ups. But he seemed to be circling in toward some other target. When he arrived at reviewing the mission and vision of the church, his flexed eyebrows shaded his deep blue eyes even more deeply. "We want to be a welcoming place, especially to people who have traditionally felt excluded by church, people uncomfortable with some of the old, cultural characteristics of church that turned them off for one reason or another." Stan took a sip of his diet soda and nibbled at his sandwich.

Philly thought he understood the cause of those furrowed eyebrows now. "Oh, well, that was one of the things that made us feel comfortable here. We both saw some of the old ways of doing church when we were kids, and we weren't really into that. We really just got into church by going to a newer-style place that was good for people who hadn't done much church before." It was way more words than he'd intended to assemble in one place, but Philly felt like he had to saturate a fairly big piece of ground in order to be sure he watered the one small plant he was trying to save. But maybe that self-critique was just the inevitable result of comparing his answer to Stan's scripted presentation.

"Oh, I get that. Yes. I can see that you have been exposed to some ... different ... ah, ways of doing church. And we here are fully affirming of a wide range of Christian experience. Some places are more into some parts of the experience of Jesus than others, and we bless them to play to their strength. Our strength, we believe, is presenting the gospel in a sort of distilled form—without some of the aspects that might put off people who are shy about faith, people who are uncertain about what they believe."

When he realized that his brow was curling hard over his own eyes, Philly forced himself to relax and to sit up straighter. That moment of worry he had suffered earlier—about why Jesus needed to assure him of his presence—came back to him.

Holly spoke up—so Stan could get a bite in, apparently. "It's not that we don't believe in lots of things that other churches are comfortable practicing, it's just that we feel we have to stay focused on what works for introducing unchurched people to the gospel."

Philly was arranging some data into new columns now and starting to add them up. Where were Sergio and Salma this week? Was Carrie going to the first service? He hadn't seen her either. All three of those folks had been so enthusiastic about Philly's healing efforts. It seemed odd that they didn't at least say hello this week. And still there had been no announcement about Thelma's healing. Jesus had said something about that, hadn't he? Philly got the feeling that Stan was reading his mind. Or maybe just reading his eyebrows.

"So, I think you can see where we're going with this, where it pertains to you." Stan had tipped his head for a "*So there you have it*" expression, a look that offered room for a response, perhaps with very particular expectations about what that response should be.

"I'm not sure what you mean." Brenda had set down her turkey club sandwich and was wiping her hands on a paper napkin.

Stan explained. "Sergio and Salma were so grateful for the unique experience they took part in with you a few weeks ago. And I think we're all grateful for what happened with Thelma. A really unexpected recovery, right? But we feel like, as a church, we need to leave those sorts of ministries to other churches to carry. We're not prepared to carry that sort of thing on a regular basis."

Philly balked at the phrase "*carry that sort of thing*," which sounded like a retail boutique deciding on what items to stock this season. "Did something happen with Sergio and Salma?" He couldn't explain what prompted that question. Maybe Jesus was feeding him some insider information.

"Oh. Well, I think they've decided to attend a different church. We recommended that they consider some options."

"This is because of the healing?" Philly was seeing it all come into focus now. But what he was seeing was something he had never viewed from this angle before.

"We've had an understanding all along that we're not going to be the best place for everyone. Other churches have more to offer when it comes to different gifts. We feel like our congregation is gifted in certain things, and others ... uh ... have gifts we haven't been assigned." As practiced and professional as Stan's presentation had felt to this point, Philly detected a tangle in his words there.

That was when he noticed a sensation like someone settling gentle hands on his shoulders. Philly needed Jesus's presence right then. At least he needed him more than usual.

Another one of those relaxation breaths helped Philly to consider how he could set Stan's mind at ease.

He glanced at Brenda. "We both got started in the faith we have now by going to a church where people prayed for healing and did other things like that. But we're not interested in messing up any church that's not comfortable with that kinda thing."

Brenda's head seemed to click a big notch forward, her mouth dropping open as she stared at her husband. She was probably less familiar than Philly with the notion of churches that didn't support the kind of healing Jesus had shown him. He had told her the story about the church people who told Theresa not to date him because he claimed to see and hear Jesus next to him. But he and Brenda had never discussed the way churches were divided by such issues. Now seemed to be the time for that conversation. Not *now*, actually. Maybe after lunch.

"That's good. I see we understand each other." Stan looked satisfied, probably relieved, that he didn't really have to spell it all out.

But Brenda, obviously, wasn't so satisfied. "Wait. What happened to Sergio and Salma?"

After glancing at Brenda, Philly switched his focus to Holly. She had softened, somehow. Maybe her bigger smile had been forced, and she was more relaxed now. Her eyes seemed much more sympathetic when she answered Brenda. "We have no problem with you attending the church. We just need to let you know that we aren't going to be providing opportunities for the sort of healing ministry we've heard about."

"You mean like the things Philly has been doing?"

"Yes. That."

"But Thelma is recovering. And Sergio was totally healed."

"Yes, we are aware of that way of seeing things. It's entirely understandable. But it's just not what we feel called to try to make happen in our church."

Philly was hearing words from Holly that seemed out of place, and he began to suspect that they were code words he would need help deciphering.

Brenda was probably even further adrift than he was. "So, did you tell Sergio and Salma they had to leave the church because they got healed?"

"No. No, we just told them they would be much happier in another church in the area if that was the sort of thing they were looking for. We gave them a couple of suggestions." Stan seemed to have dropped the script, and he sounded a bit more present. His voice had a more defensive edge now.

"You just went to them and suggested that?" Philly shook his head without meaning to.

"No. They were asking about getting training to do healing ministry. They were very enthusiastic about it. And I know there are other congregations that would probably welcome that."

"Really and truly, we are not against this kind of thing. We just aren't called to teach it. So they would probably be happier elsewhere." Holly was still playing the good cop in the scene, her voice rich with compassion. But her little pause alerted Philly that she was likely thinking it wasn't just Sergio and Salma who would be happier elsewhere.

"And Carrie? Did you suggest she go elsewhere? And Thelma?" Philly wasn't eating anymore. His appetite had checked out.

Stan looked down at the table for half a second and then at his wife. "Oh. Well, Thelma is a long-time member of the church—at least five years, I think. So, she's used to the way we do things. She embraces the vision of the church. I expect she'll stick around. Carrie was never really a part of things here. I'm not sure what she'll do."

When Philly had studied spiritual gifts at Pastor Dave's church, he had learned that the people in a congregation have a variety of gifts that work together to represent the body of Christ. Stan's notion of different churches having different gifts was new to him, but he couldn't judge whether it was right. He paused for a moment to doubt the wisdom of the woman who had recommended that he and Brenda attend this new church. But he wouldn't go there right now.

"You're not asking us to leave, you're just telling us we'll probably be happier at a different church?" Brenda seemed to be accepting what she was hearing. The shock had drained from her voice. She, too, had stopped eating.

Stan and Holly nodded in unison. Stan added a note of consolation. "You don't have to decide right away. And you can still attend the groups and services anytime you want—special events and things like the new mothers' class—even if you do choose a different home church."

Well, they were getting the boot. But it was a soft boot, gently applied to Philly's backside. He turned to Brenda and took her hand, which rested on the table near him. He grinned at her with the side of his mouth. "We'll discuss it and see what we wanna do." He turned toward Stan and Holly. "Thanks for explaining all that to us."

And that was where Philly paused to silently thank Jesus, who had generously accompanied him to what he had naively assumed would be a friendly little lunch.

Chapter 25
A Trip to See Dave

"This whole thing just makes me think I'm not really a church person." Philly was driving home after the lunch with Stan and Holly.

Brenda was leaning on the passenger door of the smooth-riding SUV. "I know what you mean. It all gets so complicated when you have to know what all the different churches believe about one thing and another."

"Of course, there are people who go to graduate school to learn all that."

"*Somebody* has to understand it. Pastor Dave probably understands it."

"Yeah. I should go talk to him. We haven't talked lately, and things were kinda confusing there around the wedding ... and me not really going back to church regularly before that."

"He understood. He told us that he understood almost every time we met with him about the wedding."

"Yeah, I know. But you know how people are—they say what they know they're supposed to say." Philly paused over a suspicion that that probably didn't apply to Dave so much. "Anyway, I'd like to see him and talk about some of this church stuff."

"That sounds like a good idea."

Neither Naperville nor Schaumburg were close to their old church in Chicago, but Philly was a city guy and didn't hesitate about driving into the city one afternoon that week. He took advantage of his flexible work schedule and left before the evening rush had built to a crescendo of honking horns. An intermittent rainfall slowed his progress a bit, but the slowdown didn't bother him as much as the prospect that the rain might threaten the game scheduled at Wrigley that night.

"How are you, Philly?" Dave laughed his greeting and grabbed Philly for a muscular hug. Dave's church was where Brenda had become a hugger.

Philly suspected his pastor of hugging him hard now to impress him with how devoted he had become to his weightlifting. Philly didn't try to compete.

"I have a whole new life now. And there are some parts of it I need help sorting out."

"Marriage issues?"

"Not so much. Really church issues."

"Where did you two end up? I don't think we discussed your plans for a new church."

"No. That's the problem—we should have gotten recommendations from you. We went to a 'seeker-sensitive' church that just told us this week that we might be more comfortable at a church that believes more in healing and stuff."

Dave asked the name of the church and nodded sympathetically when Philly told him. "Who recommended *that*?"

"I don't want to say. I'm still working on forgiving her." Philly laughed half-heartedly. He was pretty sure his resentment was nothing serious. And he wasn't feeling all that bad about having to start looking again. They hadn't fully settled in at their new church.

"Well, there are a couple of churches near you that do things like we do here, so I'll give you contact information for those. Has something happened where you are now?" Even with the high level of trust between them, Philly could sense Dave beginning to circle in a holding pattern over the real question he wanted to ask.

Philly told Dave about the healings he had been part of at the new church.

Dave grinned through the whole telling. Clearly this was part of that unspoken question. "That's some awesome God stuff. Can

I tell people around here about those? I think it'll be really encouraging."

"Encouraging because of how messed up I was before? I never would have thought I could ever see anyone healed again."

"Actually that's not what I was thinking. I just assumed you would get back into doing healing sooner or later. It's a gift. You just *have* it. It goes with you. Wherever you are, you're a healer. No, I just like the variety of experiences you described and especially the lack of expectations of the people around you. I mean, those are some clear examples of different levels and different kinds of faith."

To balance out the scales, Philly told Dave about Mr. Bowers and the failed healing there. Then he reversed the timeline and told about healing his ma.

Dave was doing his quiet belly laugh before the stories had all ended. "That's awesome. Let me tell those stories too, will ya?"

Philly nodded. "But why do you need *my* stories? You guys must have new stories of your own here."

Sucking in a deep breath, Dave scratched the side of his goatee. "We haven't seen so many healings lately. These things sometimes come and go for reasons I can't explain." Then he leveled his eyes on Philly. "What you still don't appreciate is how powerful your gift is. Sure, we see healing around here on a regular basis, but the gift Jesus gave you is very effective—as powerful as any I've seen even among churches that do this stuff all the time."

Of course Philly wasn't looking to establish his ranking among healers. And he had never had this conversation with Dave. At least not like this. Dave had tried to impress him with the responsibility he carried because of his visit from Jesus, but it had always sounded like the kind of thing you would expect a pastor to say to anyone in his congregation.

"You wanna move to another church?" Dave switched subjects while Philly was still contemplating what he had just said. "Or are you considering shaking things up where you are?"

"I wasn't even considering sticking around there. Though it would be nice for Brenda to go to the new moms classes."

Dave nodded and narrowed his eyes a bit. "Are you talking to Jesus these days?"

"Talking and listening." Philly spent a few minutes trying to summarize the conversations and interventions he had experienced lately. "Lots of times I know it's him. It sounds just like him and not like me talking to myself. Other times it's not so clear."

"That's normal. How can we know if it's him all the time when he's talking to us inside our own heads? His thoughts come from some of the same places that ours come from in there, right?" He quirked an eyebrow. "You have the mind of Christ, Philly. It's built into you now."

Maybe Dave had said all that to Philly before, but it sounded fresh and newly relevant now.

And Dave personalized it a bit more. "All this is available to all Christians, Philly. But you have to realize how rare your experience has been. Having seen and heard Jesus so clearly, you have a significant head start on the rest of us. Anyone who's had a mountain-top experience with God has the advantage of being able to go back there, at least in their memories. It can be a good place to get your spirit renewed." He allowed his eyes to drift away from Philly. "I tell you this to make it easier to understand the folks who don't quite believe what you tell them about your experiences."

Philly clenched one corner of his mouth. "Well, that's just it. I try *not* to tell people what I'm experiencing. I don't like those zombie stares I get when I do tell."

Dave laughed and held a smile for a few seconds. "That's probably wise in lots of situations. But you may be called to tell your story sometimes—so others can believe more."

That reminded Philly of something. "I found a book in a bookstore about a guy who sees Jesus in his living room. I just skimmed a few pages, but it sounded really familiar."

"You think someone stole your story?"

"It wasn't exactly my story, but it sounded like someone who had the same sort of experience as me. Do you think that's possible?"

"Sure. What happened to you is rare, but it's not unprecedented. I've heard a bunch of stories from the Muslim world where people seeking God get a personal visit from Jesus that starts their conversion to Christianity. It's often in places where Christian missionaries aren't allowed. So Jesus just shows up in person—or in dreams. There are enough different stories like that to make it believable to me."

"Huh. So, was Jesus converting me, like I was in some place where missionaries couldn't reach me?"

Dave grinned and shook his head. "I discovered a long time ago that I can't explain lots of things God does. Mystery is an inherent part of faith."

"Huh." For some reason, Philly thought of Gladys. "I don't think I told you about the woman I met a few years ago—a grandma from Wisconsin who saw and heard Jesus pretty much like I did."

As much as Dave believed in all this stuff, that little introduction seemed to trip something for him. He didn't speak, just stared at Philly as if he were recalculating. And he kept that attitude as he listened to Philly's description of meeting Gladys and getting to know her online. When Philly outlined his renewed relationship with Gladys, he realized he hadn't introduced her properly when he told the story about Mr. Bowers.

"Wow. Okay." Dave seemed to still be recalculating, or maybe recalibrating. "What are the chances that you would meet someone with such a similar experience?" He spoke as if his throat was slightly clogged.

"Well, I just think Jesus knew I needed to meet someone like that to help me recover. That was true when she talked to me that first time and this recent time too. And maybe *she* needed to meet me to feel more sure that her experience was real."

"Why didn't you tell me about her before?"

"I met her during the time when I stopped going to church—after Theresa. And it just always seemed like you and I had plenty to talk about whenever we got together after that."

"Of course. Like me telling you that God wanted you back in our church." Dave grinned at a joke he had made with Philly many times during his break from church attendance. Then he got a bit more serious. "You really should look into joining one of the more like-minded congregations out in the suburbs."

"Yeah, that seems like a good idea. I'm not gonna do some covert Jesus thing at our current church. I'm not that kind of activist or whatever."

"It probably wouldn't be a healthy situation for you and Brenda even if you were inclined to try."

So Philly left Dave's office with names and addresses on his phone for two churches near Schaumburg that would welcome his gifts. And he and Dave agreed to stay in touch.

Dave stood on the stairs outside the front doors of the church building and waved, a spring breeze mussing his hair slightly when Philly drove away.

Chapter 26
Neglecting Gathering with the Saints

The prospect of introducing themselves to a new church did nothing to warm Philly. And Brenda was still waiting for her moods to stabilize. The initial voracious hunger and queasiness had almost passed, at least on most days. But her emotions were like a stormy day on Lake Michigan.

"An empty stomach is going to be less stable." Philly was reading from a new parents book on a Sunday morning three weeks after their lunch with Stan and Holly. They were sitting together on the back deck enjoying the sun heating the little parking lot behind their townhouse. And they were *not* visiting a new church.

"That's easy for some guy sitting in his medical office to say."

"Mild food. Moderate amounts." He kept reading but allowed his volume to peter out. "Well, this guy isn't alone—there's a woman who wrote it with him. Maybe she tried it herself."

Brenda batted her eyes at her husband. "Thanks for trying, Philly. You're such a good birthing coach. I'm lucky to have you."

She still loved him, he knew. And, right now, she was feeling it. That might change in a few minutes—the feelings might. But she would still love him even when she didn't feel it. He was pretty confident of that. "When you feel better, we can visit one of those churches Dave told me about." He was testing the idea, half hoping Brenda would pull up on the brake so she could be his excuse for staying away from church for a while.

"Yes. Let's be sure we do that. We need to get back to church."

Nope. She wasn't going to support his sloth or his timidity.

Hosting Jesus

Back when Theresa died and Philly abandoned his church in Chicago, Brenda had been silent about his absence. She could certainly tell that he wasn't open to correction or even pointed questions.

To a large extent, Philly had been following Theresa when he evacuated his life in those days. He died to the world. He had woken up the next morning after leaving the hospital that one last time, and he couldn't convince himself to go to work even briefly. He couldn't hoist himself out of bed for anything more than a bathroom visit. Facing the people at work, just like encountering the people at church, would require leaving part of himself open to the world. That was out of the question. How could he trust anyone back inside his heart? And Philly was no good at faking things. He couldn't fake being okay.

After more than two weeks of absence from his computer job at the community center, not to mention the chess club there, his employer had begun to offer alternatives. Unpaid leave, paying for him to go to grief counseling, filling his position temporarily until he was ready to come back. Later he regretted it, but he didn't respond to any of their kindness or concern. Listening to Carmen on his voice mail the first time had started him crying, so Philly began deleting his boss's messages without listening. By the time he was ready to listen, the messages had ceased. He never blamed them for giving up on him. He had given up on himself.

All of that was perhaps more intensely true of Philly's contacts with Dave. After the funeral, Philly even refused to answer the back door when Dave stood outside knocking. He had hoped Dave would think he was gone, maybe staying with his parents—which Philly would never consider doing. He hadn't responded to his ma's calls for nearly three weeks after his numb interaction with her at the funeral.

Looking back on all that, Philly felt as if he had died, as if he could look back on his own death and learn from it. Or maybe it was more like a stroke victim who loses a part of his brain function. Returning to life after that loss was like learning to survive in the world with part of himself paralyzed.

During those dark months, Philly found temporary computer support work which required little human interaction. Certainly nothing personal or deep. Only his relationship with his old friend Ray persisted through those days. That friendship was less demanding than the more heartfelt and spiritual bonds he had at church and at the community center. Ray didn't seem to mind the hollow version of Philly. He just talked on and on about his latest dates or his latest sales figures. And Philly just listened out of the shell of himself he allowed to interface with the world.

Dave didn't give up on Philly during those days. He kept calling, texting, and emailing. And he even showed up at the back door a few times. One of those times he caught Philly in the kitchen. Philly had just helped Mrs. Kelly, his downstairs neighbor, with getting rid of some boxes, and he had forgotten to close the back door on a warm summer day.

"Hey, Philly." Dave spoke through the screen door as if nothing had happened, as if no time had been lost between them.

Even that normal greeting scared a year off Philly's life. His jumping startle was probably intensified by bundles of guilt over neglecting all his relationships for so many months. In fact, instead of responding to Dave's greeting, Philly had rushed out of the kitchen to conceal the hail of tears that surged out of the shock of that sudden voice on the back porch. Philly wondered later whether being startled was some sort of therapeutic method intended to help him release those pent-up emotions. Dave had never admitted to doing it on purpose, whether he knew of such a therapeutic approach or not.

For several weeks, Philly refused to meet with Dave again, only communicating electronically after that first back door encounter. Then he started meeting Dave in coffee shops around the north side of Chicago. After that it was at Philly's apartment and then Dave's office. And, finally, Philly agreed to try going back to church.

There was probably a special crown waiting in heaven for Dave—for extraordinary patience and compassion. During the first days, he very rarely asked Philly about coming back to church. Most of all, Philly felt that Dave was devoted to his survival, the survival of his soul.

And he succeeded, of course. Philly came back to church, even if the man who first attended wore a wrapper that only looked like him. That wrapper wouldn't be peeled back for many months. And that attendance wasn't consistent or sustained. Several times during those recovery years, Philly escaped for a month or two—or more.

He had never admitted it to her, but Brenda's presence at the church had repelled him several times. When he saw her, a pulse of pain would threaten to revive part of his heart. He wasn't ready for that resuscitation yet.

Those were the days when he began to see church as a sort of emergency room for his heart. He went there for healing, but stayed away when he just wasn't ready for one of those healers to press too hard and say, "Does that hurt?"

"Yes. It does. It hurts. Stop pushing on that."

When Mrs. Kelly didn't respond to his knocking on her back door one day that year, over four years ago now, he called 911. They found her in her bed. She had been dead for a few days by then. And that sent Philly back into hiding. But hiding in his apartment was difficult—his bedroom was just above hers. It was February, too cold to hang out in parks, so he went to the movie theater and paid for movies he didn't want to see, just to be alone in the dark and away from people who would inevitably hurt him.

He even felt the loss of his parents' dog in the following months, which only proved how raw his soul had become. The dog was never his. He and Blacky were never close. But the dog's death was just one more thing.

When he looked at his life back in those days, Philly knew he didn't even have any bootstraps with which to hoist himself up. Who wore that kind of boots these days anyway?

His church was using a method for emotional healing back then that involved sitting with a couple of people while the wounded person pictured Jesus coming into the room and sitting down beside him or her. A part of Philly's brain had registered that method as a natural fit for him. And then he tried it. The first time he imagined Jesus entering the room, Philly had literally screamed. Why, exactly, he couldn't explain. But the presence of Jesus in that prayer room was very real to him and deeply terrifying.

"I know you're not gonna wanna hear it, but I think that reaction means this kind of emotional healing is perfect for you, Philly." Once again, Dave had been in the position to try and convince Philly of something that he would later credit for saving his sanity. Dave somehow managed to persuade Philly to try that emotional healing again. What Philly didn't know then was how much Dave had to cajole the healing team to give it another try with that crazy guy who started screaming when he imagined Jesus coming into the room.

During the year that followed, Philly knew that he was being healed, being restored. But he didn't instantly return to the life he had known before. For one thing, Theresa had been a big part of his life before. And his role in the church doing healing ministry didn't come back automatically. Philly held back. Dave let him hold back. Brenda also let him hold back when they started dating. And Jesus had let Philly stay retired from healing for quite a while.

Until now.

Chapter 27
More Than Philly Can Handle

Late in May, Philly and Brenda finally resolved to visit one of the churches Dave had recommended. Philly was thinking about it—worrying actually—when he walked out to his car in the parking lot the Friday before. Across the lot, a husky guy was leaning over with his hands braced against his legs. At first Philly thought it was his coworker, Alvin. But then he realized the guy was too tall and was balding more than Alvin. The guy, whoever he was, was clearly in some serious distress.

As Philly approached, the big man pressed himself up to a standing position. He grimaced in a way that might have reflected more than the physical pain. He seemed embarrassed at attracting a stranger's attention.

"You okay?" Philly slowed his approach a few yards away from the man.

"Oh, yeah. It's nothin'. At least nothin' new. Bad knee is all."

"Acting up on you?"

"I forgot I wasn't twenty-one anymore and tried to skip up that curb." He waved a hand toward the yellow-painted curb next to a black SUV. The car was parked close to that curb, making it easier for the large man to step up there before getting in the vehicle.

"Really? You're not twenty-one?" Philly tried a joke his dad would have made in a situation like this. The guy had gray hair around a shiny forehead that was expanding toward the top of his head.

"Times two, at least." The guy laughed and tried to step closer to the SUV without going up the curb. He winced. "*Ooooh.*"

This was one of those times where Philly felt like he was being set up. Most folks could get away with words of sympathy and a "Have a nice day." But Philly was starting to think of himself as a healer again. "You know, I've actually seen a bunch of people healed of knee pain. Would you mind if I pray for you?"

The guy lowered one eyebrow and pursed his lips like he was trying to find the humor in what Philly had said.

"Seriously. I don't have to do anything weird. Just a few words and then see if it gets better." The déjà vu injected by his own reassurances slowed Philly's delivery.

The man still regarded Philly with obvious skepticism.

"I can do it from over here." Philly was still eight feet away. "Thank you for healing, Lord. Now let your kingdom come. Knee, be restored. All pain be gone."

"What?" The man recoiled, but then seemed to be distracted by something happening to his knee. Dropping his head to check directly, he said, "Wait a minute. What did you just do?"

"Well, I just tried to send some healing your way. And if something is happening, then that's the power of God restoring your knee."

"Is that what that is? Da—"

Philly was pretty sure the guy was about to curse but had stopped himself. "It feels better?"

"It does. It feels a hel— It feels a *lot* better." He flexed his knee and started to laugh. "My God, that's the strangest thing. I mean, I *always* have pain in this knee. I was supposed to go in for surgery, but I've been avoiding that like the plague." He laughed from his belly. "This is really weird. It's totally pain free." Then he seemed to catch a dose of sobriety. "Hey, man, do you heal people?"

It was a pretty odd question, of course. But Philly had witnessed this recovery period lots of times—the moment when people try to figure out what just happened to them without any previous experience to rub it up against. He just nodded, not sure how else to answer.

"Do you have some time to come over to my mother's house? She doesn't live far from here. She's been stuck in bed for weeks. Doctors can't figure it out."

Philly thought about whether he should take the invitation. And he thought about what would be a convenient night to visit. But the expectant gaze of the man with the new knee rearranged those musings. "You mean now?"

The man stood up straighter instead of leaning toward Philly. "Oh, well ... I mean, if you can't ..."

"Okay. Sure. Let's give it a try at least. You say she's not far from here?"

"She's just up in Lombard. You going that way?"

Lombard was between Naperville and Schaumburg. This was a setup. "I'm headed to Schaumburg. Yeah, I could stop by with you."

Then they formally introduced themselves, and Philly got directions. The guy's name was Tyler Jennings, a name that sounded familiar, but Philly couldn't place it.

Not until Philly approached the house where he had promised to meet Tyler did he start thinking again about where he had heard that name. He was intrigued by the size of the house. Lombard was a big town with a range of neighborhoods across a wide economic spectrum. This house was toward the top of that spectrum.

Tyler met him on the driveway. "Thanks, man, for agreeing to do this. I really appreciate it. My mama's been down for almost two months, I think."

That greeting from Tyler postponed Philly's questions about whether he recognized the guy from somewhere. A guy that big, it might be football. Philly could search the internet for him later. "I'm thinking God set this whole thing up." Philly said that before calculating whether it would make sense to Tyler. He generally had a hard time not just saying what he was thinking, especially when he was nervous.

He didn't have to do a web search for Tyler Jennings, as it turned out, because Tyler's mother had a living shrine to her son's football career in her front hallway.

"My mama's version of the Hall of Fame." Tyler rolled his eyes at the shallow trophy case to his left and flashed a hand toward the newspaper clippings framed on the wall to his right. There Philly saw images of a much younger Tyler in a Bears uniform.

"I thought I recognized your name." Instead of making him more nervous, this discovery settled Philly a bit, as if he knew this guy at least a little. Philly had been an ardent Bears fan his whole life, after all.

"I have an investment firm in that building you were coming out of. It's got my name on it too."

Philly snorted. That was right. He had seen the sign in the lobby along with the other major tenants listed for the building. Tyler Jennings Investments. "I never put the two together." He grinned, feeling even more comfortable with this imposing stranger. They were neighbors, at least at work.

"So, how long you been healing people?"

"A few years. I'm just getting back into it. Jesus seems to be pushing me to get back to it." Again, whether that reply made sense to Tyler, Philly didn't stop to ask himself.

"Cool."

Tyler knocked on a solid-wood door stained a rich maple brown. "Mama, I have a visitor here." He signaled for Philly to wait in the hall and then stepped into the room, closing the door behind him.

Philly could hear Tyler's gentle introduction and explanation and an older woman's faint replies. The two voices went back and forth a bit longer than was comfortable for Philly.

When Tyler came out looking apologetic, Philly was prepping his own apology and an early exit.

But Tyler's explanation was different than what Philly expected. "My mother is very religious. She's from Trinidad and has some ideas about spirits and healing and such. She wants me to ask if you respect that."

Did Philly respect that? He had no idea. Respect what? That she was a practitioner of some kind of spirituality that was unfamiliar to him? Most strangers he tried to heal were not obviously Christian, so he just assumed this was no different. "She doesn't have to believe the way I do to be healed. That's all I know."

Maybe Tyler had expected a better answer, or maybe he didn't know what the right answer was. He hesitated, his hand still on the doorknob, his eyes on the floor. "Well, she's real sick. And I know I'm feeling ready to try just about anything. Let's just give it a shot."

He opened the door and led Philly in. "It's okay, Mama. He don' mean to change your beliefs, just offerin' you some healin', or at least a try at it." Tyler adopted an island accent for this introduction, and that caught Philly by surprise.

He just stood there nodding and trying not to stare at the very large woman scowling at him from the king-sized bed. Mrs. Jennings had a mane of dark dreadlocks that were fanned out on the golden pillow on which she was propped. Next to the bed was a small table covered in little bottles. Not all of them were the kind of prescription bottles Philly would have expected.

"You don't come here to oppose my spirits, do you?" Her voice was still as weak as it had sounded through the door, but her gaze was steel, and her question was toned almost as an accusation.

"Spirits? What kind of spirits?"

"Ancestor spirits."

Nothing about her reply clarified things for Philly. He was used to people who seemed only vaguely spiritual, Christian or otherwise, letting him try to heal them. Maybe this really *was* different. He had no idea what to do—except to try to do what he had been doing since Jesus showed up on the bus one day. "Well, let's leave that part to Jesus. He's the one who leads me to heal." He was improvising, but the easiest thing was to keep stumbling down the path he had already started.

"I can trust in Jesus. And I can see dat you have some gifts. So, you can go ahead. I appreciate you comin' to make de attempt."

"You're welcome. I guess I get this feeling that you have a sort of pressure on your chest." Philly pressed his right palm to his own chest. Fortunately he had felt this type of sympathy pain before, so he wasn't worried that he was having a heart attack. And the pain wasn't as intense as he imagined a heart attack would be. It was more like a weight holding someone down.

"Yes. I do feel dat right here." Mrs. Jennings mirrored Philly's pressure on his chest.

Philly heard Tyler grunt an appreciative little noise, but he stayed focused on Mrs. Jennings. He wasn't even considering going to lay hands on her. Something about that seemed inappropriate, perhaps even dangerous. He briefly wondered whose side Tyler would be on if his mother got out of control. Why was he picturing her screaming? That picture reminded Philly of his own emotional healing session—the time he had greeted Jesus with a shriek.

"*Help me, Lord.*" It was the first time Philly had formed an internal prayer since arriving. Realizing that fact almost convinced him to surrender and retreat.

"You'll be fine." That was the response to his prayer. A curious response, which said nothing about healing Mrs. Jennings.

"Okay. In the name of Jesus, I command that pressure to come off of Mrs. Jennings's chest." He paused and felt like he needed to reiterate. "Come off her right now in the name of Jesus." He said it more forcefully this time, for whatever that was worth.

That was when the woman in the bed began to moan. Then her body seemed to rise off the bed a few inches and crash back down. She released her chest and grabbed her head. She started to howl. "*Nooooooo.*"

Philly wanted to run. He wanted to shriek. But someone was leaning against his back.

"Try again. Tell the killer to leave." The voice wasn't Tyler, so Philly assumed the presence behind him was Jesus.

"I command the killer spirit to leave right now." Philly's voice cracked slightly, but the racket Mrs. Jennings was making probably covered that up.

Mrs. Jennings suddenly fell silent. Deathly silent.

Philly's heart lodged in his throat.

Tyler pushed past Philly and went to his mother's side. By the time he reached her, Philly could see that she was still breathing, her blankets rising and falling.

Touching his mother briefly, Tyler tipped his head. "She seems to be asleep." As if on cue, she released a sigh and started to snore.

Philly nodded. He uttered a silent prayer and looked at Tyler.

Tyler spoke just above a whisper. "I guess that's okay. I don't really know what happened, but she seems to be resting at least."

"Is that unusual? Does she usually fall asleep fast like that?"

"Uh, no. Not that I've ever seen. My sister takes care of her more than me, but she's never mentioned any of this."

"Did you know about the spirits?" Philly kept his voice low.

"Well, a little." Tyler was right next to Philly now. "It's part of her religion from Trinidad. Lots of the old people still hang onto the African religions even though they go to church. Or maybe that's what they do at church. I never knew. My dad didn't go, so neither did I."

The nodding that Philly started might have been a sort of marking time, counting seconds before he could get out of there. But he thought he should put some kind of punctuation at the end of whatever had happened there. "Okay. Well, Lord, bless Mrs. Jennings with freedom from pain and from any kind of ... of ... harm." He was thinking about the killers Jesus had brought to his attention, but he couldn't bring himself to say it again. He ended the prayer in generic fashion and turned toward the door.

Tyler followed him. "Well, thanks again for coming. I guess we'll see if she's better."

"Yeah. Let me know." As they walked toward the front door, Philly told Tyler where he worked in the office building they shared. He was less than optimistic about the results of what had happened here, but thought he should leave a way to hear some feedback.

"Take care. And thanks for the new knee." Tyler laughed as they shook hands in front of a poster of him in his Bears uniform.

"Jesus gets the credit for anything good that comes out of it." Philly was still trying to sort the meaning of Mrs. Jennings's wild reactions.

Walking alone down the driveway, Philly spoke softly to himself. "Outta here."

"Thanks, Philly."

It seemed that Jesus was having the final word.

Chapter 28
Trying Out a New Church

Dave hadn't told Philly much about the two churches he recommended, but they both had websites, and Philly and Brenda chose the one with the best site. The two locations were about the same distance from their townhouse.

"Are you worried about that lady?" Brenda was riding in the passenger seat of the SUV with her big sunglasses on, the ones that made her look like she was trying not to be recognized by her public.

"Mrs. Jennings? I guess so. I mean, I wasn't worried about her before, so maybe I shouldn't be worried about her now, but I'm hoping it didn't make her worse."

"Well of course you didn't make her worse."

He didn't try to curb Brenda's confidence. She certainly had as much chance of being right as he did.

The wild scene at Mrs. Jennings's house was the deciding factor that launched them toward church on Memorial Day weekend. The holiday seemed to suggest that they could wait until a normal Sunday before visiting a new church, but Philly was feeling like a kid driving without a license. He needed a church to have his back. And maybe to provide some answers where he was without a clue.

At the door of the church sanctuary, which was in a converted warehouse of some kind, Philly recognized one of the pastors from the website photos.

"Hey, welcome. I'm Will. I don't think I've seen you here before." He stepped up close and offered Philly his hand.

He was right, he had never seen them at his church before, but Philly suddenly realized that he might have been seen by Will at the church in Chicago. When the healing stuff was taking off for him, people came to visit that church from all around the area. Philly was a bit of an attraction for a while. At least that's what it had felt like at the time.

"Yes. This is our first time here." Brenda stepped in where Philly hesitated over that late realization. She provided their names.

Will assumed nothing about them knowing who he was, introducing himself as the senior pastor.

Philly was still busy trying to figure out whether it was good or bad that Will might recognize him.

Brenda banished some of the suspense by telling Will they had attended the church in Chicago.

"Oh. Yeah. Dave and I are old friends. I've known him forever. But you can't *make* me tell you all the dirt I have on him." He laughed in a big, clownish way.

Philly's impression of Will was that the ruddy-faced middle-aged guy was as much of an introvert as he was. Will's too-loud laugh exposed a kind of nervousness that was familiar to Philly.

"Uh, yeah. Dave was the one who suggested we visit here. We live in Schaumburg now."

"Sure. That's good. Well, welcome. Make yourselves at home. Coffee is downstairs, if you're so inclined."

As they spun with the other folks headed away from Will's orbit, they met the other half of the pastoral team—his wife Mary.

"Hello, folks. I'm Mary." She was a slim, athletic woman with curls of golden hair down to her shoulders. She smiled broadly and focused her intense dark eyes on each of them.

Brenda and Philly introduced themselves again, and Mary encouraged them to get some coffee or water downstairs. The greetings seemed practiced, and Philly felt like he was on a well-oiled conveyor belt that led to the sanctuary via the coffee counter downstairs.

After meeting a few more people next to the coffee, as well as in the auditorium, they took their seats. When the service began, they sang some familiar songs, and Philly started to feel like he was back in his own territory. During the sermon, that growing comfort was disturbed just a bit by how much it seemed that Will was looking at him. Was Philly just imagining that, or had Will made the connection? Had Will visited the Chicago church when Philly was healing people at the evening services?

Even though Philly squirmed a bit at Will's apparent extra attention, he liked the way Will preached. The pastor, who had seemed a little awkward greeting them at the door, seemed comfortable in the pulpit. Maybe he was more comfortable talking to a hundred adults than to just one—especially one he had never met before. Philly could relate to that last part.

Something Will said during the teaching seized Philly's attention. He was linking Memorial Day to the notion in Scripture of remembrance. Will said that remembering wasn't just about recounting past events, it was often meant to revive a past experience, to keep it alive. He was building a case for applying that concept to their personal spiritual lives.

"I know it's tempting to think that Jesus just goes off to heaven until we remember him, until we come together on a Sunday, for example. But, really, Jesus never leaves. Once we invite him into our lives, he sticks around. We're hosting him in our lives whether we're good hosts or neglectful ones. But it's good to stop and remember the experiences we had with Jesus with this in mind—he hasn't gone anywhere since. He's still with us whether we're being attentive hosts or not."

It felt like Will was looking right at Philly. Was that Philly's imagination? Or was Jesus up there whispering into Will's ear?

Philly was realizing that he had been only a part-time host to Jesus at best. He resolved to go back to the basement and hang out with Jesus that afternoon. Before the Cubs game, of course.

By the time they left church, Philly and Brenda had met a dozen people, and they even got an invitation to stay for lunch the

Hosting Jesus

following week, something Mary referred to as the "Meet and Eat" session after the service. It was for people new to the church. The invitation, issued to them personally, assumed they would be back. Maybe their mention of their previous affiliation with Dave's church in Chicago fueled that assumption.

He would discuss it with Brenda, of course, but Philly was inclined to return there next week. He was particularly comfortable with an introverted pastor who knew Dave well. And Will's message about being a good host to Jesus had seemed tailored for Philly.

Chapter 29
With Dad in the Basement

During the ride home from church, Brenda talked to Philly's ma on the phone. They'd been trying to negotiate a time when Ma could take Brenda shopping for baby stuff. Brenda stopped in the middle of the conversation and connected her phone to the car Bluetooth. "Your dad wants to talk to you."

"What?" Philly and his dad still didn't talk on the phone much even with his dad's restored hearing and his growing comfort with a cell phone.

"Hey, Philly. You mind if I come over and watch the Cubs with you while the girls are out shopping?"

"Of course not. That would be great. Great idea." Part of him was moaning about his plan to meet with Jesus in the basement that afternoon. But that seemed like a whiny kid part that Philly didn't want to listen to. His enthusiastic acceptance of Dad's visit silenced that small, dissenting voice.

"Great. We'll be over ..." Dad apparently pulled the phone away from his ear, certainly consulting his wife. "We'll be out to your place around two thirty. A 3:10 game, right?"

"Yep, in Cincinnati."

"Should be easy."

Philly laughed. He and his dad were enjoying their evolution to being cocky Cubs fans after all those decades of humility.

"You're welcome." Brenda hung up the call.

"You set that up?"

"They said they wanted to get together this weekend. And your mom wanted to take me shopping. So we're, like, killing four birds with one stone."

"Which one of those birds is my dad?"

She punched him in the shoulder. "You know what I mean."

Philly grinned at her, the only person who could hit him and get away with it.

For lunch, they stopped at an American Chinese place where the only difficulty was deciding which delicious food to order. At the square black table, Philly tried using chopsticks one more time, determined to master the skill. "Too old to learn a new trick, I guess." He had fumbled a green bean onto the table, the lightweight wooden sticks crossing each other impotently.

"I hope not. You gotta learn to be a father."

Bobbling his head as he tried again with the stubby chopsticks, Philly agreed. "Okay. I'm up for the challenge. I just hope the kid comes with instructions. And what about a warranty?"

"Yeah. Maybe the hospital will give us one of those 'six years or sixty thousand miles' deals before we drive the baby off the lot."

Philly snickered. With very little effort, Brenda was starting to be funnier than him, though he was probably the only real appreciator of her comedy. She rarely cut up in front of friends or family.

At home, after a bit too much Shanghai beef and stir-fried rice, Philly headed for the basement. He was supposed to carry out the garbage and do a few other chores, but he was worried that if he didn't get to the basement first, his meeting with Jesus would get canceled entirely. He hoped to at least spend some time thinking about the notion of hosting Jesus in his life. The most intriguing part of that idea was that Philly might have already been hosting Jesus in his basement just like the pastor was telling him he should.

"He wasn't telling you to do it like it's some new commandment. He was just pointing out the truth that simply exists no matter what you do about it."

Sitting with his head against the cushy rest at the top of his recliner, Philly had just started to think that maybe he shouldn't get so comfy after such a big lunch. But then he heard that correction. Did he hear it because he was still awake and alert, or was that message *enhanced* by his sleepy state? Maybe he could slip back into that dream about Jesus in the basement. Or into any old dream, for that matter. He hauled his head off the cushion. "Wait. What truth? That I'm hosting you whether I like it or not?"

"Well, I wouldn't put it that way. You can meet with me if you like. You don't have to talk with me or listen to me."

"But wouldn't that be sorta like inviting my dad over to watch the Cubs and then going out for a walk or something?"

"That's a good analogy. Of course, you would never do that with your dad. On the other hand, you don't have to worry if you do something like that with me. I won't be offended. I won't go home wondering what the heck you were thinking. I know what you're thinking all the time. I understand when you're preoccupied with other things."

"Speaking of other things, what was that thing with Mrs. Jennings?"

"That was a bit more than just healing her body. Remember those times when I told a fever to go away, rebuking it? Well, it was like that. Some of those spirits she relies on are real, and they're not real helpful to her."

Philly reviewed that answer. It had to be Jesus, because it offered much more clarity about what happened than he had on his own. But was Jesus supposed to tell him personal stuff about a stranger?

"She did invite you to come in to pray for her. And her son was the one who set it up. What I just told you was information fully available to you already if you knew how to interpret what you saw. You suspected as much, didn't you?"

"Uh, well, yeah. I suppose." Philly heard a low pop of wood by the stairs. It wasn't the usual thump and creak that accompanied Brenda walking down the steps into the basement. It sounded as if she might be standing on the stairs listening to his conversation. "Brenda? Is that you?"

She snickered and then stepped the rest of the way down the stairs. When she came into sight, her entire body was already apologizing—hands raised at her sides, shoulders shrugged, and a sideways grin straining one cheek. "Sorry, Philly. I heard you talking, and I was coming to check if your parents had called you. When I figured out what you were doing, I didn't wanna disturb you." She shrugged again. "But I didn't wanna go away either."

Her obvious remorse was endearing. "So you heard me talking to myself?"

"You really sounded like you were talking on the phone. It was like there was a real person on the other end. What did he say? Or is it something you can't tell me?"

"Of course I can tell you." He forced his legs down against the footrest and stood up to comfort his penitent wife. He held her for two minutes while he tried to reproduce his conversation with Jesus—both sides of the exchange. The way she listened with childlike trust in her eyes would reinforce his loyalty to her for a long, long time.

They were both in the kitchen when, right at two thirty, Ma and Dad's old sedan pulled under the back deck. This was his parents' second visit, the first since Philly and Brenda's original moving day. On that day, the garage door had been opened and all the helpers were trooping in and out through the basement. Philly was still getting used to having guests at the new place, and had pictured his parents parking on the street and walking through the tree-lined courtyard to the front door. Instead, he had to run downstairs to open the basement door to the garage and hit the garage door button. The dimness of the garage split, and daylight graduated up the walls, reflecting off the two cars on the double-wide slab.

His dad stood hitching up his pants. He, too, had lost weight recently. Since then, Ma had complained that Dad's pants looked like a potato sack on him. Even though Philly was pretty sure he had never actually seen a potato sack, he suspected his ma was exaggerating.

"Well, *there* you are." Ma seemed to be recovering from some kind of disorientation, perhaps at the large garage door rising in front of her to reveal her son and his wife. She had on a pair of tortoise-shell sunglasses. Her hair appeared to be newly coiffed, and she wore lavender slacks and a white blouse with little pink and lavender flowers on it. Her arms were bare in the late spring warmth, and she held out her hands to Brenda, her purple purse slung over her shoulder.

Philly couldn't tell what those extended hands meant, unless Ma was being converted to Brenda's hugging culture. More likely those outstretched hands were intended to prevent an unwelcome hug in favor of clasped hands.

Dad, on the other hand, stood waiting for his hug, his shiny head reflecting the afternoon rays. He had flipped up his clip-on sunglasses and looked like an outfielder on his way to the dugout at the end of an inning. But, then, Philly was already thinking baseball.

Wordlessly, Philly directed them around his car to the basement door with a sweep of his left hand. "You guys could park on the street, our side of the street, and come in the front door like guests, if you wanted." He meant it as a hospitable offering, but it probably sounded like a rebuke. Philly was intending to reform the way he talked to his ma, hoping to discard the argumentative edge that was his habit. He still had some work to do on that project.

"Oh, this is fine for us. The servants' entrance is good enough." That was his ma's idea of a joke.

That kind of joking was as familiar as seeing his ma and dad. But this was a new place, and his parents were entering his new house in which he lived with his sort-of-new wife. And they were walking right past the basement room where Philly had recently started to meet with Jesus.

He could remember Jesus sitting in his parents' living room while he waited for dinner to be served—Jesus looking the patient house guest, amused by the black terrier that stared at him where he sat in an armchair that appeared empty to everyone besides Blacky and Philly.

During the intervening years, Philly had talked very little with his parents about seeing Jesus and about his ongoing relationship with his now-invisible friend. When he thought about it, that silence didn't feel right. But Philly had no plan to invite them into his confidence today.

They all climbed the stairs. Brenda was enthusiastically introducing his parents to the townhouse now that it was furnished and finally settled. Philly could hear the pride in her voice as she talked about the walls they had painted, the furniture they had purchased, and their ambitions for future improvements.

The baby's room was the last stop on the tour. It made sense for more reasons than just the layout of the house. Ma was probably scoping the room for things she might buy for her first grandchild. His parents were not wealthy, but they owned their house outright, and the combination of Dad's disability pension with social security was enough for them to put a little money away most months. Philly guessed that Ma had been saving up for baby shopping since they first told her the news. Maybe even before that.

After iced tea and a brief rest in the small living room, Brenda and Ma got up to head for the mall a mile to the northeast.

"Make sure she doesn't spend too much," Philly whispered into Brenda's ear during the shuffle back downstairs toward Brenda's car.

Brenda shook her head at him. Of course she was as committed as he was to protecting Ma from getting carried away in her excitement about a grandchild, finally.

That had become a familiar phrase in conversations with Ma. "A grandchild, finally." It could be inserted at the beginning, in the middle, or at the end of various topics. In Philly's mind, part of the implied protest could be forwarded to his sister in New York, still single after all these years.

"Okay, okay. Out you go." Dad was herding. "The Cubbies are starting soon. Get going." As usual, his tone was playful, but the Cubs were one rare motivator for him to look at the clock and assert his will.

Still early in the day, the men had agreed on root beer and popcorn for the game. Philly headed to gather these in the kitchen where he watched Brenda maneuver her car out of the garage beneath him and past his parents' car parked behind his. She would have taken his car if hers had been blocked in. Philly held his breath at the crucial turn where Brenda just missed touching Dad's sedan with her front bumper. Close, but no scratches.

The humming of the microwave had covered his dad's approach, so Philly startled slightly when Dad spoke. "Good to see them off together. They'll have a good time. Shopping brings women together like nothin' else."

Dad was, of course, old school. His comments struck Philly as a bit sexist. But he also knew that his dad's light assertion was at least true of Ma and Brenda. Shopping would probably be a reliable bridge between them. He even expected that they would have little conflict over how much Ma should spend on the small person incubating inside Brenda's slightly rounded belly.

Philly reached to pull two bowls out of a cupboard. "Ma was anxious enough for me to get married that she probably would have figured out how to get along with anyone I found. But Brenda makes getting along pretty easy, doesn't she?"

Dad nodded and did the rumbling hum that was his theme song in Philly's mind. "Mm-hmm. Sure. You bet. She's a fine woman, Philly. We both love her like she's our own."

Not only had they been waiting for grandchildren, but perhaps his parents had been waiting for a daughter-in-law and a son-in-law all those years. Their share in the loss of Theresa's life was probably more profound because of that long wait, though Philly was still in his thirties then. At the funeral, his dad's lips trembling uncontrollably, the hasty grab of his glasses, and his vigorous wiping of tears had been more than Philly could bear to see.

But today was a chance to relax together, to just sit down and watch a baseball game. They had watched once at Dad's house already this year, but this was Philly's first chance to host his dad in the TV room with the big, ultra-high-definition display. He had purchased that display with Cubs games and science fiction movies in mind. Dad wasn't a big fan of sci-fi movies.

"I have the game recording on the DVR." Philly led the way down the stairs again. The game had started about five minutes ago. "We can start at the beginning and speed through some of the commercials."

"Mm-hmm." Dad was moving slower than Philly was used to. There weren't this many stairs in his father's daily life. He might go to his basement to get a tool or to help Ma carry up the laundry on occasion, but most of his life happened on the first floor of his ranch-style house.

Dad was also content to watch TV programs as they happened. He and Ma *had* a DVR as part of their cable TV setup, but Philly had still not convinced Dad to use it for recording things. He was retired and didn't have so much to do that he needed to record shows to see at a later point in his week.

That line of thought unraveled a hidden thread of Philly's worries about his dad. He was getting old. This was the first time his dad had come over to watch the Cubs. Philly comforted himself with the internal promise that it wouldn't be the last. He filed those thoughts away and busied himself with settling the snacks and getting the TV turned on. Three remotes and six buttons got the recording of the Cubs onto the big screen.

Philly hadn't yet stopped to consider what the big new TV would look like to his dad. Now he held back a laugh at the childlike wonder on the old man's face. Sitting in the left-hand recliner, his eyes wide, his jaw dropped slightly, Dad stared at the vivid image of a sunny day in Cincinnati and a gorgeous green field carved by a clean infield and arrayed with players in gray and white and red and blue. Philly was about to tease his dad for staring like that, but he stopped himself and just enjoyed observing his dad's moment of discovery.

Maybe he was even hearing an appreciative chuckle from the last guy who had sat in that recliner. Jesus probably wasn't a Cubs fan any more than a Reds fan, but Philly was sure that Jesus was a fan of him and his dad.

Handing him a plastic bowl with popcorn, Philly risked breaking his dad's hypnotic trance. Philly was still repressing his laughter, charmed by the newness of this experience for both of them.

His dad grinned big when he broke out of his stupefied stare at the big screen. "Thanks, Philly. This is gonna be fun."

For Philly, it already was.

Chapter 30
Hard to Concentrate on Work

The first distraction on Monday morning, back at work, was a rare paper note from the receptionist's desk. The note wasn't written by the receptionist. It was scrawled by Tyler Jennings.

Phil,
I just wanted to let you know that my mother is feeling better. She's out of bed and moving around, says she's thankful for your help. And my knee is still great too.
Thanks again,
Tyler

That was a happy distraction. But it was still a distraction. Even as he went through the motions of starting his day, Philly was picturing Mrs. Jennings up and around. Staring at his computer, he read the same email a few times before realizing that he wasn't paying attention to what it actually said. It was from the office manager. Something about what to do with dirty dishes in the kitchen area. He probably didn't need to comprehend it fully anyway. He usually brought a lunch and rarely used any of the office dishes.

Then he was back to wondering why Mrs. Jennings might only be *better* and not all the way healed. But maybe she *was* healed. Then he backpedaled and wondered how it was possible that she was even feeling the least bit better after his rookie prayers, which had seemed potentially more harmful than helpful. This bugged Philly so much throughout the morning that he took the extraordinary step of using some of his lunch hour to ride the elevator up three stories to where Tyler Jennings had his office.

The reception area up there was impressively professional and artfully decorated. Philly had no idea how big the company was. "Hi, I'm Phil Thompson. Is Tyler Jennings in the office? He left me a note downstairs, and I wanted to see if he could talk for a few minutes." This all felt very primitive. With most of his friends and family, Philly would have texted or emailed to arrange a meeting. Here he was with a handwritten note, making an unannounced visit. Very retro.

"I'll see if he's available." The receptionist looked like a bright college girl. Maybe she was just out of college. Her combination of smooth-skinned youth and brisk competence made Philly feel a bit older than he had when he first got off the elevator.

"He'll see you in a minute. He's on the phone right now. You can go on back to the waiting area outside his office."

Tyler had his own waiting area outside his office. He seemed to be doing even better as an investment advisor than he had done as a Bears offensive tackle. As far as Philly could remember, Tyler Jennings had never made it to the Pro Bowl. And he seemed to have been injured a few times. The Bears let him go at some point, but Philly had lost track of him by then. Apparently Tyler had made the shift to this new career around that time.

"Phil, thanks for coming by. I was hoping to catch you in person this morning, but I guess I got in a bit too early."

"Yeah. Thanks for the note. It's good news, right? About your mom?"

"Yes." Tyler gestured toward a little circle of armchairs near the wall-length windows of his office. "It *is* good news, of course. A definite improvement."

Philly's feet sank into the cushy carpet as he surveyed shiny glass shelves displaying plaques and trophies under track lighting. These were investment awards, not football. He picked up on the last word Tyler had said. "An improvement? But maybe not all the way better?"

Tyler sat in a gray suede chair across from Philly. "Well, she's had a few different health issues. The thing that was keeping her in bed lately was something new. I figure she just needs to get used to being up and about again. It's probably a gradual thing." As luxurious as his office decorations were, Tyler was just dressed in slacks and a button-up shirt. Probably designer stuff, but he looked relaxed in his element.

"So, you said she was thankful. I wasn't totally sure she was happy with what I was praying there."

Grinning as if he knew exactly what Philly meant, Tyler chuckled just briefly. Then he spoke a bit more solemnly. "She said she realized that some of the spirits she deals with might not want the best for her. Makes me think of some of the conflicts she had with her mother and her aunties when she was young. Not all her ancestors were always friendly to her."

Philly wasn't going to do a radio documentary interview with Tyler. "Okay. Well, I'm not really so familiar with all that stuff. I was just curious how it all worked out."

"It worked out very well, I'd say. I gotta admit, I was desperate when I asked you to come and see her. That's the only reason I even invited you. That and what you did for my knee." He settled a hand over that knee and flexed it by kicking his foot off the floor. Tyler chuckled as if enjoying his healing all over again.

Philly echoed that chuckle. "Well, it was one of those things where it would have felt totally wrong for me to say no. I've seen Jesus do some amazing healing, and I can't imagine keeping it to myself when I see someone obviously needing some."

A distant stare and half smile seemed to signal a departure from Tyler's comfort zone.

Philly didn't press it. He just assumed Tyler wasn't a church-going man, not entirely familiar with prayers and healings. "Well, thanks for seeing me. I'm really impressed with your operation up here. Looks like you're doing really well."

Tyler stood up as Philly did. "Oh, yeah. I was a business major at the University of Wisconsin before I went to the NFL. My player salary was always gonna be the foundation for a business for me and my family. It just turned out that investment advice and management was that business."

"Cool. How much does it help that you played for the Bears? Does it get you any clients?"

"Oh, a few, I think. It gets 'em in the door sometimes, and then I just have to convince 'em that I know what I'm doing."

Philly nodded as they walked toward the office door. He understood what Tyler was saying, but he couldn't really picture what it was like to be an entrepreneur. He had followed his father's footsteps to simply working as an employee with skills, living off the wages earned by those skills.

They said their goodbyes by the reception area. But Tyler surprised Philly before they parted. "I want you to know that what you did meant a lot to me. It made me stop and think about some really important stuff. I just wanted you to know the impact it had."

Conscious of the smart young receptionist just a couple of yards away, Philly suspected Tyler was giving him a sanitized version of that testimony. But maybe the successful businessman wasn't ready to talk intimately about his faith in *any* context. Philly was just glad at the implication that Jesus had caught Tyler's attention with those healings.

Philly headed back to work, feeling good about what he had learned up in the offices of Tyler Jennings Investments. But with that feeling came a lingering curiosity about what Tyler had said about his mother's faith. A few web searches netted him a wide range of possibilities having to do with African traditions people from Trinidad sometimes mixed into their Christianity. Still distracted from his work, Philly resorted to sending a text inquiry to Dave. It was an effort to get this all settled enough so Philly could get back to concentrating on work. He often found it difficult to concentrate when there was no crisis on the network. But, of course, he didn't want there to be a crisis. For now, he occupied himself with meandering from screen to screen of his network monitoring applications while he waited for Dave to answer.

"Good news about the healing. I think I've seen some things like that." That was Dave's text response after about half an hour.

"Is it possible for a Christian to also have these ancestor spirits she prays to or depends on somehow?" Philly tried to get at the core of what was bothering him. He was still at work, and this was just a text conversation.

"It is possible I think. Lots of Christians have baggage with them and still qualify as real Christians."

Philly could think of how that probably applied to his own life, or to the people he knew. His dad, for example, probably had a real faith in Jesus now. But he didn't go to church, and he stayed pretty much in the same rut he had been rolling in before his ears were healed and before he started to read his Bible. In that example, Philly's ma was in the role of baggage his dad had brought with him. But that probably wasn't a constructive way to think about his ma. "I guess only God can say who the real Christians are." He expected Dave would agree with that one. Dave was probably the one who taught him to think that way.

"Fortunately God is more generous than most Christians."

Philly chuckled at that reply, but had to stow his phone quickly when one of the project managers stopped by to get a report on the performance of one of their in-house websites. That proved to be just enough of a crisis, or at least a focus for his mind, to get Philly invested in work for a while.

Late in the afternoon when he paused to do an internal high five over getting some work done, Philly thought he could sense Jesus's presence in his office. With that presence came a warm approval and a little bit of amusement. Philly knew Jesus was on his side. But he also seemed to provide his invisible friend with some entertainment. Philly didn't mind that part at all.

Chapter 31
Domestic Bliss for New Parents

It wasn't until Tuesday night that Philly opened the box containing the car seat his ma had bought them. This was a key piece of parenting equipment, he knew. In it, their baby would be lugged to doctor's appointments, to the store, and to church. But Philly tried not to think of the gray plastic carrier as luggage.

"Sir, will you be checking your luggage?"

Did real parents have such irreverent thoughts about their children? Would Philly ever feel like a real parent?

A warm spring evening, just under eighty degrees, invited the happy couple for a walk around the neighborhood. Part of Philly's weight loss had come from a habit of vigorous walking around a high school track near his old apartment, and then around another track near the apartment he and Brenda shared for eighteen months. This new location had won points with him for its grid of sidewalks and walking paths that encircled the cluster of townhouses.

Just enough clouds to collect the colors of the setting sun billowed in the western sky. Rays of gold and pink cut through and reflected off the small pond two blocks from their townhouse. The glory of that sunset was, however, somewhat diminished by the need to watch for goose poop near the pond. Philly didn't complain. He held Brenda's hand and allowed himself to absorb the glow of the sunset as well as the glow of his happy wife. She seemed younger and fuller of life in her maternal state. And that made him feel younger too.

"We should start a list of names. One for boys and one for girls." Brenda swerved with him around a splattering on the asphalt walking path.

"Or we could think of names that could be used for either one, to make it more efficient."

"This isn't a computer networking project, dear. This is the future of our child. We don't wanna give them a name that'll get them picked on in school."

"Is that the main thing we have to think about when we choose a name?" This wasn't just a tease. Philly was willing to accept that Brenda had discovered the key to baby naming. Did new anti-bullying laws also require parents to select names that were not conducive to teasing? Well, maybe he wasn't taking her entirely seriously.

Brenda elbowed him in the ribs where they were exposed now, his arm around her shoulders. "That's not the only reason to choose a name. But we have to think about protecting our little one from the world."

When he started to reply, he was still trying to kid around with her. "Yeah, but don't we trust God to protect our kid from the world?" It didn't come out as a joke.

That comment seemed to bump Brenda beyond rib poking and teasing. "Hmm. I guess you're right." They walked in silence for a few seconds. "Do you ever imagine him walking with us like this? Jesus, I mean."

Letting his hand slide down to rest on her hip, Philly wondered why he *hadn't* tried imagining that. "Do you want me to?"

She was quiet again. "Sure. Why not? You don't have to stop being with Jesus because you're with me. Though, if you do talk to him, you gotta let me know that's what you're doing so I don't answer instead of him."

Philly grinned big at her. Yes indeed, he could walk with his wife and with Jesus at the same time. And he could talk with them both as well, which prompted a resolve to be more faithful about praying with Brenda when they went to bed and before meals.

Prayer was a new habit, and it had made only experimental debuts in the early stages of their dating and then again in their marriage. During those dating days, when Philly was just getting back to church, Brenda had been ardent in her faith. She had become friends with some women who took their faith very seriously. They seemed to have high expectations of themselves even as they had high expectations of God working in their lives. When Brenda had suggested that she and Philly should pray together on their dates, Philly thought he heard the voice of one of those church friends. But he didn't resist, even if he wasn't comfortable with his novice efforts at praying aloud in front of her.

Over time, Brenda's relationships shifted as some of her women friends moved away or got married and were less available. And her expectations of a fervently expressed faith faded, as if it had been merely a youthful phase.

During their premarital counseling, one of Dave's assistants had asked them what they were doing to work on a spiritual life together, to go with the romance and the friendship they enjoyed. It was a question. But it implied a suggestion. Philly had taken it as a rebuke for his negligence of strengthening his own faith and including Brenda in it.

"Help me remember to pray tonight in bed, okay?" He let his thoughts mature into words as they turned the corner back toward home.

Brenda nodded, seemed to start to say something, and then paused. "Okay." That was all she said about it for now.

In bed that night, Brenda turned to him when they were done praying, each propped up on multiple pillows. "Maybe we should choose a name from the Bible."

"I always thought Zerubbabel would be a cool name."

Brenda grabbed at Philly's ribs and squealed. "That would be a terrible name for a little boy." Pillows scattered, some landing on the floor.

Philly writhed and wriggled away from her rough tickling. "I wasn't thinking about a boy's name. That was for a little girl."

"You beast." She made a sort of sideways pounce at him. "Now apologize to our little person in there. And make sure he or she knows you were just kidding." Brenda was speaking in the little girl voice that Philly had first heard during their first round of dating.

Philly stopped trying to escape. He liked the idea of talking to the little person growing inside Brenda. His enveloping love for her went deep and included the unseen person she carried.

Brenda seemed to sense his change of mood. Rolling onto her back, she pushed down the sheets.

Her belly mounded just slightly in that position. Philly could see the difference under her thin cotton nightgown, but it was subtle. His little child was in there, apparent but not obvious, present but not visible. He or she was still hiding from the world, not ready to face being teased for being named Zerubbabel or Moonflower. Philly snorted a hidden laugh at that thought, but he slipped down in the bed so he could address the third person in the room. "Hello there, kiddo. Your mom says I have to apologize for planning to name you after some weird Bible guy. And she may make me take it back when I try to name you after one of the Cubs' pitchers."

She bopped him lightly on the back of the head.

Philly laughed and persisted. "But all you really need to know is that your parents love you, and that God is gonna take care of you no matter what. And I hope that you get to see Jesus some time like I did."

Quiet now, almost perfectly still, Brenda snickered ever so slightly and then sniffled just once. "Maybe she sees him already. Or *he* sees Jesus already."

"I guess you're right. Jesus already knows this person. That's a pretty cool thought."

That thought quieted both of them, Brenda keeping her breaths small, and Philly lightly resting his head on her belly.

"Well, Jesus, tell our little one what you want him or her to know. And we trust you to take care of this life from here all the way to when we're really old." It wasn't the first time Philly had talked to Jesus like that around Brenda, but it was unusual. It felt good—somehow different than just praying together. Why that should be so, he couldn't explain.

That night Philly dreamt about Jesus and a little child. They were in his dream, but he didn't actually get a clear look at either of them. In the dream, it occurred to him that he couldn't see them because he and Brenda had decided not to know the gender before the baby was born.

In the morning, he told Brenda about it. "I knew it was Jesus, and I knew he was playing with our child, but I didn't ever see them clearly. The whole thing made me feel really good, even *with* the frustration for not getting to *see* them playing."

Brenda propped her chin on both hands, staring at Philly across his toast and coffee. She had finished one fried egg—part of her prenatal diet. Now she seemed to be venturing into that dream instead of just finishing her toast. Her nose turned red and her eyes watered instantly.

Philly was getting used to that. She cried easily these days.

She sniffled. "You know, when I first met you, I thought you were this computer nerd, all tech and sci-fi. But you're really a guy with a big soft heart and a lot of dreams." She rested her fingers against his near cheek and stared into his eyes.

Philly had to take a big breath to keep from adding to the tears dripping onto the placemats. He laughed awkwardly but didn't take his eyes off his weepy wife. He was just discovering that his wife was even more endearing as a pregnant woman. But maybe that was just *his* hormones speaking.

Chapter 32
Is This Our New Church?

Before they went to church that next Sunday, Philly remembered that Dave had recommended *two* churches in the area. Shouldn't they at least check out the other option before settling in? He logged in to his computer in the basement to take another look at the website for the other church. It looked nice. Lots of smiling people. Lots of good programs and group meetings on their calendar. It all seemed familiar from his time at the church in Chicago. But it only convinced him that he could be at home in either the church they had visited already or the other one. And why not just stick with what they had found?

Part of that resolution might have come out of his easy identification with Will. Something about a pastor who was actively pushing past his own introversion to minister to people was inspiring to Philly, the card-carrying introvert. If there *were* cards for that, he would have one.

It turned out that Brenda was just assuming they would continue going to the same new church until they found a reason to switch. "I guess it's nice to know there's another option, but I'd just as soon give this one a real try before we go somewhere else."

When they greeted the pastors in the front hallway of the church building that first Sunday of June, Philly was stunned to find that Will remembered his name. And Will gave something away when he called him by his *full* name. "Phillip Thompson, right? Good to have you back." Will did seem truly glad about it.

Had he looked Philly up? What would he find? Philly hadn't searched for himself online recently. Had Dave said something?

Philly was too shy to ask Will those questions. Instead, he just exchanged an overly long smile with Will before moving on to greet others around them. When Will had to ask Brenda to remind him of her name, Philly counted his suspicions confirmed.

It wasn't a creepy feeling, really. In a way, it was a relief. If Will knew about Philly's past healing ministry and wasn't barring the door, that was good. Healing had been a big part of who Philly had become back in the day, and it was making a comeback. So, all the better if the pastor of his new church knew about it and wasn't forming a mob to run Philly out on a rail. The notion that Will knew something about him was good. Those smiles seemed genuine. Maybe Will was as happy to have Philly's healing gift in his church as Dave had been.

Did pastors talk about stuff like that? "Hey, we're sending you one of our first team healers. What do we get in this trade?" Later, looking at Will introducing Mary for the morning sermon, Philly could imagine trade talks between Will and Dave. Was Will a Cubs fan? A Bears fan? Well, those didn't have to be deal breakers.

That morning, Philly discovered that Mary was at least as comfortable talking to a hundred adults from the stage as Will was, and she brought an exciting message with lots of entertaining personal stories and insights. Philly could tell that Brenda was enjoying it, and probably not just because it was a sermon by a woman. The warm inclusiveness of the message that Mary brought was like home cooking to both Philly and Brenda, who knew little about church beyond what they had experienced in Dave's church.

After the final song and an invitation for people to go up front to get prayer for anything they needed, an older couple introduced themselves. "I'm Mindy, and this is Roy." Mindy was a bird-like woman with curly gray hair and wide blue eyes. Roy was probably close to sixty, his hair thin and gray, and his face a bit jowly around his short-cropped goatee. This church reminded Philly of his old church in the number of men who wore goatees. But, of course, that wasn't really important.

"You two are new here, right?" Roy's handshake was tight and warm. "You have plans for lunch?"

The "Meet and Eat" that had been announced the previous week was being postponed. Too few people had signed up. Philly hadn't noticed that they were supposed to sign up. Brenda just shrugged when he had looked at her during the announcement of the rescheduling.

"We were gonna go to that lunch for new people, but I guess we're free now." Brenda's answer was bright and upbeat. Food generally made her happy these days.

"Wanna join us, then? We're getting together with another couple at Gigio's." Mindy said the name of the restaurant as if Philly and Brenda might have heard of it. But then she probably read the blank looks on their faces. "It's just around the corner. You could follow us."

And it was arranged. Philly followed Roy and Mindy's little white hybrid out of the church parking lot, through the residential neighborhood, and onto the first commercial street to the west. When they arrived, the parking lot of the little Italian place was practically empty. One car squatted under a mulberry tree in the back of the lot, and that car might have been abandoned there. This didn't look like a famous or popular place. But it wasn't noon yet, so maybe it was too early.

While they were still filing through the entryway, pushing open the second set of doors, Will and Mary caught up to them, opening the outer door.

"There you are. Right on time." Mindy sang her greeting and turned back to step into a hug with Mary.

So this was the other couple Mindy and Roy were meeting? Shouldn't they have mentioned that the other couple were the pastors?

"You got away pretty fast." Roy was shaking Will's hand.

"Oh, that's the beauty of a church where everyone helps out. We did our part. Now we're free to go have a yummy Italian lunch. Hey, Phil, good to see you. You joining us, then?"

Now Philly saw the irony in this lunch arrangement. The original plan had been lunch with the pastors and a few other new people. He and Brenda had missed the part where they should tell someone they would be attending, and that probably caused *that* lunch to be canceled. That cancellation freed them to get together with this other couple ... and freed the pastors to join them. Philly tried to keep his head from spinning around in those thoughts and answered Will. "Yeah. Uh, Roy and Mindy invited us to come along. I hope it's okay."

"Of course it's okay. Roy does lots of questionable things, but inviting you guys to join us for lunch isn't one of them." Will grinned like a satisfied fox, and Roy chuckled a low protest. Then Will turned more serious. "Phil and Brenda were at Dave Michaelson's church in Chicago before this."

"Oh, so you're already part of the family. Very good." Roy was leading the men into the restaurant now, the women ahead of them talking in cheerful tones.

Mindy heard what Will had said about their previous church. "Oh, that's nice. So, we don't have to indoctrinate you over lunch."

Without thinking about it in advance, Philly offered what felt like a confession. "Well, we could probably use some indoctrinating. We haven't been in church very long. Dave's church is pretty much the only one either of us have been part of."

"I wouldn't count that as a handicap." Will clapped Philly on the shoulder. "Folks at our church come from all types of backgrounds, churched and unchurched. You'll fit right in."

Was that just friendly pastor talk? Maybe Will said things like that to everyone. Or did Will know something about Philly's past? How long would it be before Philly could figure out the answer to that mystery? He told himself to stop obsessing. Instead, he let his stomach take over. The saucy aroma in the restaurant was beckoning to him. He was ready to answer the call of oregano, garlic, and pepper. "Man, I'm suddenly hungry." He hadn't meant to say that aloud.

But Brenda echoed Philly. "Yeah, me too." She rested a hand on her belly.

That hand seemed innocent enough to Philly, but Mary's eyes turned to lasers, and she aimed them at Brenda's tummy. "Wait! Are you ...?"

Philly had been trained to never ask that of a woman. It was a minefield full of craters and wrecks. But Mary seemed to have special powers in those laser eyes.

Brenda giggled. "I'm pregnant. Our first. Almost four months. How did you know?"

Even as they slipped into a booth by the windows, everyone but Philly made an appreciative noise, a quartet of baby news celebrations. The baby conversation flocked and fluttered around the table for several minutes, like a gathering of birds just begging to settle down. Ordering food helped them transition from baby talk. They had probably reached the threshold where Brenda wanted to talk about food more than she wanted to talk about babies.

Hearing the two other couples recalling their many years of parenting experience, Philly put a bookmark there so he could come back for help in the future. And he got the sense that he would be welcomed when he and Brenda did cry out for help.

Eventually, their conversation looped around to Philly and Brenda's experience at the church they had attended in Chicago. The other two couples apparently knew each other very well, so their curiosity about Philly and Brenda blew past any need they had to catch up with each other.

"You said you didn't go to church before you started at Dave's church. What brought you there in the first place?" Mary asked the question, but the harmony of attention from all four of their lunchmates hinted that they all had been wondering the same thing, as if they were sure it would be a good story.

It *was* a good story. Philly thought so. He knew Brenda thought so. Would these people think so after they heard it? If they were good friends with Dave and close affiliates with that church on the north side of Chicago, then wouldn't they love

Philly's story of encountering a touchable Jesus? It felt like such a big story. Did they really have time? Would any of these people really be ready to hear all that Philly had to tell?

Brenda grinned at Philly. Her mouth was full of pizza, so it was a tight-lipped grin. Philly could tell what she was thinking. It was Philly's story that had started them both attending church. He should tell. Besides, she had her mouth full. She took another bite just in case he had missed this latter point.

"Well, Jesus told me to go and talk to Dave, because Dave could help me figure out what was going on with me." That was Philly's introduction.

"Jesus told you? How did he do that?"

"What *was* going on with you?"

Philly grinned at the willing listeners. Then he told them his story, about meeting Jesus on the bus and Jesus following him to work, about Jesus mooning over Brenda there, and about Jesus coming home with him. It was, of course, convenient to omit some parts of the story—the part about Philly getting engaged to a different woman, and the part about that other woman dying, for example. He kept the telling focused on the times when Jesus hung out with him and the ways Dave had helped him figure out what to do about that.

If Philly was the kind of guy who wanted to impress people, to wow them with a good story, that lunch would have been a very satisfying experience. But he was nervous even as he told it, draining his water glass repeatedly to keep his mouth from drying out completely. The little gasps and the big smiles he received from his audience kept him going. More than once, Philly noted a red nose, a teary eye, or a breathless pause among his listeners. He could even tell by Brenda's satisfied eyes that he was doing a good enough job.

After he finished, the two couples sat silent. Mindy looked out the window, and Will drilled his eyes into Philly's head. Roy spoke first. "Even just hearing the story is like witnessing a real miracle.

I mean, I've seen a few miracles over the years, but this feels like witnessing a real miracle even just to hear you tell it."

To Philly, reliving the miraculous beginning of his faith was well worth all the nervous energy he had spent in baring his soul to these strangers. His fear of doing so was entirely about himself, he realized. He didn't get a clear answer to how much of this Will had already heard, but he was guessing that Will had heard a summary, at least, from Dave.

Philly was certain that his relationship with all these people had been forever transformed by telling his story. That was good. The visit from Jesus defined him. His story about seeing Jesus was the best way to introduce himself to these new friends.

Chapter 33
Gladys Recommends Jason's Jesus Book

An occasional message from Gladys arrived on Philly's phone. A new theme of some of those messages was her enjoyment of a novel she was reading. It was the story of a young man who sees Jesus in the college library and then in his apartment. His girlfriend can't see Jesus, but she starts to believe when some minor healing miracles happen.

Philly guessed it was the same novel he had found in the bookstore a few weeks before. He hadn't bought the book. He wasn't really a reader, and he certainly didn't read novels. He read an occasional biography, often baseball-related, when on vacation. But Gladys's enthusiasm was making him curious.

"You don't think he's writing about *you*, somehow?" Brenda flipped pages in the newly purchased paperback on the way home from the mall. They had purchased some curtains for the baby's room, and the novel purchase had been a sidetrack from their main mission.

"Me? No. How could he? I don't know who this guy is."

Brenda turned the book over. "Nice picture. Young guy. Maybe he's writing about himself."

"Gladys saw Jesus at her place. Maybe this is another guy who really saw Jesus."

"Or it could just be a guy with a really good imagination. Maybe it's just a coincidence, and he's just imagining the same sort of thing that happened to you."

Philly wasn't worried about how this Jason Stivers came up with his story. It was fiction. It didn't necessarily have to happen.

Maybe *something* had happened to him, but maybe it wasn't exactly as described. That it might have actually happened to the author wasn't why Philly had bought the book. Gladys was stirring a longing in him with all her starry reviews of the novel. The fact that she found it profound and encouraging made Philly wonder if it would help him with some of his doubts.

That Friday night, instead of watching the Cubs or a movie streamed from the internet, Philly read the first eight chapters of the novel. He suspected that Brenda moved upstairs to do her baby book reading and decoration planning because she got tired of his little exclamations. While reading chapter four, he had paused to comment on something he found in the book. That was when he discovered that Brenda was gone from the living room. He smiled and rocked his chair. The late sun of a summer day, the breeze that pushed the thin white curtains toward him, and the reassuring affirmation he was finding in the book were putting him in a good mood.

"You really seemed to like it." Later, Brenda was lying next to him in bed idly rubbing her tummy through her nightgown.

The way she often petted herself like that used to bother Philly, but he was used to it now. He also liked the idea that now she was petting their baby, soothing the little one from the outside.

"I found a lot of it really familiar. I think the main thing that gets me is that the Jesus in the book is familiar. The way this guy describes Jesus talking and doing stuff is so much like what I saw."

"Makes you feel like what happened to you was even more real, right?"

Philly hummed a faint agreement. He thought of the response of the two couples at lunch this past Sunday. Their friendly reception of his story had been positive reinforcement of his faith in what Jesus did for him. And the best part of that was the way it strengthened his confidence in what Jesus was still doing. That thought inspired him to take one of those relaxing breaths and listen for Jesus, right there in bed.

"He's here, ya know. Jesus is right here." He hadn't planned to say anything. He was just feeling so full that he couldn't keep his hope inside.

Brenda stopped rubbing her tummy and rolled to her side, stretching an arm across Philly's chest.

For a moment, Philly was annoyed that she was interrupting his awareness of Jesus. But that vanished quickly when he received a little electric charge that seemed to start where her arm rested on his chest. That tingle reminded him of times when Jesus had touched him. Could Jesus be touching Philly through Brenda?

"Did you feel something?"

Brenda lay perfectly still for a second. "Like a little sort of buzz or something?" She was whispering.

"Yeah, when you touched me. I felt something. When I was saying that Jesus is here right now."

Brenda shuddered. "Oh my. That is so ..."

Maybe she was going to say *weird* or even *creepy*. Through all of Philly's descriptions of his experiences with Jesus, Brenda had stayed in the audience—watching appreciatively, even enjoying it vicariously. Of course, Philly couldn't explain why those things happened to him, which also meant he had no idea why they *didn't* happen to Brenda. Though it had been a small and subtle sensation, they had just shared a touch—what felt to Philly like Jesus revealing his nearness to them.

As had usually been the case for Philly, this new experience got shuffled under a pile of rewinding and second guessing. Even if he'd never been able to explain why these things happened, that didn't stop him from trying one more time.

Before he had climbed into bed that night, Philly had sent a response to Gladys regarding her book recommendation. On Saturday morning, he found her up early and messaging him about the joy and hope she had found in that story. She said it seemed very much like what had happened to her. She, too, found the

Jesus portrayed in the book very similar to the man who showed up in her little house in Wisconsin.

"I just wish I could get him to heal me these days. No matter how close he feels, I don't get that healing touch anymore." That was Gladys midmorning, when Philly had consumed a couple more chapters of the book and had messaged her about a healing story in one of those chapters.

"Gladys needs some healing." Philly said this as Brenda padded through the living room on bare feet, carrying dishes she had left by her bedside upstairs.

"Oh. Well, you could go see her and give it a try." For Brenda, it was as simple as that.

Of course Philly could offer to go see Gladys. He was a little annoyed at the new thought that Gladys was hoping he would offer, and was hinting instead of just asking. But that, too, was something he couldn't really know.

It would be encouraging for both of you. That wasn't a voice. It wasn't Brenda. It was a thought—one of those thoughts that seemed like something Jesus would say. This one contained a promise.

Philly answered aloud. "Is that a guarantee that she'll get healed?"

"If you want a guarantee, go ahead and buy that new stove Brenda wants. Ninety days money back."

That really sounded like Jesus. Complete with a little laugh at the end.

Okay. Philly was convinced. He would get the stove sooner rather than later. And he would offer to visit Gladys.

Even back at work on Monday, Philly was thinking about the book. He had finished it over the weekend. It inspired him to pay attention to Jesus beside him during the day. He closed his email and waited quietly for a few seconds to try and sense Jesus in the room.

"Hey, Phil."

Philly jumped in his chair.

"Oh, sorry. Didn't mean to startle you." It was Michele Masterson from accounting. She and Philly had been working on troubleshooting the online accounting software access.

"Oh. No. My fault. Was just ..." What was he doing? "I was just taking a breath to relax." That made him laugh. "I guess it didn't work."

Michele seemed more baffled than amused, but Philly didn't try to solve that. He just landed back where they had left their conversation via email. And that was how the day got rolling. Philly only diverted his mind away from his work a few times. Once, he paused to wonder if the young guy in the book was supposed to be at a college in Illinois. And he only wondered a little about what would happen when he went to visit Gladys.

Philly found Gladys in her apartment building lobby, which was full of chairs and sofas. Philly hadn't been in Gladys's apartment, but the lobby décor made him imagine that her place was cozy and charming. Though maybe that had more to do with his overall impression of Gladys than the room in which he met her.

"Hello, Philly. Thanks for coming to see me." She pushed off the arms of the tan microfiber chair she was sitting in.

Standing seemed to be no problem, but Philly could detect a stiffness about the way she held her head. "I'm glad to see you. I really enjoyed that book. Thanks for recommending it."

"Oh, you're welcome. Wanna take a walk? I like to get in a mile or so before dinner." She lifted her arm on which she wore a slim smartwatch or fitness tracker.

"Sounds like a good idea." He wondered whether he could actually do healing while walking, which led to a bit of mental rummaging for memories of trying that in the past. He couldn't think of anything right off. "So, how long has your neck been bothering you?" He followed her out of the building and down the sidewalk.

"Well, the headaches have been here for a while, but I finally realized the problem was my neck. Or rather, my nurse practitioner figured it out. The chiropractor gave it a few twists, but that didn't really seem to help. I got the feeling he was afraid he would break my neck, so I don't think he tried very hard."

"Maybe that's a good thing."

"Yeah. Don't need a broken neck."

Philly instantly saw a mental image of him walking with his hand on the back of Gladys's neck. That would be strange. But maybe it was just symbolic. Nevertheless, it seemed like directions coming from Jesus. With Gladys, he felt like he could speak freely. "You know, I have this sort of picture of me putting my hand on your neck back there." He pointed to the back of her shirt and wondered whether he was reporting his picture accurately.

"That sounds about right. Should we stop somewhere?"

When she worded it as a question, Philly got a bit bolder. "I really think the picture in my head was of me doing it while we're walking, though that might be too strange."

"In my experience, the strange ones are usually him givin' me a leading on how he wants to do something." She kept walking, looking straight ahead.

Philly interpreted her posture as his chance to imitate that mental picture, awkwardness and all. Gladys reminded him a bit of his grandma, but he hadn't even touched his grandma very often, certainly not walking along with his hand on the back of her neck.

Gladys would have loved Philly's grandma. The thought nearly choked him up and gave him a bit of distraction from how weird it was to touch her as they walked. For just a few steps, Philly rested his right hand at the top of Gladys's collar on the back of her dark blue blouse with white leaf patterns on it.

Still walking face-forward, Gladys laughed, and Philly dropped his hand.

Though he was, of course, wondering what she was laughing about, he was devoting a lot of his attention to just putting one foot in front of the other.

Gladys kept laughing. "That was a little odd." She laughed a bit harder and tipped her head to the right, then back to the left.

Then she stopped walking. Maybe she was laughing too hard to keep up the pace.

"It feels better?" Philly wanted to be in on the joke.

"Oh, yes. It feels *completely* better." She gasped and then started to laugh even harder, wheezing a little and holding her hand over her mouth.

"Is that sound in your breathing okay? Like a wheezing sound?"

Gladys decelerated to a humming chuckle. "Oh, I don't know. Maybe not."

Philly put a hand on her shoulder and spoke this time. "Breathing, be free. Wheezing, go away." He just realized that he hadn't said a word for healing her neck, so he covered both healings with one thanksgiving. "Thank you for all you're doing, Jesus."

A woman in pale green scrubs approached, pushing an old woman in a wheelchair. The caregiver looked concerned.

Gladys stopped laughing. She took a deep breath. "My breathing feels really good. And I didn't even know I needed *that* fixed." She started laughing again.

Philly just smiled at the short, dark-eyed nurse or nurse's aid. She slowed, as if to check on Gladys before pushing past.

"Having fun, Gladys?" The hunched woman in the chair spoke up in a scratchy voice.

"I am, Mabel. I'm feeling great. How about yourself?"

The worker pushing the wheelchair stopped completely, looking down at the woman in the chair.

"I still have trouble with my stomach. I can't eat a thing these days."

Philly and Gladys exchanged a glance that required no subtitles. Gladys spoke first. "I've been feeling much better since this young man prayed for me. Wanna have him give it a try for your stomach?"

The slight recoil from the young woman behind the wheelchair caught Philly's attention. But he saw her brighten, her eyes alight and her head tilted slightly. Was that expectation? Maybe it was just shock at the craziness she had found out on the sidewalk.

"What do I have to do?" Mabel was straining to look up at Philly.

"You don't have to do a thing. I'll just say a prayer, and we'll see what happens." Philly stepped closer. He was still monitoring the caregiver. She could, of course, turn and speed away with her patient, preventing more craziness here. But she looked at least curious, if not fascinated.

"It won't cost me anything, then. How could I refuse?"

Philly offered a little prayer of thanks for Jesus's healing power. At the end of what was more of a habit than an inspired connection, he thought he felt a little surge of electric tingles up his spine. "In the name of Jesus, I tell Mabel's stomach to get right, to straighten out. I bless her digestion to work fine from now on." It was one of those times where it felt like it didn't really matter exactly what he said, but the words he chose were probably good enough not to embarrass him, at least.

Giving herself to another round of little chuckles, Gladys wriggled a little, as if she had felt something when Philly got that tingle. She restrained her merriment just enough to speak. "What do you say, Mabel? Feel anything happening?"

All eyes were on Mabel now, including the health care worker's.

"Ah. Well, I feel okay. I do feel a bit hungry. Maybe that's something. I think I could try to eat something." She sat up a bit straighter. "Hey, my back feels pretty good too. Guess that was extra." And she seemed to catch some chuckles from Gladys.

"Excuse me, sir. Do you think you could pray for my uncle? He has a heart problem and is gonna need surgery. Maybe you could say a prayer for him?" The caregiver looked even smaller to Philly as she humbled herself for that request.

He first wondered how far he would have to drive to heal this uncle. But then he realized that she was asking him to pray, to intercede for her uncle's healing. That wasn't really what he was used to, but the momentum of what felt like two or three successful healings made him optimistic. "Okay. Lord Jesus ..." He realized he had skipped a few steps. "Uh, I'm sorry. What's your name? And your uncle's name?"

"I'm Rosalia."

Mabel spoke up. "Where are my manners? I should be making introductions."

Rosalia persisted. "My uncle is, uh, Armando."

Philly returned to his prayer and sent blessings for Armando's health. He also paused to add something for Rosalia. "And bless Rosalia's faith in you. Let it grow and prosper." That last part just came to him in the flow of things.

Wiping first one eye and then the other, Rosalia thanked Philly and looked gratefully at Gladys.

Philly was sure Gladys would follow up on his prayers for each of these women. And that thought brought back Jesus's promise that both Philly and Gladys would be blessed if he went to pray for her.

Jesus may as well have offered that healing guarantee, as it turned out.

Chapter 34
Finding Jesus in the Suburbs

Despite all that Philly had seen or done, he still didn't think of himself as a church person. As far as he was concerned, his role in church had been a lot like working as a consultant. In his computer consulting work, he had driven to a few different offices and performed the work of a network administrator. Strangers walking through one of those offices wouldn't know that he was just a consultant, but Philly knew. He knew he was only there temporarily. He knew he ultimately didn't belong at that company. In his heart, he had been a sort of church consultant as well.

Maybe that feeling was supposed to change now. So he agreed when Brenda suggested they go to one of the midweek meetings offered by their new church. The one advertised for this Wednesday was in a suburb right next to Schaumburg, in the house of one of the church members. But it was being billed as a worship and prayer time, not just a small group or Bible study.

The GPS on his phone led them to a large brick multi-level home just short of what he would call a mansion. With everyone dressed casually at Sunday church meetings, no one stood out to him as being rich in that congregation, just like in their old church in Chicago. But, in Chicago, Philly had gathered the impression that probably no one there was well off. He was in the suburbs now, and he wasn't sure how he felt about Christians who lived in big houses. Wasn't there some kind of commandment about that?

Then a thought accompanied him up the stone walkway. *"Jesus is welcomed here."* That thought probably didn't come from Jesus. In Philly's experience, Jesus didn't talk about himself in the third person, unlike some famous people he could think of. But the truth of Jesus being welcomed in this house seemed real, and it energized him right up the steps to the front door.

Brenda started to knock, but Philly stopped her when he noticed that the interior door was open a few inches. That seemed like a signal to walk right in. The ten cars parked in the huge driveway and along the road out front implied that other visitors were already inside.

The first face that greeted them as they stepped onto the hardwood in the front hall was familiar. "Well, hello. Oh, so great to see you two here." Mindy sang that greeting in a way that was also familiar.

Philly was glad to see someone he recognized, but he was hearing a lot more voices than he had expected, men and women talking in animated and jovial tones from the room at the end of the front hallway.

A blonde woman in her fifties turned toward them and floated down the hall. She arrived on bare feet to greet them with a smile. "Oh, hi. Welcome. I'm Karen. Welcome to our home. I think I saw you guys in church on Sunday. Am I right?" The slightly hushed excitement in Karen's voice implied intimacy. Where Mindy's greeting had been comforting, Karen's was compelling.

Brenda looked like she might start crying, a blissful float to her movements as she greeted Karen with wide eyes and high eyebrows.

After they gave her their names, the hostess talked them through some of the usual details about the facilities and the meeting. But Philly couldn't pay much attention to the location of the restrooms or the refreshments.

"Come on in. Come on in." A barrel-chested man with a gray and white beard beckoned with both arms from farther up the hall. "Let's get started." Guitar chords rose from behind him, as if the jolly guy came with his own little band of troubadours. A bongo drum joined in, and then a bass guitar. And the music bloomed to fill the house all the way to the two-story ceiling and the balcony above the great room into which Philly and Brenda were being led.

Philly was still feeling the shy awkwardness that he always carried into a gathering of strangers, but that burden had become lighter. He felt as welcomed to this gathering of believers as he could ever remember. It was almost like arriving at his grandmother's house on one of those dinner nights with just the two of them—and Jesus.

The three young musicians parked in front of the fireplace were playing with their eyes closed, as if the music was making them, and not the other way around. People were settling into armchairs and couches and onto the floor. Others were standing from their seats in stacking chairs arranged in the center of the room. The big bearded man directed Philly and Brenda to a pair of seats in the second row of the padded stacking chairs, right in front of the guitarist who was starting to lead a familiar worship song.

Though he had just arrived and nothing that he could clearly identify had happened yet, Philly's heart swelled. He looked at Brenda and snorted a laugh. She looked like she was high on something. Maybe that was hormones. But if that was the case, then pregnancy would be more popular, he guessed. Silly thoughts. He was feeling like he did at the end of a Cubs game when they pulled it out with a walk-off home run, him punching his fists into the air to celebrate.

Hands all around him were reaching into the air. Maybe they were reaching up to grab handfuls of whatever was floating around them, mostly invisible, but certainly real to Philly.

In Sunday services at church, Philly had come to love worshipping to modern songs with deep lyrics about an intimate and infinite God. This meeting in the big house in the suburbs was starting to intoxicate him like a double shot of whatever he had felt in Sunday worship settings. It was a party feeling. It was a sense of *home*. It was rest. And Jesus was definitely here.

For at least fifteen minutes, no one addressed the group. No words were spoken, only sung. The only prayers put to words were low and private. The folks gathered had all slipped behind a lavish curtain, welcomed without any ceremony or hype.

Maybe this was what Philly had needed all along. He had gotten comfortable at the church in Chicago, even if he had still felt like he was just a consultant there and not a member of that company. He needed to find a place, a welcoming place. A place he belonged. Right now it was easy to believe that all the limitations that had kept him exiled from such a place were contained entirely inside himself. There had probably been gatherings just like this one at that other church. He might have even attended some. But now he was finding in his hand an invitation that he hadn't recognized before. Jesus was helping him to make himself at home.

A guy who Philly didn't recognize joined the musicians in front of the room and welcomed the new folks. But he didn't make anyone stand up and introduce themselves. The people around Brenda and Philly had already started exchanging names with them and shaking their hands or patting their backs. And that, too, was like home. It was like being welcomed by other people who were entirely in their element, and who saw the newcomers as mirrors of themselves—just people who needed a place to rest like they did, people who also fit right in here.

Another round of songs started up without Philly noticing any kind of announcement about it. It just seemed to flow. And so did the prayers, the petitions people offered between the songs. One called out for more awareness of God's presence. One prayed for their church leaders. Another prayed for neighbors who still needed to meet Jesus for the first time. And then the musicians set down their instruments.

A bald man with olive skin and shining, dark eyes followed the big bearded man to the space in front of the fireplace. The bearded guy was Max, and he introduced Kamal, his neighbor from across the back fence.

Kamal greeted everyone with a pristine set of white teeth. "I am so glad to be here. I am so happy that I found these people. And so full of joy that I found Jesus as my Savior." And he told his story of meeting Max and Karen, his neighbors, and asking them dozens of questions about the gatherings they hosted at their house and the church they attended. He told about his little girl being healed of allergies that had made her life miserable for many years. He gestured to a woman with long black hair seated to his left, and told about his wife's conversion to Christianity and then about his own. "It was right back there," Kamal pointed to the seats just behind Philly, "that I saw Jesus holding out his hands to me. He wasn't hating me for who I was or what I had believed all my life. He wasn't angry at me. He wasn't judging me or condemning me. He was inviting. And that was an invitation I did not want to refuse."

When Philly turned toward Brenda, he saw the shine of tears on her cheek. She was entranced. The utter ecstasy he saw in her eye worried him for just a second. How could it really be this good? Were they being sucked into some kind of cult? This whole experience was overwhelming.

"If Christian faith is really this good, this pure, this attractive, then how could anyone refuse? If it's really this good, everyone would believe." He was arguing with someone—maybe himself.

"You've been to church meetings before—meetings that weren't like this." Was that Jesus? Was he arguing back?

"I think I'm looking for proof that this is too good to be true."

"With mere humans, apart from me, that is a real possibility. Advertising is almost always too good to be true. But this is not advertising. This is real. More real than you can even recognize."

"But why isn't it always like this in church?"

"Everywhere? All the time? That's a pretty high bar."

"Was it like this at other meetings I went to, and I just didn't notice?"

"Didn't notice. Didn't connect. Weren't as willing to be aware—to be aware of me. To host me in the world, in the room, in your life."

Philly brushed away a tickle on one cheek and then the other. Tears were dripping off his chin, flowing on their own.

"I can help you be more aware. More aware of everything."

"*I want that.*"

"Me too."

He surely wasn't just talking to himself. Jesus *was* here in this place. Philly tried sniffling as quietly as possible when Kamal finished and Max led the clapping.

Max was directing everyone to turn around, or reach across, to form a little prayer group with the people near them. The last course of this spiritual feast involved people receiving prayer for personal needs, including healing.

Brenda and Philly looked around. They both focused on a woman who was pushing her way past the folks standing and milling around them.

"You wanna pray together?" She looked expectantly at them. A bit shorter than Brenda, with a medium-length Afro and black-rimmed glasses, the woman struck Philly as a confident professional, whatever her profession might be. In this context, she was taking the initiative to invite them into the next stage of the prayer and worship meeting. She was inviting them to join her for whatever came next.

A skinny guy in his fifties who had been sitting next to Philly turned toward the three of them and raised his pale hands slightly as if to request inclusion in their group. Two women also pushed toward them, one tall with black hair and caramel skin, and the other short and blonde.

Philly got the feeling that the first woman was a magnet. She had picked the new couple, and that had attracted others. Her name was Heloise. The skinny guy had already introduced himself as Harv, and the other two women were Marlena and Joyce. Besides Philly and Brenda, the others all seemed to know each other.

First, their little group prayed for Joyce's marriage, with Heloise adding some sort of encouraging insights into God's vision for that marriage. Her insights seemed to start Joyce crying cathartically.

They all prayed for Brenda's pregnancy, and Philly felt a warmth over his whole body when Heloise declared future blessings over their baby.

"This child will be a miracle. Not that the pregnancy is especially miraculous, but I believe miracles are in the future of this little life. And God's glory will shine on ... this child."

Philly paused to wonder if Heloise was about to say *him* or *her* instead of *this child*. She seemed to have some kind of prophetic gift that the other folks in their group understood. He forced himself to squeeze past that thought in order to stay with the group and move to the next prayer need.

Harv was rubbing his jaw and explaining how he ground his teeth in his sleep and that his jaw was suffering from it. He also had frequent headaches and was feeling one right now.

When he finished this summary, Heloise looked squarely at Philly and said simply, "Go ahead."

Only briefly, Philly paused over how strange her prompt would have been to the average newcomer who wandered into this meeting. But for him it was the exact opposite of strange. In fact, he felt another dose of that *welcome home* in Heloise's opening for him to go ahead and do his thing. How did she know?

He glanced at Brenda with half a smile. She seemed satisfied with this turn of events.

Philly asked Harv for permission to put a hand on his head. Philly usually avoided doing that particular move because it reminded him of men he had seen on TV, healers with whom he didn't want to be associated, though he actually knew very little about any of them. He cleared his throat softly. "Peace. I speak peace to the part of Harv that does this teeth grinding without him knowing about it or wanting it. Peace, in the name of Jesus. Jaw, be restored. No inflammation, no pain. Off, now." And Philly pulled his hand away.

Harv stood perfectly still with his eyes closed tightly. Then he opened his eyes and shook his head as if shedding water after a dunk in a pool. "Ha! Oh. I felt that. That was something. Oh. My headache is gone. Yeah! Thank you, Lord. That was good."

As Philly stepped back and observed Harv's reaction, he could see that both Marlena and Joyce were starting to speak, a request in words while pointing to something in their body that hurt. He caught a glint from Heloise's eye. She looked proud of herself, or maybe just satisfied at a connection completed. But he didn't let that distract him long. He and Brenda teamed up with the others to pray for healing to Marlena's sore ankle and a painful problem in Joyce's lower abdomen.

The healings that happened in their group, and in the groups around them, were cause for rejoicing. And Philly could sense that people in that room had seen healing before, but maybe not as often as he had. Most of all, he sensed that this prayer time sealed his invitation to come in and join the family. No longer just a consultant, he was a member of the team, a member of this church family.

It didn't hurt either that the people were friendly, and the refreshments were creative and tasty. Brenda kept saying, "Eating for two," when she went back for another sample of the snacks laid out in the kitchen.

Philly just tried to signal permission with his eyes as he smiled at her and then turned to meet another member of the family.

Chapter 35
In the Face of Promises

Thursday at work was different. Philly was an employee. He was welcomed there. He belonged there. Nothing about his employment status had changed, really. But Philly had changed, or at least some sort of bubble he carried around him had popped.

Bubble?

In some mysterious way, the discovery of a "church home" had spilled over to his work. And, instead of distracting him from his work, he now focused on the tasks on his to-do list with less diversion or distraction. Had he received some healing that he hadn't even requested? The idea was rich and satisfying. That feeling lasted most of the day.

Around four o'clock that afternoon, Brenda called him. She rarely called him at work.

"Hello, dear. Is something wrong?"

"Philly, I need you to come home right away."

"You're at home? What happened?"

"I felt sick, so I left early. When I went to the bathroom here, I saw some blood."

Philly froze. The world around him froze. The air, the building, the city—everything stopped for one second, as if preparing for something. Then it all pounced. "Blood? Okay, I'm heading out right now." He probably said goodbye before he hung up. He probably remembered to log off his computer. His office door automatically locked, fortunately. He walked fast. Someone said something to him. He might have answered, at least with a noise of some kind. He speed-walked through the parking lot to make up for the slow ride down in the elevator. He was running to the rescue. He was supposed to make things right. Wasn't he?

His phone rang over the Bluetooth system in his car. Brenda again. "I have cramps, but the bleeding is less. I just don't feel right."

"Should you go to the hospital?"

"I don't know. Maybe."

"Did you call your doctor?"

"She's out. I left her a message."

Philly drove quickly and precisely. He needed to get home, and he needed to get home fast. His adrenal urgency was better than caffeine. He hoped the cops would understand if they caught him sailing past them at eighty miles an hour. It still seemed to take forever to get home.

He left his car on the drive outside the garage and hustled in the door and up the stairs.

Brenda was sitting in the kitchen fully dressed, including her shoes. "The doctor says to go to the hospital right away."

"Do you need anything? Should I grab something for you?"

"Just bring your wallet with the insurance card."

"Okay. Got that. Let's go." His head swam as he helped Brenda to her feet. He willed himself to stay upright, to stay strong.

"It's gonna be okay, isn't it?" She was clinging to his arm as they both walked down the stairs toward the car.

"Of course it will." Philly focused a silent prayer to Jesus. When he slid into the driver's seat, he suddenly realized that he didn't know where the nearest hospital was. He pulled out his phone.

"What are you doing?"

"Where's the hospital?"

"Find the one in Elk Grove Village. My doctor sees people there."

Philly expected her doctor would go wherever Brenda was, but the hospital in Elk Grove was probably the closest one anyway. He searched in the maps app and found directions to the emergency room.

Now he was driving fast again, this time with confidence that he could convince the police he had good reason. The woman in his passenger seat clutching her stomach was his pass to breaking the speed limit.

"Slow down, Philly. I feel sick."

He eased off the gas and took the next turn more carefully. They would arrive soon. They would arrive safely. That was all that mattered, all that he dared hope at this point.

He parked near the emergency room entrance and helped Brenda toward the wide sliding doors. A woman in scrubs was walking into the hospital away from that door. For just one second, Philly thought it was Theresa. One insane second. He hesitated, gasped, and then called ahead to the anonymous woman, "Can we have some help here? She's pregnant and having some bleeding."

Brenda added to that list of complaints by bending over and vomiting onto the speckled white tile.

The woman started calling out in a sharp, alarming voice, saying something that must have been meant for someone else. Philly didn't catch it. But he did hear her more comforting voice aimed at Brenda. "Okay, dear. Hang on. We'll get you a place to lie down right away."

A gurney coasted to a stop just up the hall. Philly had been thinking wheelchair, but he helped Brenda over to the gurney without comment. A big young man in purple scrubs helped her onto the narrow, rolling bed.

Now Philly was following. He was answering questions. He was no longer the one who was going to save Brenda and their baby. Others had taken charge of that. He just stayed close and answered whatever they asked him. He shook himself free of a crazy question he wanted to ask about who was supposed to clean up the mess Brenda had just made near the entrance.

"Get her in number eleven." Someone was taking charge. Until now, it had seemed that they were all being swept along by the momentous emergency, the will of that same urgency that had focused Philly's driving on the way home. He could tell who was in charge now, and what they wanted. They were no longer just a bunch of pebbles rolling in the surf on a Lake Michigan beach.

A nurse with a stethoscope tucked in her breast pocket pulled Philly toward a desk. "Why don't you get her registered, and we'll get her situated in a bed."

"Brenda. Her name is Brenda."

The nurse hesitated a moment, as if she didn't understand why Philly was telling her that. Then she seemed to realize the point of what he had just said. "Okay. We'll take care of Brenda. You get started on the paperwork. Do you know her doctor's name?"

"Harrison. Brenda talked to her, and she said to meet her here."

"Good. Thanks." She pointed him to the registration desk again and hurried back toward where Philly had left his wife.

For a second, he stuck to that spot. Moving one foot farther away from where he had left Brenda seemed wrong.

The woman behind the little registration desk pulled him out of that ditch. "Let's just get started on the paperwork. You can get back to her right after that."

"Okay. Yeah. Sure." He took a seat and suddenly felt as if he would start to cry. Just relaxing enough to sit down seemed to release the latch on his emotions. He pulled a few quick breaths and tightened down the shutters once again.

The registrar asked for his driver's license and insurance card, and he answered all the questions thrown at him. Maybe they weren't all perfectly correct answers, but Philly just did his best imitation of surety and pushed on. He had to get back to Brenda as soon as possible.

It was probably only a few minutes, but every delay for the computer to process information, every pause to print a document, every new screen full of questions seemed to stretch as long as an entire dental appointment.

Hosting Jesus

"Okay. She's in number eleven. You can go see if they're ready for you in there. If not, they'll show you where you can wait."

He wandered up the wide hallway to where he hoped to find bay eleven, or room eleven, or whatever that was called. Curtains in some patient areas stood open a foot or two, some revealing solemn scenes of families hunkered by a bedside, or of still forms lying on high beds with wheels at the ready, poised for moving the occupant to some other source of help in this huge hospital. He finally noticed where the numbers were posted by each of the patient bays and followed them up to eleven. But he wasn't allowed through the curtain when he arrived.

"Hold on. Just wait here a minute." A young woman with short, streaked blonde hair had pushed ahead of Philly and was peeking in behind the curtain. "Just hang on a minute."

"Is her doctor in there?"

"No. A nurse practitioner is seeing her now. Her doctor called in. She's on her way."

And that was when Philly suddenly felt like he was an intruder in a land exclusively for women. He had glimpsed one old man in one of the other patient bays, and had heard a male voice somewhere along the way, but Brenda was surrounded by women. Women protecting her. Hopefully saving her and saving the baby. That was good. He felt safe having those women all working together for the good of his wife and the life of his child.

But he wanted to see Brenda as soon as possible. What had happened? What was this about? How serious was it?

As he stood there, Doctor Harrison arrived. She was a tall and erect woman with fine, medium-brown hair and nearly black eyes. She grasped his arm. It was the first time she had ever touched him, he was sure. "Mr. Thompson. I'm glad you got her in here so fast. That's very good. Hang on a minute while I go see what the situation is with Brenda."

He nodded and stood still before doing a sort of circular shuffle. There was nowhere to sit down, nowhere obvious to go. He just stood outside that curtain. He could hear noises from inside, but the clutter of sounds from the nurses' station and the other patient bays obscured the voices. He heard Brenda say something, answering a question, maybe. There were so many questions to answer.

When they finally let him in and two of the caregivers left the scene, what he found was surprisingly peaceful. Brenda was smiling weakly at him. She wore a very pale gray gown with some sort of tiny shapes printed on it. She had a blanket or two draped over her from the waist down. Her doctor stood examining paperwork and checking a small metal box that looked sort of like an ancient computer.

"Hey." Brenda seemed a bit spacey.

"Hey. How are you, honey?" He slipped into the slot next to the bed, opposite the doctor and most of the medical equipment.

"I'm fine. I'm not in any danger." She said it calmly, reassuringly.

And Philly *was* reassured. But what she said called out to what she *didn't* say. "The baby? How's the baby?"

Brenda looked at the doctor.

Dr. Harrison stepped to the side of the bed and looked first at Brenda and then squarely at Philly. He felt her attention, her focus on him. And he felt her focus on the crisis that lay among them.

"The baby is under some distress. We are monitoring closely right now, trying to figure out what's causing that distress."

Philly tried to fit that explanation into something he could understand. "Is the baby coming too soon? This is too soon, isn't it?"

"The baby's due around the first part of November, we believe. This is much too early. But I don't think the baby is really trying to come early. There was some bleeding, but so far we have no evidence of placental abruption or cervical dilation." She paused, as if aware that she had thrown more medical terms at Philly than he could catch. "The baby is fighting something, and we'll have to keep Brenda in overnight, at least, to see what's going on." As the doctor finished her statement, the monitor behind her started to beep.

Philly watched the doctor deftly reach for the button hanging on the edge of the bed.

"Please step outside, Mr. Thompson."

Step outside? What's that beeping? What does it mean? He didn't speak. The questions just ricocheted around in his head and landed against his heart. Was his heart still beating? What about the baby? Was the baby's heart still beating?

And then Philly felt hands leading him out through the curtain and down the hall toward a waiting area. Did someone say *waiting area*? How did he know that was where he was going? Where was the person who led him there?

He sat in the corner. Then, as if someone slapped him awake, he knew he should be calling people. He needed help. He should call for help.

Chapter 36
He Cannot Escape His Past

Philly had never been admitted to a hospital for an overnight stay. He had been in hospitals many times, but always to stand next to the bed of someone he loved, to worry and to wait. The most recent of those crises had been with his late fiancée, Theresa.

The first thing Philly had heard, when Theresa got sick, was that she was in the hospital. He had seen her for dinner just two nights before, and they had a date to go shopping that Friday. When your fiancée is a nurse, finding out that she's in the hospital doesn't seem very alarming.

"Hello, Phil? This is Clarice. I work with Theresa at the hospital. You should come here as soon as you can. She's being taken to the intensive care unit."

It seemed fortunate, at the time, that Theresa's symptoms had started becoming obvious at the beginning of a shift on the critical care unit where she worked. And it seemed *very* fortunate that her colleagues prevented her from simply going home sick when they saw how high her fever was and how frequently she was rushing to the bathroom. At least, people kept telling Philly how fortunate all that was.

All those consolations wore thin by the time Philly stood outside Theresa's isolation room with her mother. Her mother held her hand over her mouth, certainly unconscious of that pose, certainly not trying to protect herself from catching whatever had infected her daughter.

Doctors assured them eventually that it wasn't something they could catch through the air, not something Philly might have caught from her the last time he saw Theresa. But what they couldn't say for sure was how Theresa had contracted the infection. The patient from whom she'd caught it had a clear clinical history that doctors could articulate, though perhaps too late for Theresa's benefit. But they couldn't say for sure how the contact-borne disease made it into Theresa's digestive and blood systems.

Whenever they recited for Philly the technical term for the infection, something with the word *resistant* in the middle of some much longer words, he just shook it off. He didn't need their Latin name for it. Robber and killer were all the names he needed.

The killer began strangling Theresa, robbing her of breath. And, in doing so, it was defying the best wisdom of infectious disease experts from around the Chicago area. When the patient from whom Theresa contracted the disease died, Philly tried to isolate that fact from his fiancée's story. That death was news, but it didn't tell the whole story. It didn't tell Theresa's story.

People from the church had begun to show up. Maybe they were working in shifts, praying with Philly and trying to bring healing to Theresa's failing body. Dave seemed almost clinical in his calm and intensity, but he proved powerless in his prayers for healing.

Philly tried then to quarantine those failures—the failures of the doctors, and the failures of the healing prayers. He tried to isolate them from Theresa's story as well. But all that isolating closed him off, shut him down.

Every interaction he had ever had with Theresa's mother before this crisis had been cheerful and pleasant. He had discovered that the mildly disappointed look on his future mother-in-law's face had nothing to do with him. It was just the curve of her mouth and the slant of her eyes. She had usually countered those disappointed facial cues with an easy smile and a chirpy tone. That was, until the bad news began to pile into an overwhelming stack, the weight of which couldn't be moved by a smile or an upbeat word. It was then that the disappointment on her face began to appear real and permanent.

"I don't want to lose her, Philly. I just can't lose her." In her late sixties, Theresa's mother had lost a son to drug addiction and a marriage to infidelity. Her own new marriage and her daughter had been her consolation. Would the marriage be enough if Theresa left her now?

Philly's disappointment had become profound, but remained silent. Once they began allowing him to sit next to Theresa in the ICU, Philly started trying every version of healing prayer he had ever heard. He didn't stop when others were around—nurses, Theresa's relatives, people from church. He just kept repeating his pleas, retrying his commands, and often resorting to begging—something he had been taught was unnecessary with a loving God who wanted his children well.

By the end, it felt to Philly like the machines were forcing Theresa to breathe, but they weren't ever going to be able to force her to live. He only nodded when Theresa's stepfather told him that her mother had decided to shut off the respirator. She apparently didn't want to be part of forcing her daughter to breathe. Nobody did.

That was the end of Theresa's life on earth, but it was not the end of Philly's loss. In his heart, Theresa continued to die. He lost her every morning when he awoke to realize that his crushing nightmares were daytime reality. He wanted to go back to work and forget the nightmares, to get lost in the glare of living needs among living people. But he couldn't get himself out the door. Not for weeks.

How many times did he replay those healing prayers? He searched for the flaw in what he had said or how he had said it. And, when he couldn't identify that flaw, he gave up. He knew at the time that he should be talking to Dave about all this, but that was no different than knowing he should be going back to work at the community center, that he should be going on living his life.

He just couldn't do it. At least, not for a long time after that great loss.

Chapter 37
The Hope of Things Unseen

In that hospital waiting room now, waiting for word about the fate of another person he loved, Philly remembered the time Jesus accompanied him to see his grandmother. Jesus had been there with Philly more than once, but Philly focused now on the time after he finally knew that Jesus was offering to heal Grandma Thompson. That was also when Philly had met Theresa.

He knew where Theresa was now. He knew where his grandma was.

Where was Jesus?

The last place he had been certain that Jesus was present was at the midweek worship service in that beautiful suburban home. Was that yesterday? He started seeking help by sending an email to Max, the owner of that house. Philly hadn't gotten Max's phone number, but had added his email address to his phone. Pastor Will was next. Philly had his email address as well as his phone number. He was glad for each of these links to rescuers, links to Jesus's presence in this situation, in this hospital.

Will called in response to Philly's text. "Hey, Phil. Mary wanted me to tell you she's on her way. Let me give you her number. She's gonna text you when she gets to the hospital."

No preliminaries. No arrangements that Philly had to decide about. Just "Help is on the way." Already on the way.

Dr. Harrison came out to see Philly a minute after he hung up with Will. "Mr. Thompson. Brenda is doing fine. We are rehydrating her a little through an IV, but that's mostly just a precaution. The baby is struggling. The monitor has been showing an irregular heartbeat. But what concerns us most is a series of seizures. In one so small, it is very concerning to see seizures. And these may be the cause of the irregular heart rate."

Seizure was a medical term, but not one that Philly had to strain to understand. More than that, he understood the look on Dr. Harrison's face. Brenda was going to be okay physically. That was the good news. The bad news was about their child. The little person hidden inside Brenda was suffering, struggling.

"Can you do anything to help the baby?" It was the question he was supposed to ask, wasn't it? He was forcing himself not to cry.

She shook her head slightly. "I've contacted a specialist at Lurie Children's Hospital. I'm not ready to recommend any action yet. We don't have a lot of options."

Did that sound generic? Was she answering in a void, trying to sound like she was in charge even though the fate of their child was out of her hands?

Philly just nodded. Right at that moment, he was counting on the arrival of people from his new church, not a call back from specialists in a distant hospital. But he knew even less than the doctor did about what was needed, so he knew he might just be grasping wildly at mere wisps of hope.

The doctor gripped his upper arm briefly. "You can go in and be with Brenda." Then she walked away.

He would go in and be with Brenda, and he would be with their baby. He wasn't counting this baby out yet. Philly took a deep breath to prepare himself for facing his wife.

"What did they tell you?" Brenda's eyes seemed abnormally large, like a frightened animal about to run for cover.

Philly tried to figure out if there was a reason not to tell Brenda everything he knew. Didn't she already know everything? He just did the natural thing. He told her all that the doctor had said.

She wasn't surprised at his summary of the situation. Maybe she was sifting it for some new fragment in the version he had heard, something better than the news the doctor had given her.

"Mary is on her way. Mary from church." He wasn't sure Brenda would recognize who Mary was in this situation. "She'll text me when she gets here."

"You called her?"

"I texted Will and emailed Max." Philly remembered then to check his email to see if Max had gotten back to him.

I'm on my way. Karen's in the city. She'll come later. Here's my phone number ...

Again, no hesitation. On the way. His new church was on the way. Maybe just two people, but they were people who knew Jesus. Mary had even believed Philly's story about Jesus walking around with him and healing people. These folks weren't just coming to sympathize with Philly and Brenda. They were bringing something of Jesus with them.

That's what Philly was hoping. In the meantime, he decided to try praying for the child. Again, Philly slid up to the side of the bed where he could be closest to Brenda. "Let's ask Jesus to heal our baby." It felt like those might be his last words. Saying that much choked him for a few seconds.

Brenda's tears were pooling and spilling down her cheeks. She slipped her hands over her belly, around the circles at the end of the fetal monitor cables.

Philly worried that her hands might disturb the monitor. But his desperation to see this baby live outweighed that caution. "Lord, we rely on you for everything. For life, and health, and healing. Bring your power right here, right now." Philly took a deep breath. "In the name of Jesus, be restored. Be well. No seizures. No heart problems. Live. Live. Live." His voice squeaked shut at that point.

As he struggled to recover control, he felt his phone buzz in his pocket. He fumbled with getting his phone out of his jacket. It was a text from Mary. He sniffled hard.

"Me and Cassey are here. What room are you in?"

Philly texted directions to Brenda's bed and hoped no one would stop Mary and whoever Cassey was.

A minute later, the curtain stirred. "Phil? Is it okay to come in? It's Mary."

Checking first very briefly with Brenda, Philly stepped to the curtain. He pulled it back after she nodded her approval. There stood Mary and a teenage girl who looked a bit like her.

"This is my daughter, Cassey. I hope it's okay. She's seen some powerful healing, especially with babies."

How could Philly refuse that? "Come in. Thank you. Thank you for coming." Then he knew he needed to update them. "The baby is having seizures. The doctor doesn't think there's anything she can do about it. It's very serious." In other circumstances, he would have tried to sound less panicked. He would have regretted the strained rush of his voice, his words squashed and coming in surges.

"No problem. Jesus can deal with it." Mary patted Philly's shoulder. She was headed for Brenda. "How are you doing, Brenda?"

"I'm okay. I'm just scared for our baby." And that broke her open again. She started to sob.

Without hesitation, Mary put a hand on Brenda's head. "Of course you're scared. Of course you are." She turned to Cassey and nodded the girl toward the side of the bed that Philly had vacated.

Cassey was an even slimmer version of her mother with large blue eyes and long blondish hair in a loose braid down her back. Though she moved carefully and landed gently, Cassey showed no hesitation. She was already praying under her breath, from what Philly could tell.

When he drew close to Brenda, brushing shoulders with Cassey, Philly could feel warmth radiating from the bed. Was that from Brenda? Was it from the three women united here for the life of this child? Maybe it was their little one, their baby. Maybe he or she was glowing, radiating.

"Healing. Healing. Wholeness. Peace. Peace. Calm. Peace." That was Cassey's prayer, or her blessing for the child.

"Total healing. Complete recovery. We tell this little one to live. Live. Live." Mary spoke more clearly than Cassey, but her voice cracked with emotion.

Philly heard Mary's echo of his own prayer.

Brenda was panting, no longer sobbing.

For a moment, Philly was worried about that panting. Was she going into labor? The doctor said it was too early.

But her breathing began to slow. It seemed to only be about recovering emotional equilibrium. Brenda settled more deeply into the bed, as if she had been rigid with tension before.

Both Mary and Cassey stood silent, hands gently resting on Brenda. Cassey's thin fingers stretched over Brenda's belly. Then she withdrew one hand, stood up, and withdrew the other. She looked at her mother and nodded.

Quiet nodding might mean something good between mother and daughter, but Philly also thought it could mean that the doctor's assessment was true. There was nothing that could be done. No one could save this child. He studied Mary's response.

A small smile. She stroked Brenda's head and then turned to the fetal monitor. She acted as if she knew what she was looking at. Philly hadn't even taken a moment to try and interpret what the little display was saying.

The radiating heat continued. It was comfortable, not sweaty or feverish. That comfortable warmth seemed to fill the room.

"I felt Jesus's hands rest on me, on my belly." Brenda was whispering, but Philly could hear her clearly. And the smiles on Mary and Cassey's faces confirmed that they heard it too.

Or did those smiles confirm something more? Had they felt those invisible hands?

Mary looked at the monitor again. "Steady heart rate. But I think it was already steady when we got here."

"Yeah. I really felt like the healing had already started." Cassey nodded softly and then turned to look at Philly. She offered a subtle, dimpled grin that might have been her way of hinting that *he* had begun the healing process.

"As long as Jesus got involved, that's all I need to know." Philly had never seen a healing situation with a less than wonderful result when Jesus clearly made his presence known.

A tap on the wall outside the curtain preceded it sweeping to one side. A nurse scooted in, followed by Max. "Well, quite a gathering in here." The middle-aged woman with a squarish face stopped and stared at the monitor. Then she regarded Brenda curiously. "How are you, dear?"

"I'm feeling better. Less scared." Maybe that wasn't right at the center of the nurse's responsibilities, but Philly knew Brenda's fear level was a good gauge of what was happening.

The nurse paused as if sensing something, perhaps something she wasn't ready to name. "Well, the baby has very good cardiac rhythm now. Solid and steady. No sign of seizures for a while. That's good." She took Brenda's temperature and blood pressure while everyone else watched silently.

Philly was holding his breath, as if a laugh was building inside. Maybe the others were feeling it too, holding it in while the nurse did her work.

"Okay. Looks good." She scanned the four other people standing in that small patient bay. "Don't stay too long. She could use some rest." That sounded like a prerecorded message, one she didn't really expect anyone to respond to immediately.

That's how Philly took it. He let out the air he had been holding when the nurse swung out through the curtain. And he smiled at the other people who were all looking at him now. He turned to Max. "Thanks for coming, Max."

"Sure. Of course. But maybe I missed the excitement." His brow was flexed just a bit as he looked with a sort of humorous suspicion at the faces around him, faces optimistic in the greenish hospital light.

Mary described all that had happened since she and Cassey arrived. "And we may have just been here to witness the miracle that was already happening." She looked at Philly. Was she remembering his stories about Jesus accompanying him? Did she know about the healing ministry Philly had done even after Jesus went invisible? Or was she just reflecting some intuition or revelation she had received right there at Brenda's side?

Philly took Brenda's hand. "Jesus is the reason we're together. He is the reason this baby exists. And he seems determined that this baby will live."

One miracle in that room, at that moment, was the unanimous peace those five people felt in the face of an ominous diagnosis. They had made no pact declaring their rejection of medical science. Philly had not rallied them in opposition to Dr. Harrison. But they all seemed to sense the relief that comes when the fever breaks, when the pain disappears, when the seizure ends.

Dr. Harrison was the next person to slide that curtain aside and step in. Max excused himself, and Mary and Cassey followed his lead.

"We'll hang out in the waiting area for a little while, Phil." Mary spoke quietly with a hand on Philly's arm. "Just text me and let us know if you want us to come back in."

Philly nodded and smiled at her. Her quickly composed arrangements lacked the triage feeling that had filled that room before she arrived. Even if the healing started before those two women joined him, the peace settled on Philly and Brenda only after Mary and Cassey brought it in.

"So, we haven't seen any more seizures for almost half an hour, and her heart rate is good." The doctor seemed to slip a gear and then to speed past something. "Uh, so that's good. I don't want to give you a false hope, but stable and steady is good, of course."

"Is our baby a girl?" Brenda hadn't missed that hitch.

Dr. Harrison quirked a little smile in one corner of her mouth. "I know you didn't want to know until the birth. Sorry."

"I'm not sorry," Philly blurted. The new hope he was feeling about the life of this unborn child flashed sharper. The baby was more real to him for having been identified as a daughter, and not just a child. She was more real, and she was more alive.

"Well, we'll get you up to a room so you can be more comfortable, and we'll keep an eye on her as well as on you." She patted Brenda's hand just below the IV.

"Okay." That one word seemed full of meaning for Philly. No longer was his wife a terrorized victim of an attack on her unborn child, she was a cooperative patient with much less worry about the life of her daughter.

Okay. They would stay to assure the doctors.

Philly and Brenda needed little more assurance.

Chapter 38
Mother and Child Doing Well

Like lots of his experiences with healing, Philly couldn't prove conclusively that the baby had been healed. The fact that she had no more seizures didn't prove that she would never have another one. None of the evidence satisfied the doctor's requirements to declare a miracle. But that evidence did help the medical personnel feel more hopeful, hopeful enough to agree to let Brenda go home after one night in the hospital.

Philly came to pick her up with a bag full of toiletries and a change of clothes. He was just outside Brenda's room when the door to the next room was easing shut. A scene in that other room printed on his mind in one brief instant—an old man attached by tubes and wires to various medical equipment, and a woman sitting next to him holding what might have been a Bible.

"Offer to pray for the man." That was the idea that formed almost as automatically as the instant image burned onto his mind's eye.

With that picture, and the accompanying idea, Philly carried Brenda's stuff into her room.

"Oh, good. I just saw that other doctor. Uh, Doctor Justacarryon, or whatever his name is. He's all worried and thinks I'm dumb, but at least he's not gonna stop us from leaving." She was sliding off her bed, only a disconnected IV port still taped to her hand.

"Justacarryon?" Philly couldn't remember the correct name either, but that didn't sound right.

"Whatever." Brenda kissed him on the cheek.

He got a little whiff of her need for the toothbrush he was handing her. "Are we crazy for feeling like the baby is fine now?" Philly watched her toddle to the bathroom.

"Will and Mary said to listen to the doctors, but to continue to feel encouraged. The doctors haven't proposed anything risky, so it's been easy to do both." She swung the door halfway shut. "Gotta get cleaned up. I feel gross."

"You could never be gross. But go ahead."

Her smile was the last thing Philly saw as the bathroom door closed.

He checked around the room to judge how much junk they needed to haul with them. And then he admitted to himself that he was avoiding the thought that had come with the picture he captured of the room next door.

Snorting at himself, Philly answered the call. "Okay. I'll try." He turned back toward the hallway, slowing as he walked by the bathroom. "I'll be right back, Brenda."

She said something monosyllabic in return, already in the midst of her ablutions.

His heart rate rising and breathing getting tighter, Philly was glad he wasn't hooked up to a patient monitor. If he had been, a team of medical professionals would be rushing toward him after an announcement blared from the speakers in the hall. "Attention all personnel. Code chicken. Code chicken on the fourth floor." He snorted at his own joke.

Philly knocked on the dark wooden door, closed but for a slim inch of invitation. That's what it felt like to him, though it was too narrow to provide him another one of those snapshots of Brenda's neighbor. After the knock, he pushed the door open wider, like the doctors and nurses had been doing all day at Brenda's door. Knock, and then open when no protest follows.

"Hello?" Philly stepped into the room like it might be wired with booby traps.

"Hello." The woman beside the bed looked at him with her eyebrows raised. But it wasn't consternation or even curiosity that Philly read on her face. It seemed to him like hope.

Maybe that was just his imagination. Though, his imagination tended more toward doom and retreat, not hope and welcome. "Hi. My name is Phil Thompson. My wife is in the room next door. We're getting ready to go home. To take her home. I'm taking her home. That's why I'm here ... now." Ugh. Gotta pick up the pace. "I was just wondering if I could pray for him." He noticed that the man in the bed was staring at him. "If I could pray for healing for *you*."

"Really? Who did you say you were?" That welcome on the woman's face might have been meant for someone else. She seemed to be pulling it back.

"I just had this feeling that I should try for some ... to pray for healing for you, when I was walking to my wife's room just a minute ago." He wasn't really finding a welcome on the man's face either. The elderly man seemed a bit lost. But Philly was in the same boat.

"What was wrong with your wife?" The woman had turned fully toward Philly somewhere in there. She asked the question with the intonation of an experienced interviewer.

That tone made it easier for Philly to sort his thoughts. "She's pregnant. The baby was having irregular heart rhythm and seizures. But she's okay now. Both of them. Mother and baby are both okay now."

"Oh, that's good to hear." A tilt of her head and a small smile softened the reception the woman was offering. She must have been near seventy years old. She looked alert and healthy compared to the man in the bed. Her husband, was it?

"Actually, we prayed for the baby and the seizures stopped. Some people from my church came to the hospital, and the baby has been fine since. I was wondering if I could sort of pass it on. Maybe I could pray for healing for ..."

"Oh. This is my husband, Andre." She stood up and approached with her hand out. "I'm Sophia."

Philly shook her hand. Generally, for Philly, it was the *offer* of healing that was the hard part, the part he had to boost himself over, like an overweight kid trying to climb a fence. But Sophia hadn't accepted his offer yet, so he felt the need for another boost. "You mind if I give it a try?"

For a second, he feared that he would have to introduce the topic all over again. Sophia's eyes twitched. Not quite a blink, she seemed to falter just a moment. Then she relaxed visibly. "Well, I do believe in miracles. And that's what it would take for Andre to get better, they tell me."

"Sure. At least we can try, right?" Philly sidestepped Sophia just a little, not doing an end-around, but also not wanting to have to ask for any more permission. "Hi, Andre. I'm Phil. My friends call me Philly." Whether another introduction was needed, and why he told this stranger his nickname, Philly didn't know. But it was out there now. No turning back.

Andre smiled. "I'm a *Phillies* fan." His voice came as a phlegmy croak.

Without hesitation, Philly poked back. "A Phillies fan this close to Chicago? Well, I'll forgive you for that. I guess God can heal you anyway." Philly breathed a laugh through his lips, sending a fleck of spit flying in Andre's direction. He hoped the two other people in the room hadn't noticed that.

At least they laughed at his joke. Certainly they had heard some version of it before.

"Okay, I'll just pray a simple prayer." That was something he had learned at his church in Chicago. People might worry that you were about to begin a loud, long, and generally embarrassing prayer. His "simple prayer" comment was meant as a relaxer.

"Thanks for your love for Andre, Lord. I welcome your healing power here now, Jesus. I welcome your presence, Lord." He took a breath and then said, "Be healed. Breathing restored. Every unhealthy cell and organ be healed." It was one of his more invasive healing commands, but he managed to say it calmly and without a lot of emotion. It felt good. Philly felt that he had done what he was supposed to. That was a good feeling. But he was also feeling that something might have just happened.

"You were just next door, and you decided to come and pray for my husband?" Sophia was on the other side of the bed looking across at Philly. The light from the window was cutting across her maroon and gray top—an old warmup jacket. The room was well air conditioned.

Now that he had done his part, Philly felt like he could see the couple more clearly. Maybe his fear and anxiety had blinded him a little, stretching a foggy filter over his eyes. Or maybe he was just seeing them better from the sunny side of the room. "I was bringing her stuff for getting ready to go home, and I just had this thought that I should come over and give it a try."

Andre cleared his throat and then did it again. "Ha. Well, I'm not gonna argue about it one way or the other. I'm feeling pretty good right now. It felt like I was gettin' a shot or something—like something was just pumping right into me."

Philly smiled at him. "That sounds good." He let some enthusiasm fill that last word.

Sophia looked startled. She stared at her husband. "You feel *good*? You feel better?"

Andre laughed. "You keep prayin' for me all the time. Why are you surprised when it works?" He laughed some more as if he was having fun with her, not really rebuking her for her little faith.

A rebuke about little faith might have been in order for both Philly and Sophia, but Philly could feel a sort of lift in the room as Andre's wife bent toward him, the sunlight illuminating her face as she leaned in.

The loving connection between those two old folks reminded Philly that his wife was next door and that she would expect him to be back by now. "Well, I hope you feel better and get out of here soon." He was looking forward to that last part for himself.

"Oh, that *would* be a miracle. We weren't expecting Andre to go home from here." Sophia had a bit of that stunned animal look in her eyes that Philly had seen on Brenda the previous afternoon. Perhaps the version he saw on Sophia was good. A good surprise.

Philly returned their smiles and acknowledged their thanks on his way out the door.

"Philly." Andre caught him before he closed the door behind him.

Sticking his head back in the room, Philly waited for Andre's final word to him.

"Thanks, young man. You have saved my life. Bless you."

Now it was Philly's turn to clear his throat. "Uh, wow. That's great. I didn't even know what was wrong. I just thought I should offer to pray."

Back in Brenda's room, she was blow-drying her hair with the bathroom door open. "Hey." She shut off the dryer. "Where did you go?"

"Just next door."

"Next door to the hospital?"

"No, next door *in* the hospital." He pointed toward Andre's room.

"Why?" She lifted the dryer toward her head but delayed turning back it on. "Wait. Did you go pray for the person next door? Who *is* next door?"

"Andre and Sophia. I saved Andre's life." He laughed with one of those ratchet inhales at the end. "Or, at least, Jesus did, according to Andre."

"Oh, wow. Cool." She returned to drying her hair, a blissful smile on her face as her brown locks flailed around her head.

When they had finally collected all their stuff and the hospital orderly arrived with Brenda's ride to the exit, Philly had to stop right outside her room. He waited for a pair of women in scrubs who were talking animatedly. Philly recognized one as a nurse who had stopped in Brenda's room that day.

"I don't know what else to call it but a miracle. Totally impossible otherwise."

That little fragment of conversation, and some elevated voices and laughter from inside Andre's room, gave Philly a smile.

"Philly, is that the room? Is that where you went?"

He nodded and caught up to Brenda's wheelchair.

" 'A miracle,' she said."

"A miracle." He smiled at the slice of good news.

Chapter 39
Becoming Part of a Community

Philly's introduction to the church in Chicago had been primarily through his healing ministry. He had met Dave because Jesus suggested it. And Dave had brought Philly up front in a meeting the first time because of the healing Jesus had taught Philly to do. Now, in their new church in the suburbs, Philly and Brenda were being introduced through healing once again. They let a week pass before allowing themselves a victory lap. With no more bleeding, no more cramps, and no more of those hiccuppy little seizures—they were ready to declare the crisis passed. To Philly and Brenda, it was a miracle story.

Word about the baby's emergency had been spread through the church's social media site to the praying faithful. Lots of people were giving thanks for the continued health of their baby, even if it wasn't something anyone was going to publish as a verified miracle.

On Brenda's follow-up visit with Dr. Harrison, she received the impression that the baby being born healthy, without epilepsy or other seizure-causing ailments, might be considered a miracle. Apparently the doctor had never seen a baby entirely recover from prenatal seizures. She expected side effects sooner or later, but she didn't tell Brenda not to feel relieved that their little girl was looking perfectly healthy on the ultrasound.

Every passing week would advance their little girl one step closer to being the miracle child Philly already believed she was—even before she needed to be healed of something so scary.

"Hi, Brenda. Hi, Philly. I'm Nicky Martin. This is my husband, C.J. We're so thankful for your story. We had a baby who was supposed to be mentally handicapped according to the tests they ran while I was pregnant. She's an honor student in middle school now. It's a wonderful feeling, isn't it? Jesus has our back no matter what we face as parents."

C.J. shook Philly's hand. He was a big guy with a strong grip. These were the priceless benefits of being initiated into the church via a healing miracle. A lot of people just came up and introduced themselves, and most of them told their best healing stories.

The friendly smiles of this couple, who seemed about the same age as Philly and Brenda, gave Philly a feeling of permission to tell his most recent story. The previous day, a rainy Saturday, he had received a phone call from an unfamiliar number.

"It took us a long time to track you down," said the woman's voice on the other end. And a man's voice joined her on the line, chuckling in harmony.

"Sophia?" Philly stalled over trying to imagine the logistics required for the people he had met at the hospital to find his phone number.

"I know there are all those privacy rules and such, but the hospital staff is calling it a miracle, and we finally found someone to bend the rules for us."

"Okay. So, Andre is feeling better?" That was still how Philly thought of it, despite what Andre had said about saving his life.

"Better?" Andre's voice cracked incredulously. "I'm feeling totally well. And, more than that, the scans show no sign of the lung cancer."

"Lung cancer?"

"Yes. You didn't know, did you?" Sophia's voice hummed warmly. "I thought you didn't realize what it was you were praying for. Andre had lung cancer. He was just in the hospital to get help breathing and to get pain meds while he waited to die." She choked up at that point.

Andre chuckled again. "It's okay now, dear. I'm okay now." He elevated his tone a bit. "Did you think I was kidding about saving my life?" He was nearly shouting. Maybe he was enjoying strong lungs for the first time in a while.

"Wow. I didn't really know. I wasn't sure you weren't exaggerating, you know. Just a figure of speech, sort of." Philly wasn't shouting.

By the time he finished telling that story to the couple he and Brenda had just met, C.J. and Nicky were both grinning at him like intoxicated department store mannequins. And Philly was regretting that he had just one-upped them with his healing story. All he had meant to do was let out the great news, to bring someone else into the celebration of what Jesus had done for Andre.

"Makes me wanna go to the hospital and start praying for all the sick people," Nicky said upon breaking out of her plaster mask of surprise.

For Philly, that seemed like a crazy idea. And it made him pause to consider whether he should tell his story to anyone else. He didn't want people to get the wrong idea about him, as if he liked going up to strangers and offering to pray for whatever ailed them.

"Don't you like it, though?" Was Jesus interrupting his thoughts.

That night, Philly had a dream. He was running through the townhouse looking for something. Then he was in the hospital, still in his pajamas, running down the hall looking for something. He found his phone at the nurses' station, but realized that the phone wasn't what he'd been searching for. With one of the women behind the counter staring at him, he looked down to make sure he was wearing his pants. But then he found that he was fully dressed. Still, he felt that he shouldn't be there. He had to look somewhere else, though he still wasn't sure what he was looking for.

Turning to run away from the nurses' station, he caught a glimpse of a sick man through an open hospital room door, and then he was back home. And that made him anxious, because he realized he had left the hospital without praying for the sick man. So he ran downstairs to see if Jesus could help him fix it.

When he hit the bottom of the stairs and turned toward the TV room, there was a door where there normally wasn't one, and it was locked. Or he didn't know how to open it since it wasn't supposed to be there. Behind him, people from church—mostly his new church—were shouting instructions. But the instructions didn't seem to address his problem with opening the door. The frustration made him frantic, his heart racing and his face sweating.

"Philly!"

And suddenly he was awake in his bed.

"Philly, you were having a dream." Brenda rested a hand on his shoulder and spoke right into his ear.

He sighed and pulled at the sheets where they were tangled around his arm. "Oh. Sorry. Go back to sleep." He felt bad for waking Brenda, still concerned that she should be getting plenty of rest.

Saying no more, Brenda turned over and seemed to fall right back to sleep, a skill that Philly had often envied. But he was still awake. And he still had that feeling that he wanted to talk to Jesus, to get him to help with ... something. Checking that Brenda's breathing had returned to a sleeping rhythm, he untangled himself further and rolled slowly toward the side of the bed. By the time he was standing, he realized that the collar of his T-shirt was damp. He tugged at it to get it unstuck from his neck and staggered out of the bedroom.

Downstairs, Philly creaked over the nighttime floor into the kitchen for a glass of water. He leaned against the counter and sank into thoughts about the need to upgrade the counters and the floor. Then there were the appliances. Not now. This was no time to think about that. He wanted to talk to Jesus. The basement seemed to be the place to do that. It was the farthest point in the house from where Brenda was sleeping, and maybe it was where Jesus hung out these days.

"You asked me for help. I gave you a church community."

That thought hit Philly in the face as soon as he stepped onto the cold tiles by the garage door. He padded onto the carpet in the TV room and decided to skip over the question of where those words had originated. "*So, the new church will help me find what I was looking for?*" Philly responded inside his head.

Jesus chuckled.

Maybe he was really there, in that recliner.

Of course he was really there with Philly, though not necessarily sitting in that chair.

"Don't overthink it, Philly."

He took a deep breath and sank into the other recliner, flipping the lever and raising the footrest. "It still scares me that they're gonna expect me to go to hospitals all the time and pray for all the people with cancer or something."

"Yeah. That would be a lot to take on."

Was that sarcasm? No. Jesus wasn't sarcastic. Was that really Jesus?

"I never asked you to save everyone or heal everyone."

"No. You never did."

"No one else is asking you to either."

"Except maybe myself. Isn't that what I should do, though? Even if I can't heal everyone, shouldn't I try?"

"Of course you're not really the one who heals anyone anyway."

Something about that thought sounded sensible and religiously correct, but he had once heard Dave argue with someone who said something very similar. "If you say things like that about healing, then when I give a teaching I should say, 'No, it wasn't me who did that teaching, it was Jesus.'" And then Dave quoted some passage where it said that the apostle Paul healed everyone on this one island. *Paul* healed them. Not Jesus. Not God. That's what it said.

"I'm not insecure, Philly. I like sharing my gifts with my people. I'm not worried that you'll steal the credit from me. My glory cannot be robbed from me."

Was Philly saying those things to himself? It seemed unlikely. Maybe it was his old pastor, Dave, invading his thoughts. Or maybe the devil.

That thought reminded Philly of when Jesus chased the fear and darkness out of the basement. He glanced around the dark room now, not having bothered to turn on any of the lamps. A sliver of light was cutting through a gap in the curtains, the street lamp in the courtyard illuminating a strip of the wall like a shining stalk of bamboo. It was easier to believe that Jesus was there with him in the basement than that the devil was.

"So, this new church is the right one for me and Brenda?"

"What do you think?"

"I guess so."

"It feels like home, doesn't it?"

"Yeah."

"Feels like family?"

"Yeah. Sort of." When he thought about that idea, Philly had to admit to himself that his new church family actually fit him better than his natural family did in a lot of ways.

Chapter 40
A Visit with Their Families

In an unprecedented show of unity, the two mothers had organized a gathering at Philly's parents' house. Brenda's mother had just sold her house, and her impending departure to the West Coast was the motivator for a big gathering. With only five of them getting together, it was only *big* in significance. And that significance mostly derived from the fact that it was a first—the first time Brenda's mom had seen Philly's parents since the wedding reception.

"We can celebrate the new grandbaby together, knock on wood." Brenda's mother knocked on the end table next to the couch.

Sparks barked at her. He didn't seem to favor that pagan tradition. At least he didn't like the confusion over whether there was someone at the door.

"Sparks!" Philly's ma barked at the dog.

Brenda rebuked her mother. "Mom, we don't believe in that kind of thing. God is going to protect our baby. We don't need to knock on wood." She was sitting on one of the dining room chairs Philly had dragged into the living room. It had been Ma's idea, as if they were expecting more people.

"That's right. We prefer crossing our fingers around here." Dad laughed at his own joke. He was in rare form.

Philly wondered if his dad could possibly be flirting with Brenda's mom. Dad didn't get out much and didn't often meet attractive women around his age. But maybe it wasn't really flirting.

Hosting Jesus

Trying not to laugh at Dad's joke, Philly exchanged an eye roll with Brenda.

Dad had been standing near the front door taking in some of the breeze venturing off the lake to cool the city. It was ten degrees cooler here than it had been at Philly and Brenda's place in Schaumburg. Still chuckling at his little joke, Dad turned toward the kitchen and his preparations for their picnic supper.

When he heard the back door open, Philly knew that Dad had taken the dog out and was probably going to light the gas grill on the patio by the garage. Philly got up to join the males outside.

Brenda caught his hand on the way by, and they slid their palms and then their fingers across each other as he passed.

Philly grabbed a cold root beer from the fridge on his way outside. He would save the iced tea for dinner.

Standing up after clipping Sparks on the chain that the dog could drag around the backyard, Dad turned and smiled when Philly approached. That little moment reminded Philly of what it had been like when his father was hearing-impaired. Philly and Eileen had learned to try to catch their dad's eye before getting too close so as not to startle him. Grinning at the difference, Philly crossed the driveway to the patio.

Dad lifted the lid of the gas grill and used a wire brush to clean something left from its previous use. "Got your root beer, I see. Glad to be done with that diet stuff?"

Philly snorted at the reminder and nodded. "I still have to be careful. Only one root beer on the weekend, and hardly any beer."

"That's okay. Good to take care of yourself. When was it you lost that weight?"

This was typical. Dad remembered that Philly had lost weight, but he couldn't place it on a timeline. Philly feared this might not just be from being retired and having so many days in a row that looked the same as the one before. Philly reminded his dad of the general time frame and resisted worries about Dad's mental health.

Without warning, his father launched a new topic. "I'm thinkin' of gettin' some kinda work—to keep me busy, to get out once in a while. I tried looking on the internet on that computer you gave us, but I don't think I know where to look. I got all crossed around to some kinda advertisements for enhancements and replacements for this and that. I gave up."

Trying not to laugh, Philly ventured a look at his dad to see if he was teasing. He found no sign from the man intent on cleaning his grill. "I can help you find the best sites for job searching. I'll show you how to use them and then leave you some shortcuts so you can go there when you want."

Dad nodded. "Shortcuts sound good. I think I took the long way around and got lost somewhere in the woods or something." He chuckled as he turned the lighter switch to get the flames going.

The gas hissed for a bit longer than Philly expected before the lighter kicked in. His dad recoiled at the flames that jumped up through the gunmetal-gray grill.

"Whoa. Be careful."

"No worry. I don't have much hair left to singe anyway." His dad picked up a metal spatula and began scraping at the grill again.

"Maybe you could start going to church somewhere to get out of the house sometimes."

Dad squinted one eye and looked toward the house. "Well, it's one thing for me to go off to some kinda job once in a while. I don't expect it would go well with your ma if I went off to church without her."

Though Philly was still repenting of thinking his ma was baggage weighing down his dad's faith, he allowed some regret at her power to hold the old man back. That thought added some weight to the worry Philly cultivated about his dad's happiness, if not his mental health.

Looking up at Philly, his dad seemed to sense his mood. "Don't worry. I'll find something. And maybe we could come out to your place to watch a Cubs game again soon."

"Yeah. Let's do it next weekend. I bet we can talk the women into going shopping again."

Dad laughed deep in his throat.

Philly followed him back into the house as his dad let Sparks inside. He watched as Dad sorted things in the kitchen, getting the burgers and bratwursts ready for the grill. This was familiar territory. And what was wrong with days that might melt a bit into each other? Truthfully, that was what Philly would prefer. At least, part of him would prefer that.

Brenda's mother, on the other hand, seemed to thrive on change and movement. Her plan to move to Spokane was no surprise from that perspective. And she had become especially restless after her husband died a few years ago. Before that, she just dragged Brenda's dad on a cruise or on a drive halfway across the country a couple times a year.

Philly had met Brenda's dad only a few times. Mostly Philly's impressions of him came from Brenda's stories. Even the brief visits Philly had had with her dad during their dating days included a short litany of complaints from the man who swore his wife was trying to kill him, or at least trying to lose him in baggage claim. "Comes a time when a guy should be able to sit back and rest and not have to ask a lot of people where to find the nearest bathroom."

Philly knew exactly what he meant.

"I found this darling little apartment near a golf course, just a mile away from Sharon's place." Brenda's mom leaned back in a plastic folding chair and smoothed the paper napkin in her lap. "I could even walk over there. I might just do that sometime."

When Dad set the burgers and brats at the end of the table, Brenda's mom delicately extricated a burger and its bun from the pile on the oblong platter. "Don't mind if I do," she said under her breath.

"Walking would be healthy. But what's the neighborhood like in between?" Brenda reached for a burger and carefully avoided elbowing her mother in the face. "Excuse me."

"Oh, it's just a neighborhood. Nothing to worry about. Just by a golf course."

"Nothing to worry about except stray golf balls. Get ready to duck when you hear someone yell *fore!*" Dad had closed the grill after turning off the flames and was taking his place at the other end of the sturdy folding table.

"Oh. Yes. I hadn't thought of that. I wonder if it really is a problem. Maybe it's not safe for guests to park their cars around there either."

"I thought you were going on an adventure. You can't be too worried about being safe if you do that, now can you?" Philly's ma was probably teasing, but that was a rare occurrence, so he couldn't tell whether to laugh along.

Brenda bumped the discussion along as she squirted mustard on her cheeseburger. "Oh, Mom isn't gonna wrestle any alligators or climb Mount Everest. She likes to keep moving, but she knows when to duck."

They all laughed when Brenda's mom led the way. "There's enough mountains in Washington. I won't need to go to Mount Everest for that."

Philly liked the idea of mountains. He had little experience with actual mountains, so he wasn't sure he would enjoy one in real life. But now it occurred to him that he would have a chance to see for himself when they went out to visit his mother-in-law. "You'll have to be our guide up a mountain when we come out to see you."

"When are you coming? You can't fly halfway across the country with a little baby."

"No. You'll have to come back here to see *us* until Hannah gets old enough to travel." Brenda was talking with her mouth full.

"Did you say *Hannah*?"

"Oh!" Brenda swore. "I knew I would do that." She swore again.

Philly was belly laughing. He dropped his bratwurst on his plate, scattering potato chips into the coleslaw and onto the plastic tablecloth.

"Don't *laugh* at me. I'm a pregnant woman. You can't laugh at a pregnant woman." Brenda pouted at him and shook her head at herself. "I blew it. I'm so sorry."

He wasn't laughing because she had given away their secret plan for naming the baby. It was her instant resort to foul language that tickled Philly. She was still his girl, even if she was about to be a mother. He didn't mind that his wife was bad at keeping secrets either. It was an endearing quality most of the time.

Philly's ma spoke through the laughter. "Hannah? That's a nice name. Hannah Thompson. That's gonna be my granddaughter's name." She looked more wistful than Philly had seen in a long time.

Brenda's mother folded right into that wistful mood. "Oh, my. It *is* a sweet name. I'm so messed up about going away. I promise I'll be back for the birth."

Philly had already been wondering how that was supposed to work with flight reservations and uncertainty about the due date. But probably it just meant that she would be back soon after the birth.

Still recovering her dignity, Brenda added, "I'm not gonna give away her middle name, and you can't make me."

Philly had just begun to resettle his bratwurst into the bun, but lost hold of it again when that set him laughing even harder.

Dad laughed with him.

And Brenda joined them.

After dinner, they all trooped into the house. The mosquitos would have chased them in soon if they hadn't already planned to phone Eileen for a family conference call. That call was Eileen's idea. She couldn't get away from New York for the weekend, but she promised to be at her place this evening to join her voice with those gathered in Chicago.

"Hello, Eileen," Ma shouted at Philly's phone, which rested in the middle of the dining room table. The five of them sat there for the phone call, to be followed by dessert.

"She can hear you without shouting, Ma." Philly scowled across the table at her.

"Hello, Ma. Is everyone there together?"

"Everyone but you," Dad said.

"My mom and I are here, Eileen." Brenda raised her voice a bit too much and then made an apologetic face at Philly.

"Hello, Brenda. Hello, Brenda's mom." Everyone laughed at that.

Philly asked Eileen questions about her work, and Ma chimed in with follow ups. For a moment, it felt like his sister had come to visit just for this picnic or maybe just for the ice cream dessert.

Eileen reported that there was nothing big going on at work, just some minor personnel problems. And she assured them that there was no romantic news. "Who has time?"

Philly looked around the room at some elderly people who had quite a bit of time. But he didn't say anything about that.

Instead, Dad prompted him. "Hey, Philly, do that trick where you tell Eileen something about her life that you couldn't know." His dad grinned as if he were describing a game the family used to play together.

"Uh, well, that's not really a thing I do. Jesus was the one who did that, really." Philly paused over how much this sounded like that argument in his head about whether he actually healed people or if Jesus was the one doing it.

"Yeah, he can't do anything like that." Ma was trying to rewrite family history as far as Philly was concerned, but he still didn't want to perform for the family in this way.

"I think I know something." All eyes in the room turned toward Brenda.

"Brenda? You know something?" Eileen sounded more excited than scared about that prospect, even though Jesus had revealed that her boyfriend was lying to her about being divorced back when Dad had witnessed the trick he was talking about.

Brenda nodded. She looked at Philly. Was she asking for permission? Maybe she thought she was treading on his territory.

He just shrugged, adding a small smile meant as encouragement.

"What is this about?" Brenda's mom hadn't been there six years before when Philly and Jesus had dropped that previous bomb on Eileen.

Brenda bypassed her mother's question. "Well ..." She seemed to be sorting information. "I just suddenly had this idea pop into my head that one of the women who works for you—maybe an Indian woman—has been inviting you to church. And you think it's not for you, but really you would like it there. Maybe there are some single men there, even. Though I might just be adding in that last part myself."

Eileen forced a laugh into the phone.

Everyone in the dining room sat perfectly still, though Philly could tell that Brenda's mom was perched on the edge of reiterating her question about what this was about.

Philly tried to help. "Well, Eileen, does that sound familiar?"

"I just don't know how you could know that, Brenda. I mean, Jesus isn't sitting there next to you, is he?" Her voice trailed off at the end, as if it wasn't a real question.

"So that's right, then?" Ma seemed suddenly interested in this game. "At least the part about the Indian woman inviting you to church?"

Dad was smiling broadly at Philly and Brenda. That smile started a line of questioning in Philly's mind about what his dad knew, and when he knew it.

"Uh, yeah. She works for me. She says she thinks I would like her church. There are lots of single men there."

"Ha!" Brenda sounded a bit more triumphant than Philly would have in her place, but her reaction made him chuckle.

He took her hand, and she just grinned and bounced her eyebrows once.

Chapter 41
Thank You for Hosting Me

Wednesday night of the following week, they decided that Dad and Ma would come visit on Sunday. This meant they could accept Gladys's invitation for Philly to bring Brenda to visit her Saturday. "Her family is coming to pick her up to go out to supper, so it's not like we'll have to stay there all evening or anything."

Brenda stopped brushing her hair and bent her head in rebuke of Philly. "I'm not afraid of spending an entire evening with a nice old lady who wants to meet me. That's the kind of thing *you're* afraid of, not me." She snickered at him.

"Oh, okay. Just in case. I didn't want you to feel trapped."

"If she tries to trap me, you can just hold her back while I make a break for the door." Brenda resumed brushing her hair without relaxing the smirk on her face.

"Yeah, I can probably do that. And I know this former Bears offensive tackle with perfectly good knees who could help us out too." Philly didn't want to be out teased by his wife. He picked up his phone. "I'll let Gladys know."

That Saturday was one of those violently rainy days of summer. Philly loved days like that. And their new townhouse had a covered porch where he could sit in a red Adirondack chair and watch the rain if the wind was from the north. He got a bit wet that afternoon when the wind shifted to the west, but the temperature was warm both outside and inside, so he didn't mind so much.

Hosting Jesus

"You better change before we go. You'll smell like a wet dog otherwise." Brenda was cleaning up in the kitchen. Philly had made them omelets for lunch.

"I think Sparks would be insulted if he heard you say that."

"Well don't tell him then, poor sensitive little guy." She joked sharply over the noise of the running water. She was rinsing and scrubbing the dishes before putting them in the dishwasher as usual.

He didn't make fun of her for putting so much effort into washing this time.

The rain let up during their drive down to Naperville, then it surged for a few minutes while they waited in the parking lot. When the deluge diminished again, they scampered into Gladys's apartment building.

Before this invitation, Philly had assumed that Gladys's place was too small for guests. She hadn't invited him up. But it occurred to him on the way up that she might just be conscientious about having a man up to her apartment. That explanation made Philly smile.

Gladys opened the door to her second-floor apartment. "You two don't look too wet. Did it stop raining?"

"It just let up a minute ago." Brenda extended her hand. "So glad to finally meet you, Gladys."

"Oh, likewise. I've been fascinated by Philly since I met him years ago, and I was so curious about his wife."

Philly assumed those were just polite words. He couldn't imagine Gladys staying up late at night wondering who he had married.

Gladys stepped back. "Come on in. Do you like lemonade? I made some this morning out of real lemons. I haven't done that in years."

"Oh, I would love fresh-squeezed lemonade. What a treat!" Brenda led Philly past Gladys.

The freshness of the apartment seemed to go beyond the strong scent of lemons in the air. Philly guessed that the building couldn't be more than twenty years old, and it seemed to have been painted recently. Most of the pictures on the walls were photos of Gladys with multiple generations of people—people Philly had never met. That reminded him of what Brenda had said about him fearing getting stuck hanging out with people he didn't know.

When Gladys came back into the living room carrying a small tray with three lemonade glasses on it, she resumed their earlier discussion. "Anyway, I would think *you* would want to meet this strange woman your husband sneaks off to see after work." She waited while Brenda paused to look at her smiling face before taking a glass.

"Oh, I trust Philly. And he's told me all about you."

"Oh, so he's told you about this crazy business of seeing Jesus and about the healing things?"

"Oh, yes. We were friends when Jesus was walking around with him. I first thought Philly was going crazy, but then Jesus told him something about my past, and I knew Philly was really seeing and hearing a higher power of some kind."

"Higher power? You didn't believe in Jesus before that?"

"No, not really. I guess I thought some of what people said about him was probably true, but I wasn't really what you'd call a believer or anything." Brenda looked at Philly, her brow furrowing just slightly.

Was that a rebuke? Was she troubled by the discovery that Philly had told Gladys hardly anything about her? He started to assemble a defense for that oversight, but Gladys was still asking questions.

"So, do you believe Jesus is still around us even when we're not seeing him?"

Maybe Gladys was being a bit pushy, but Philly wasn't worried. He knew that Brenda believed, and that she wouldn't be offended by the innocent cross examination.

"I would love to see and hear him like you and Philly did, but I'm glad to just believe in him even when I can't see."

Gladys was seated now in a rose-colored armchair, her feet flat on the floor, her torso gradually reclining closer and closer to the back. "Sometimes I think I don't have as much faith as I should. I really wanna see him again. I even pretend that I *do* see him, once in a while." She sipped her lemonade and glanced toward the window. Thunder rumbled low and long.

Now Philly was curious. "How do you pretend?"

With her head at a slight angle, Gladys reminded Philly of one of the Easter Island statues, a slight grin on its face and a considering air offered to all who found it perched there. She had relaxed against the back of the chair now, setting her glass on the little brass lamp table next to her.

"He told me to close my eyes and picture him being inside me when I'm at home alone. And that's usually pretty good. That's *really* good sometimes. But I like to imagine him with me when I'm visiting folks around the home here, or when I'm shopping, or when I'm visiting my kids at their place. I look at an empty chair and imagine him sitting in it. And I imagine what I would say to him and what he would say to me, and what his eyes would be doing, the smile on his lips always so peaceful, always so happy." She sighed and turned her attention more directly on Philly. "You think I'm losing my marbles?"

Shaking his head, all Philly could think was how well he understood Gladys and how he might just try imagining Jesus in more places from now on. "No, you're not losing anything. I think you're right on, Gladys."

Gladys checked with Brenda and then went on. "When I'm home alone, I like to sit and talk to him like he just came over for a visit. I ask him how he's doing and what he's concerned about. Sometimes I get religious about it and pray about whatever I think he's telling me, but other times I just set a cup of tea out for him like he was my guest and I'm a good hostess." She looked from Brenda to Philly and back. "The teacup is still full when he goes away though."

Without even looking at her, Philly knew Brenda was thinking melancholy thoughts about what Gladys was saying and the way she was saying it. He turned his head toward his wife and then back to Gladys. For whatever reason, he felt like he should tell her about healing Andre in the hospital, and about Brenda and baby Hannah, and about Brenda having a word of insight for Eileen over the phone last weekend. He didn't mean to be changing the subject. It was supposed to be all part of the same subject. And he wanted to connect Gladys's longings, which he felt deeply when she confessed them, with the living experience of Jesus still in his life. He expected Gladys would understand, and he hoped she would be encouraged by all of it.

When Philly was done recounting their experiences, Gladys replied with a story of her own about a woman with hand tremors who used to be an artist. "It was sad to hear her literally crying in the craft shop where she was just trying to paint this ceramic pot, not even one of the beautiful paintings she used to do. I've seen the paintings in her room, and she was a real artist when she was younger. So I just got this feeling that it wasn't right, it just wasn't right that the devil could do this to this poor woman and her wonderful art. And, before I really even thought about it, I put my hand on her shaky one, right there in the crafts room where she was just crying and crying. And I said, 'In the name of Jesus, let peace come to these hands.' I only had one of her hands, but that was the way I said it anyway." She reached for her lemonade. "And the shaking just stopped."

As Gladys sipped, Philly glanced again at Brenda. She had this dreamy-little-girl look on her face. He suspected she was relieved to hear that story from Gladys. Before that, their hostess had seemed on the verge of depression at Jesus's invisibility, especially with that comment about the tea still being full in the cup. Philly was glad to hear that Gladys was still meeting with Jesus and still doing the things Jesus led her to do.

That evening, back at home, Philly went downstairs to the TV room while Brenda talked to one of her friends on the phone. For just a moment he thought about going to sit on the porch instead, but he had been assaulted by mosquitos the last time he tried that in the evening. He recalled the dream about Jesus in the recliner, and especially the handprint on the arm of that chair. Then he was standing behind the chair in his basement, the same chair where he imagined Jesus sitting to talk to him.

"Have a seat, Philly."

"Are you hosting *me* now?" He took his usual seat on the right, not the least tempted to reach for the TV remotes.

"It's a beautiful evening."

Philly noticed now that the windows were open behind him, a bit of the birdsong from the courtyard chirping into the basement. Brenda must have opened the windows to air out the room. It was a cool and fresh evening after the thunderstorms.

"It's nice."

"I'm glad you visited Gladys today. You two are good for each other."

"And Brenda loves her, that's for sure."

"Yes. They are both beautiful and kind, a very lovely pair."

"Lovely? That sounds like something Gladys would say." He thought about it for a moment. "And maybe Brenda too."

The silence that followed seemed agreeable.

"When Gladys pretends you're sitting with her in her living room, you're there, aren't you?"

"You think I should drink the tea?"

Philly laughed. "I don't know." His laughter softened. "Maybe not."

"I'm always there with her. I'm always here with you."

"Yeah."

"But it's one thing to be here or to be there. It's something else entirely to be welcomed."

Philly sat with that agreeable silence. Cicadas began their plaintive call and drowned out the crickets. Brenda's voice upstairs was animated for a few seconds—a joke between friends, perhaps. In all of it, Philly wasn't alone.

"Philly."

"Yes, Lord?"

"Thanks for hosting me here."

"Huh. Well, you're welcomed, of course."

Hosting Jesus

Made in the USA
Monee, IL
24 October 2025